FOR A BETTER LIFE

FOR A BETTER LIFE

JULIA REID GALOSY

atmosphere press

FOREWORD

Four years ago at a low ebb in my life, Cece, the heroine of this work, entered my imagination. She was the embodiment of all of those strong women whom I had met here in Mexico. These were my neighbors and friends, those women who keep the family strong and on track while their men are elsewhere—north of the border, working three jobs, in the arms of others. Cece captivated me, taking my heart and asking me to come with her, to write her story, as she, like so many before her and not by choice, fled a life that she felt offered little to her unborn child. She is another of these heroic Mexican mothers and I hope I have done her justice.

I have been an immigrant for more than half of my adult life. By choice. As an immigrant, I feel the excitement of beginning again. All of my former culture with its laws, rules, customs, food, and festivities is left behind to be replaced by those of the new culture. I have had to look at everything in my life with fresh eyes, holding judgement at bay. It is thrilling. As an immigrant, I am going toward.

On the opposite spectrum from my experience are the refugees. They do not feel the thrill of the new, they live the terror of the unknown. Where immigrants are challenged, refugees are humiliated. Where immigrants are filled with anticipation, refugees are filled with dread. Immigrants have choices, refugees have none. Refugees are running from, not moving toward.

In all of my experience here in Mexico, as an immigrant, I was welcomed, embraced, included. Cece begins her tale as a refugee but she prevails to become an immigrant and brings her daughter into the world where she is an American citizen of Mexican heritage: proud of both.

I dedicate this work to my own mother, Kathryn Lambrechts Reid, and to all mothers around the world who share the same single hope for their children: for a better life.

I

I couldn't feel my arm. I knew it was folded under me at the bottom of the trunk but I still couldn't feel it. The car was on a very bumpy road and each bump threw a bolt of electricity shooting through my body. I wanted to scream out but I knew the slightest sound could stop me; could stop all of us. I wondered how this terrible journey could be the start of a better life.

I thought of my village in northern Mexico, so near to the resorts where I never got to go. We would see the cars full of people and suitcases on their way. Bikes were attached to the back or surfboards were roped overhead. Everything about those vehicles signaled a golden trek to pleasure. As the cars whizzed past, we villagers knew that these places were not for our kind.

Our kind gathered firewood and sold it to local bakers. Our kind caught snakes and sold the skins on the roadside. Our kind raised chickens whose eggs we could eat daily but the flesh had to be saved for special occasions. Our kind had no wells or access to drinking water. Our kind made the weekly trek to the market to get the big water bottles for our families' needs.

My father had died long ago, worn out by scratching at the ground like a rooster, trying to get anything to grow from the dry desert. He left us in one second saying he was tired and lay down never to get up again. My five brothers and my mother and I buried him on the hillside next to the big tree. Shortly after, two of my brothers left for a better life. We never heard from them again.

What did this mean? They were in the States, happy and rich, and no longer wanting to be in touch with the poor relations they sought to escape? Did they have American families now with chubby kids glued to their videogames or their phones? Or did something terrible happen to them, trapped as they were in the hands of the coyotes? Were they tossed on the side of some road like bags of garbage to rot in the sun? Did some redneck vigilante with a rifle from Star Wars come out in the night and pick them off like targets in an arcade game, high-fiving his friends for "gettin' one of 'em?" Years have passed now so our family will never know. My mother keeps the three remaining men close to home. They have families here and struggle to make enough for the special chicken occasions to be more frequent. Their wives are from here too so they know what life is like.

I am the youngest. Just 20 years old and so wise that I knew Guillermo was the love of my life. I couldn't take the birth control pill because this would have meant that Guillermo and I were planning to have sex. Catholics who are not married cannot plan to have sex. If it happens, it is just something like a tsunami of the soul which runs at the lovers with waves of passion so intense that nothing can stop it. This is what happened night after night with Guillermo as we planned our life together far away from this place.

My mother carried the face of guilt into the conversations between us as she warned me not to take such a choice at so young an age. She pointed to herself with her first child at fifteen and now buried under the burden of lifelong obligation when not even fifty. Did I want this to happen to me? Did I want to live like this forever? I was smart. I was being educated. I could be a doctor or a lawyer or a teacher. I was a very good writer. Didn't I want to be a writer? I even spoke English. Why throw it away for a moment's passion? But it was so much more than this. It was like heaven.

Then, as suddenly as he had appeared in my life, he was gone. *Collateral damage,* it was called. He was in the way when two gangs fought over the rights to kill each other in their efforts to deliver poison to the children of wealthy Americans. When he left, he left a small messenger who swam into me and there he stayed these past weeks, growing our baby.

How could I not go for a better life? How could I bring this baby into the world of scratching the dry earth and watching the rich go to resorts and burying the people who were in the way, while we made our tortillas and prayed for a future that would never arrive? Some looked to the government. Some prayed to Mother Church. No angels arrived from either source to save us. We had to save ourselves.

There was no possibility of my telling my mother. She had already lost a husband and two sons, how could she lose her only daughter? I went to see Antonio, the son of the baker—my only hope. For the love of me, he gave me the money.

The choice had been made and the preparations were as well. The coyotes would be the easy part. They were well known and their tactics were clear. Money was their only concern, not you, not your comfort, not your welfare. You were a package to be delivered and they would do it; or maybe they would not. It was, like everything, a roll of the dice.

I had made a special plastic purse that fit inside of the sole of my shoe. I had to take off the sole and slip in the purse and then re-glue the shoe. I couldn't think of another place that would be safe to hold cash. There would be rape, so even my own vagina would not serve as a place to safely store funds. Women making the trip usually took birth control for several months before going. We knew what was going to happen.

The shoe was sturdy and had three sets of straps so I knew that it wouldn't fall off along the road. I took three large pointed pins with me to secure my hair as well as to serve as weapons. I had small packs of water so that I could discard them as I went and everything would get lighter. I made up a protein powder so that food was at a minimum but strength would be at a maximum. I faced the trip with the sense of dread that had been haunting me my whole life. It welled up now with a fierce strength; I shoved it aside, I had to go.

With a note to my mother on the kitchen table, I left the house that night. I had written her telephone number on my stomach in permanent marker. If they found my dead body at least they would know how to return me to my mother. I had a tiny flashlight to lead me out of the village onto the highway to wait for the truck. After twenty minutes, I heard the old engine whining as it pulled into view, its passengers silhouetted against the bright moon. The back looked full, but people re-arranged themselves to give me space. No one spoke.

We drove until the beginning of the new day. Just before sun up, the truck ground to a halt in the middle of the campo. Nothing was visible as far as we could see. The coyotes got out of the cab and came around the back of the truck rousting us from our shallow sleep. They had long poles which they thrust through the slats poking those who had been able to get some floor space on which to stretch out. We groggily climbed down into the dirt.

"*Dinero, dinero!*" they shouted. We were all confused, as we had had to pay in advance and now the coyotes were shouting for more money.

"*Joven*, we have already paid," one middle aged farmer said, addressing the young coyote as a youth. His words were met by a sharp punch to the stomach with the pole. He tumbled over into the dust.

"*Dinero, dinero,*" they shouted again. No one was making any moves so the coyotes plowed into the crowd. They pulled backpacks off of us and threw our belongings onto the ground, seeking money. They groped the women on their breasts and their pants looking for the tell-tale bulk of hidden funds. They did the same to the men seeking money that had been stashed behind their balls. They grabbed women by their hair and held them while they screamed as their little children were searched in places that should never be touched.

Little by little money started appearing, raining down into a great pile, as everything was ransacked or violated. Through this orgy of greed we cried out against the attacks happening to us. What were we to do? I had put small amounts of money under my breasts and in my pants and when my turn came the coyote took his time examining me for money. He searched, and although he was satisfied with his discovery, he still put his finger up my vagina seeking more. His face carried a lewd smile and his eyes held me in the grip of dominance. I was his puppet.

The attacks continued for many minutes while the children cried and their parents screamed and objected, but no one had the power to stop it. Finally satisfied, the coyotes gathered the money and told us to get our things together. I hoped for a place to wash the filth of that man's touch from my body but there was none. We put our clothes back into order and picked up our belongings and re-mounted the truck. It was a lesson in power and we knew who the alpha dogs were.

All of us were aware that now we had no money. We had to find some somewhere and I had to pretend to need it as well. The coyotes let us out near the edge of the town and told us we had until dark to replenish the money we had lost. We spread out along the town. At this point begging was the only option and many of the people, proud workers their whole lives, were reduced to beggars with hat in hand. I could not look into the eyes of the townspeople as I asked for money. Most hurried past us horrified by the dust clinging to our clothes and the desperation clouding our eyes. But the women dug into their purses and their bags and shared with me. As always, the women knew. By the end of the day I had enough for a big meal and more to hide in the not-so-secret places all of us used.

We made the connection at the truck, each person hoarding his food, hunching over it to form a protective shield. How could we be Mexicans and not be sharing? Had we so soon become the Americans we wanted to copy? None of us believed we would be getting a meal in the next few days and this one was precious. I ate in silence savoring the three enchiladas filled with meat and cheese, covered in pico de gallo. I mixed the refried beans into the rice and added some chili to make it spicy. I didn't know when my last meal would arrive so I took my time.

I used this opportunity to study the two coyotes. The first, called *El Tamí* when the other one yelled at him, was young, maybe my age. He must have named himself because he didn't look like the *Big Tamale*. He had one of those deep beards that Mexicans have: black and coarse. His chest hair peeked out of his t-shirt neck. His arms were heavily tattooed. I guess he was in a gang; the symbols meant nothing to me. His face was a perpetual snarl as if this way of behaving would strengthen his power over us. He walked around the camp kicking people's meager belongings out of his way. He smoked copious numbers of cigarettes, tossing the butts into the air. Cigarettes were hugely expensive in Mexico and this display of wealth was not lost on us as we sat in the dirt. He wore heavy jeans and a white t-shirt with a bandolier strapped across his chest. Maybe he thought he was Emiliano Zapata, the father of our revolution, instead of a reviled trafficker in human misery. The other coyote called *El Gordo,* earned the name through what seemed to be years of overindulgence. His t-shirt strained to cover his protruding stomach and low slung jeans. His short stubby legs bowed out like a circus ring and each step left a deep imprint in the dirt with the weight of his stride. His face was swarthy with patches of hair and the same on his head. He stood guard on us while we ate.

El Tamí circled around the back of the pack of us looking for a straggler he could cull from the herd; he found one. Suddenly he grabbed a young girl from the edge of the circle. Her mother leaped up to protect her.

"Joven, joven, please, please leave her. She is no good to you. She is only fourteen." The girl screamed and struggled in his arms. He continued dragging her across the dirt.

"No! No! Mami, Mami, help me!" She spit the words out into the air. Her face was contorted and her eyes shone with fear. We were all on our feet now. El Gordo pulled his gun and pointed it at us.

"Sit down. All of you. Fuckin' sit down! I don't give a shit about any of you. I'll blow your fuckin' brains out! I fuckin' mean it. I'll fuckin' blow your brains out. Sit down. Now!" He pointed the gun at us. One by one we sat down. *El Tamí* continued to pull the girl into the bushes.

"Take me! Take me!" her mother cried. She leaped up and ran after her daughter. The shot rang out and we all ducked farther into the earth. The mother stopped. Bits of dust had leaped from the earth at her feet.

"*No mames! No mames! No fuckin' way*! The next one will be at your head. Sit down now!" He pointed the gun at her.

"Mami, Mami, help!" We heard the sound of the slap.

"Shut the fuck up, you little cunt." The girl stopped yelling now, only crying. We heard the sounds of the scuffle as he threw her to the ground. Next came the piercing scream as he took her virginity in a dust-filled valley out in the middle of the desert with only us as silent witnesses. Shame must have penetrated inside all of us. Her mother cried quietly. El Tamí rejoined El Gordo, the older coyote.

"That's one of the real benefits of this job." El Tamí

smiled, tucking his shirt around the bandolier and buckling his belt. He slapped the older man on the back.

"Si, joven, for you, an endless supply of virgins! You are a blessed man." They laughed, enjoying the moment. The mother ran to her daughter and held her in her arms as she cried. We all hunkered down and looked away. The mother and daughter returned to our circle of humanity, which had not provided the protection they might have thought it would. A hand reached up to help them sit in the dust. Mostly we avoided their accusing gaze. The girl wiped away the blood running down her leg and continued to whimper.

"You all shut the fuck up," El Tamí cried pointing his gun at us. "You too, bitch. It had to happen sometime. You got lucky. *Vales verga.* You're worthless." He leered at the mother. She turned her back on him.

The dirt had already ground itself into our pores and we put out a strong aroma all around the campsite. The ground was a sea of white where pieces of toilet paper had been discarded by the crowds of people who had already made this journey. Their fresh urine smell wafted into the breeze. Individuals and families closed in on themselves setting up an invisible barrier for privacy and safety. I rolled myself into a ball hoping to catch some sleep.

"*Andale! Andale!*" The coyotes' shouts woke me with a start as everyone clamored into the truck. A hand reached down to help me inside and I found myself again in the circle of strangers who did not speak and did not share. I wondered how I could still even be in Mexico; there was so little connection among us.

"*Andale! Andale!*" shouted El Gordo, the Fatty. I got a

closer look at my two traffickers then. El Gordo was a short Mexican with a very square head and bushy black eyebrows. He had a square body to match his head. I thought he was probably about fifteen years older than El Tamí. He was much shorter than the younger man, no taller than me. He made up for his height in strength. Bulging muscles showed under his t-shirt and he held the heavy guns and poles like they were matchsticks. He seemed a bit nicer than El Tamí but not by much.

His approaches were more subtle. I felt his hands on my breasts and my ass as he passed or pushed us into the truck over the next hours. I saw him cup the breasts of the older women as they climbed up into the truck and often just brushed against them as they climbed down. He didn't drag anyone into the bushes as El Tamí did, but he never let a woman pass without getting something.

He especially enjoyed doing this much more openly if a woman was accompanied by a man. He took pleasure in his power. I caught him several times with his hands on a woman's breasts and his eyes staring directly into the eyes of her man. Once there was an objection.

"Please, Señor." A gentle man put his hand on the hand of El Gordo. The short man spun around, dropping his hand from the woman's breast.

"*No vale madres!* I don't give a fuck." His words were strong but his reaction was one of surrender. He walked away kicking at the dirt without looking back as the man encircled his wife tenderly.

The truck rumbled through the night jostling us as it had before, until we reached a place where we could see lights along the horizon. Was this the Promised Land? The truck stopped. We reached a location with ten cars lined up in the desert.

"*Afuera, afuera!*" screamed El Tamí and we all began to jump down from the truck as he ordered. The coyotes moved us roughly, creating a series of smaller groups of three, four, five people. I think it depended on size as I was a small woman and was connected with three men. I saw a group of five: three children, a man and a woman. It seemed to make sense.

"*Dentro! Dentro!*" barked El Gordo pointing to the inside of the trunk of the car and indicating that I should get in. My heart sank. I was to be stuffed into the very back of the trunk which had been a bit hollowed out so that we could fit into it. With no choice, I folded myself into as small a package as I could become and climbed into the trunk.

Three sweaty, stinking men then climbed into the trunk on top of me. Four people crammed into the tight trunk were all the car would hold. A piece of wood was put on top of us with tiny holes for breathing and then things were piled in. I guessed these were some obvious souvenirs from Mexico which would likely be in the trunk if it weren't full of smuggled people. From the outside, all would look normal.

Coming back to the present now, I was on the inside, it was suffocating. I fought down the gag response and concentrated on my breathing, being very slow and being very deliberate. I breathed through my nose and my mouth. I felt my arm go numb. For someone who never did this, I began to pray.

Shadows played inside the trunk. We could hear the sounds of the traffic lining up at the bridge. It moved slowly but at least it was progressing. I felt that we were part of the procession as we crept along. All of a sudden, we stopped. From what I could hear, a car which had been in front of us was moving forward but we were not. We waited for what seemed an eternity and then we drove forward over a *tope*, a speed bump in the road, and were stopped again. We heard the driver talking to someone and then we moved forward again. Were we through? My heart raced for a minute. No, we were making a turn. We stopped. I heard the door of the car open and close.

It seemed we were in the middle of a burst of activity. All of the doors of the car were being opened. We heard the latch of the trunk click and light streamed into our hiding place, temporarily blinding us. We heard the rummaging around of the souvenirs above our heads. Then a fist pumped hard on the floor of the trunk above us. Now everything was thrown out onto the ground. The tempo was accelerating. I heard the souvenirs being hurled out with fury. Finally there was a scratching around the edges of our false bottom and it sprung open. We were caught. The men above me shifted as we were hauled out of the trunk. Their shoes and elbows and knees dug into me until finally I was lifted out.

"You're lucky you didn't suffocate in there," a border guard said. The driver of our car had his hands behind him and he had handcuffs on them. We were put into a huddle and guards were all around us. They took us through a gate and into a hallway. Everyone was staring at us. Finally, we arrived into the parking lot behind the building and we were put into a van which left immediately.

We bumped along in silence. I thought of the lost dream and brooded to myself. We traveled a ways into the desert and the van left a trail of dust behind it. I could see a building in the distance and figured this would be the detention center, not the hoped-for nirvana.

We stopped at the gate and the guard opened it for us and we drove through. The van came to a halt and the engine was turned off. The guards opened the doors and we got out. They took the driver into another area and motioned for us to wait with a hand up like you do with a dog. We stood around. Waiting. Not talking. Finally a few guards came out and they took the men to one side and me to another. I was brought into a small office and sat across a desk from a woman. She spoke to me in Spanish.

"I am Señora Granados." She was not smiling. She did not say anything cordial like Mexicans would always say: *Mucho gusto, encantado; nice to meet you, enchanted.* Instead she barked at me, "What is your name?"

I knew what to do now. The coyotes had instructed us for this. When we made the deal to come to America they told us to prepare a story. A lie really. A story about who we were and where we came from. I had my little story with the wrong name and the wrong town and the wrong reasons for trying to come to the United States. I thought it was a pretty good story and I repeated it for Señora Granados right now. It wouldn't really matter what I did or didn't say. It was the end of the story anyway. She typed my story into the computer.

"Come here now and put your face into this machine. Yes. Stand still now." The machine made a scan of my eyeball. I didn't like this. It seemed scary to me, like a science fiction movie or something.

After I told my story and she scanned my eye, she fingerprinted me and Señora Granados printed it out and gave it to me to sign. Another guard took me into a bathroom and gave me a towel and let me take a shower. The water felt so wonderful and washed off all of the grime from the road. There were so many girls speaking Spanish that I could forget where I was and think I was still in Mexico. *Mexicanas* were everywhere: in the center, in the yard, in small cells, in the bathrooms. After my shower, Señora Granados came and took me to a cell where there were already two other girls. She told me I would be deported tomorrow.

"Where you from, chica?" a tiny little señorita asked me. She had the deep brown chiseled face of a Central American, not the soft mocha color of Mexicans.

"The North." I didn't want anyone to know my business.

"Oh, Miss Uppity Mexicana," the little one said. "*Culera.*" Asshole was not a usual greeting for Mexicans.

"Leave her alone, Elvira. You sure look tired honey. How'd they get you?" said a smiling, middle-aged woman. "I'm Lupita." Her eyes were kind.

"We were in a false trunk under some packages," I said, moving across the room near Lupita. I sat on an empty top bunk closer to her and farther away from Elvira.

"Dumb idea," Elvira said, admiring herself in the mirror while she experimented with different hairstyles. "The border guards can tell by the weight of the car that something's not right."

I moved to the lower bunk next to Lupita. She put her arm around me. She reminded me of my mom.

"You paid a coyote for that idea?" Elvira faced me with a snarl of disgust on her face.

"Don't pay her no mind. She's going back just like the

rest of us." Lupita tightened her arm around me.

"Did you both get picked up today?" I looked around at the two of them.

"No. We got picked up at different times. We are waiting to be sent back. Sometimes it takes a while for paperwork. Nobody explains it to us. We just wait. What did the guard say to you?" She smoothed my hair.

"She said I would be sent back tomorrow."

"You're so lucky. You can come right back." Elvira pinned her braid to the top of her head and looked like a Mexican Dutch girl.

"Maybe not so lucky. I didn't get in, did I?"

"No, but you didn't get killed neither." She pointed her finger at me.

"Well, that's something, I guess."

"Let's go get some food. It isn't too bad really." Lupita took me by the hand. "Anything would taste good right now. Thanks so much, I'm Rosita." I was amazed how easily the lie came to my lips.

I supposed this is what it feels like to go to college and live in a dormitory with other girls. Lots of chatting: some nice girls, some mean girls. We washed our faces and brushed our teeth in long sinks in a huge bathroom with about twenty cubicles. It was the biggest bathroom I had ever seen. The toilets flushed and the girls could put the toilet paper directly in the toilet. I couldn't believe how clean it was. Under different circumstances, it would have been nice to be here.

The beds were flat and hard but they were clean and everything worked. There was a little light near each bed so we could read. I was in the upper bunk and the light was in the wall over my head. I took a few minutes to look at my mother's picture before I went to sleep. I thought I would be sad but like the lady in the bunk below had said, I wasn't dead. I knew what I had to do.

They woke me early, first light. Señora Granados was already on the job and came to get me.

"Get up, Rosita," she called. For a second I forgot that I was Rosita. I jumped out of bed. "You've got thirty minutes to get something to eat and get ready. I will come for you here." She stomped away before she was finished with the sentence and it trailed after her.

"*A la verga. Oh shit!*" Elvira woke in a foul humor. Probably every day, I thought. "Can't get no sleep here."

Lupita waved at me from her bed as I was leaving the cell. I waved back, grateful for her kindness.

After breakfast I was waiting near the door to the cafeteria when Señora Granados came along.

"Let's go, Rosita," she took my arm. Where was I going to run?

II

They put us in the van. There were about ten of us. I thought the van would take us to airports and fly us to our fake destinations but it didn't. They drove us right across the bridge. When we got to the other side, they just let us out and drove back over the bridge. For a second, I had a thought that I could crouch down under the seat and just be taken back to the USA, a stowaway in a government van. I smiled at the idea.

We scattered along the streets of the seedy border town. I felt more unsafe here than I had in the trunk. I didn't even stop to think, I just started walking. There must be someplace where I could swim across the river. It was very early in the morning and I had all day. I walked parallel to the river for a while. If anything, I knew I had to find a place that was some distance from the town. A bus ambled along the dirt road on which I was traveling. I hailed the driver and climbed aboard.

It must have been market day because the bus was filled with women loaded down with food from the *tianguis*. There was a seat in the middle and I took it. I knew it was going to be a tough day. The woman next to me smiled.

"*Buenos dias*," she said. I smiled back.

"*Buenos dias, señorita*," I said. I moved my backpack to my lap. "You have a lot of food. You must have a large family." I showed my interest.

"Yes, thanks to God. We are ten."

"Everyone is well?" I asked.

"Yes, well. Happy." She re-arranged the packages at my feet, giving me more room.

"They must be very young because you are so young." I smiled.

"The youngest is four years old and the oldest is twelve. My in-laws live with us too. Everyone works or goes to school. It is a lively home." The woman moved the packages in her lap.

"It sounds very nice." I meant that too. It did sound nice: a family working together. I had had that, too, until my father died and then Guillermo. Things change so fast.

"Are you a *mojada*?" she asked, using the term Mexicans used for people trying to get to the States: 'wet ones.' Her eyes were so clear with truth that I had to tell mine.

"Yes," I said. I searched her gaze for compassion.

"It is very dangerous," she said. The compassion was there.

"I know. I have already failed. But I can't fail." I pointed to my stomach.

"Ah," she said, understanding. "Is the father with you?"

"He died."

"Oh, so you must go?"

"For a better life. For her. For my Nely." I pointed again.

She smiled. I wondered if this woman, like me, had always known before her babies were born if they were girls or boys. She seemed so kind.

"There is a place near my village where people have come to swim the river. Shall I show you?"

"Yes, please. I need to try. Don't they patrol this area?"

"There are so many places to cross, they can't patrol them all. For some reason this place seems to be ignored by the border patrol. Maybe there is danger on the other side to stop people. I don't know about that. I only know this side is safe."

We rode in silence then. I wondered if God had sent this woman my way. He seemed so seldom to be answering my prayers that I had virtually stopped asking. The bus came to a stop in the middle of the dust. I got off with the woman. She motioned for me to follow and I took some of her bags away from her to help her carry them.

In a short while we came to a small village, maybe twenty homes. There was a small store and a taco stand but not much else. The woman wound her way along the paths and I followed. We arrived at a small adobe home with an old woman sitting out front shucking corn.

"*Buenos dias.*" I smiled at her.

"*Buenos dias,*" the woman said. I followed my guide into the home and put her groceries on a concrete counter.

"Wait a minute." She put down the rest of her purchases. She became a burst of activity. I didn't know what was happening. The woman moved rapidly around the kitchen putting things into old plastic containers. I realized that she was getting something ready for me.

"*No, señora, no necesito nada.*" I didn't need anything. The woman had so little. My host smiled at me but said nothing. When she had finished her work she presented me with a water-tight package wrapped several times over and secured with many rubber bands. I was very grateful.

"Thank you so much," I said, knowing so clearly what Mexican hospitality meant.

"Come." She led the way out the back of the home and I followed. We walked for a while along the river until we came to a deserted spot. She pointed to it and turned to hug me. I held on to her for the hug I should have given my mother and did not. She waved me a good-bye and left.

I sat down to assess the spot that I hoped would lead to my freedom. There was a rock ledge that looked like a platform jutting out into the river. The river itself looked to be no more than 300 feet wide. I could see the far bank clearly. I waded in a short distance and felt the heavy rock under my feet. The current did not feel so strong. I knew I could swim across here. What choice did I have? Judging by the clothes and backpacks and shoes discarded on the shore, plenty of people had tried to do the same. I was amazed I was alone. I lay down on the bank behind some brush and looked for sleep. It was going to be a long night. The voices woke me. The sun was just going down, silhouetting the three men in front of its light.

"What about here? We could wade out here and then swim," the first voice said.

"I think it would work. What do you think, Anselmo?" A second voice.

"I think so but let's keep looking; this is so important."

I could see the men from my hiding place. They were *mojados* like me. This would be my first risk, talking with strangers, but I felt I had to take it.

"*Compañeros,*" I said. I hoped they would be my partners so I chose my greeting carefully. I came out of my hiding place. They stood still, trying to determine if I were friend or foe. "I have looked at the river for several hours today and I think I have found a good spot." I walked along the shore just assuming they would be following me. They did.

"Here there is a rock ledge and, if you look, it seems there is one on the other side as well. You see the large rocks jutting out over there? It looks like we will not have so far to swim if we can walk out here to the end of the ledge and then walk for a while on the other side too."

"*Bueña, Chica, gracias.*" The tall one smiled at me. I actually did feel like a good girl at that moment. We walked along the edge of the river.

"What do you think, Tomás?" The tall one was talking to the shortest.

"I think she's right. We can do it here. We have to try somewhere. The first of us across can bring a line and that will help the rest. Juan Pablo, you are the best swimmer. What do you say?" He looked at his middle brother.

This man hardly looked at us. He spoke to the ground when he finally answered. "I can do it." Such an easy declaration for such a difficult task. I marveled at his confidence. I had put on my brave front but I was grateful for the help and the company. We walked along the edge now together, looking for signs of danger.

The tall one was Anselmo. He was about 6'4", unusual for a Mexican. He was very lean and his long legs made him appear even taller. He had a full black beard and deep black eyes. There was a silver tooth in the front, which caught the light of the moon. He squatted in the dirt while he talked.

"*Hermanos.* We will cross the border tonight. The girl has helped us find the perfect place and Juan Pablo, our brother, will lead us. Let us pray to Jesus, our Lord and

Savior, to lead us." He bowed his head and his brothers did the same. I followed reluctantly as I felt that God and His son seldom helped the Mexican people. "Lord Jesus, please protect this small group as we search for a new life. Protect us from all of the harms waiting to hurt us. Deliver us to our families on the other side. Amen."

"Amen." Tomás made the sign of the cross and kissed a rosary which he returned under his shirt.

"Amen," Juan Pablo echoed. He walked toward the water's edge and stared out into the darkness. Maybe he was visualizing his swim, like all of those Olympic athletes do.

Tomás sat in silence. He was the shortest. He wasn't really that short, maybe 5'10", but he seemed short in comparison. He had black hair like Anselmo, matched by giant tufts peeking out from his chest. He wore jeans so dark that they disappeared into the night and an equally dark shirt. His vest was so overloaded that I worried he wouldn't be able to swim. He still hadn't looked at me directly but rather turned his face away from me and looked at me sideways.

Juan Pablo carried the largest bundle and laid it alongside the water. He moved with the grace of an athlete. His manner was gentlemanly and shy as he walked along checking for my safety at each step. He wasn't as dark as his brothers but he was nearly as tall as Anselmo with the muscles of Tomás. He followed Tomás to the water's edge.

"*Que pedo, Juanpa?*" What's happening, Tomás asked his brother. I had the same question.

"Don't worry, Tomi, we are going to be fine. I have swum in rivers far stronger that this one. We are ready.

Are you worried?"

"*No hay pedo.*" No problem, his brother answered him. I thought there might be a lot of problems but I wasn't going to start by making trouble. I tried to look confident.

At about 9 o'clock, Juan Pablo began to walk on top of the rock ledge. He had the line tied around his waist. It was a nylon cord because a big rope would have weighed him down. Just before he entered the water I yelled at him.

"I am Rosita, at least you deserve to know my name if you are taking this risk for us." I still didn't trust that there weren't vigilantes waiting on the other side for us. He turned, smiled, and waved to me.

He waded as far as he could into the water and then began to swim. He rose to the top of the water like a dolphin and it churned with the strength of his stroke. His long arms cut through the water, supplemented by his strong kicks. He seemed to glide across the river like those Olympic swimmers you see who were all about six inches taller than him. Still he swam and swam. We could barely see him now in the moonlight. We purposefully wore dark clothing because we didn't know what awaited us on the other side. All of the asylum seekers knew that the Americans couldn't patrol such a long border. We hoped that this spot would be lucky for us with no vigilantes lying in wait. Juan Pablo swam on. Some time later, there was a pull on the end of the line which Tomás held. We let up a silent cheer, pumping our hands in the air.

"You go now, Rosita," Tomás said. I smiled at him and walked along the ledge, careful to watch where the cord was, so that I could grab it if I needed to. I waded into the water. I was amazed at how warm it was. The current didn't seem too strong and I used it to give me some buoyancy. I swam and floated and touched the cord for support and struggled but I made it to the other side. Juan Pablo was waiting.

"Good girl, get out of those wet clothes," he said. We couldn't have a fire because it would attract attention. I went to the other side of the clearing and changed into something a bit warmer, then went back to Juan Pablo.

"Thanks for the line." I put the wet clothes on the outside of my backpack. "I needed it a few times as I went across." He smiled but stayed focused on the river, straining to see which of his two brothers would arrive next. It was Tomás. Of course it would be Tomás. Anselmo, the tall one, would wait until last.

"Ah, Tomi," Juan Pablo cried as if he had been without his brother for years. They clasped each other on the back and hugged tightly, their wide smiles visible in the dark night. Tomás turned to me and made the same movement toward me, *compañeros* all now. He caught himself before he hugged me.

"Ah no, Rosita, I am too wet. We will have our victory hug later." He walked toward the brush to change into dry clothes. Juan Pablo tended the line, holding tight, waiting for any sense that something was amiss. At last Anselmo came across and Juan Pablo greeted him as he had Tomás. "Papí," he cried, letting himself be gathered into the arms of the taller man. "We are here!"

We were so happy and so relieved. I found it hard to share in their joy as we had only reached the shore of the Promised Land. There was so much more we had to do. Right now we were under the treasured darkness and time was precious. Anselmo changed into his clothes and the three were now prepared to move on.

"Thanks so much. Good luck to you." I turned and waved.

"But wait, Rosita, do you know where you are going? Do you have a plan?"

"Well no," I admitted, a bit embarrassed, "I thought I would just go."

"Come with us then," Anselmo said. "We are going to the house of a cousin in Fort Worth, Texas and we have a plan. Do you have family here?"

"No one."

"Then come, right, *pendejos?*" he said, naming the word we all used for *assholes*. They smiled at this. They nodded and we moved off as a team.

The brush was dense and tangled here, and traveling was slow. They had brought machetes and easily hacked their way through. For protection we all had to wear heavy jeans which were hot even in the night time and made our legs sweaty. We walked silently, each lost in his own thoughts. The baby was behaving very well and gave me none of the sickness I had had in the mornings. I drank my water sparingly as I did not want to depend on my boys— as I already called them inside my head—for more than they were already doing.

The time wore on and the moon shone over the desert. All of us were smart enough to have brought dark hats and we walked in a zigzag pattern following nearly invisible paths around the holes and brush which would have tripped us. My legs ached and I knew there would be blisters on my feet but we had to keep going. I could not slow us down. I should have been the last in our line but Juan Pablo was the last and Anselmo was the first. They were shielding me.

As the first rays of the sun touched the earth we stopped in a small grove of cactus that would give us a little shelter. For the first time we could rest and really talk to each other. As we dug into our meager packs for food, we began the connection that so many *mojados* who came before us must have made. We were strangers but the Mexican culture is a strong one; we were family. All Mexicans, no matter where they are in the world, know this.

"So, Rosita, where are you from?"

"I'm from the North. And you three, where are you from?"

"We're brothers from Sinaloa," Anselmo answered for them. "I am the oldest and Tomás is the youngest."

"Your mother must be so upset that she is losing three sons."

"No, she is happy. There was no work out there for us and the *narcos* are getting worse. They cut off the heads of our father and another brother and stuck them on stakes in the village. Everyone fears to associate with us. Our mother wanted us to leave because the drug cartels have targeted our family. They think we are telling the police about them. It wouldn't even matter as the police are part of the gangs anyway. You know this, of course, like all of us Mexicans do. Our mother didn't want to see our heads on stakes. Do you have this problem, too, in your village?"

I don't know what came over me at that moment, but I burst into tears. The picture of Guillermo's body full of bullet holes flashed into my mind and overwhelmed me. I played a whole movie of our embracing and our love making and his death in a split second. I made myself stop crying with a series of gasps.

"I'm so sorry; I don't know what came over me. I lost my boyfriend to the gangs. They shot him in the center of our village and just left his body lying there, full of holes. I had to identify him and he was so pale and so cold. I just got that picture in my mind again. I'm sorry."

"It doesn't matter," Juan Pablo said. "We know how terrible it is to see your family mutilated. It's the last image any of us have of them. Sad."

"Very sad," I agreed.

"So you left for the promised land to get away from the narcos?

"To get away from everything really—no work, violence, no future. To get away and find a better life."

"Yeah, it's gotta be done!" Tomás said. He did not look at me as he spoke; he just gave me that sidelong once-over.

I don't know why I didn't tell them about the baby, or why I had to escape the family of Guillermo. I had that terrible sense of dread when he was killed. I didn't trust anyone and I had to protect the baby. Nely was so important to me. The most important thing in my life. I thought that these three boys would take special care of me if they knew I was pregnant and maybe I would be a burden to them. If they didn't know I was pregnant, perhaps they would treat me as an equal and not as someone delicate and fragile.

With the camouflage tarpaulin they had brought we slept under the sun for many hours, resting our tired feet and our worried minds. One of the brothers cried out in his sleep but we were miles from anyone and likely only the armadillos and the lizards were disturbed. I turned over and laid a hand protectively on my stomach. Nely was asleep.

Anselmo, our leader, routed all of us in the beginning of the evening and helped everyone to pack up. I didn't think about the things I wanted—a hot shower, a soft bed, a big meal. Instead, I made my mind look at the things I had—a baby inside of me, three roadside companions, a chance for a better life. I knew it was these thoughts that would keep me going.

"Look, Anselmo." I pointed to some bits of Mexican fabric sticking to some cactus. It seemed so strange to see this in the middle of the desert.

"We heard about that from a *mojado* who has returned to our village. He told us that *mojados* had left tiny bits of fabric, Mexican fabric, on cacti and branches. We would find rocks turned in opposite ways to show us the direction. Stones and rocks would be arranged in a fashion that would speak to us but which would look random to gringos."

I was amazed that those who went before had left us a roadmap to freedom and we were following it, as had many others. In the morning of the second day, we came upon a little watering hole and some cacti.

"Oh, look! Fresh water." I ran to the hole, getting out my canteen as I went.

"Don't touch that, Rosita," Anselmo called. "It's poisoned." I stopped at the edge of the water.

"How do you know?" I looked longingly at the water.

"You will soon see. But there is another alternative right here." Anselmo cut some cactus into small pieces and then, with his big leather gloves, he wrung it out like a sponge. Beautiful clear water trickled from the cactus into his canteen and he filled up mine as well. He avoided the watering hole.

I couldn't understand why until a few minutes later when we found so many dead animals along the paths leading away from the hole. There were no green plants growing there either. I turned and smiled at Anselmo.

The third night was the night of the full moon. Normally such a clear night would be a blessing for *mojados* but for us it brought fear. If we could see clearly so could anyone pursuing us. We had heard about the vigilantes—armed Americans who had decided that they could help their country by killing 'wet backs.' Many Mexicans who had come back from the United States told horror stories about trying to hide from men with high-powered rifles intent on killing them. Anselmo told us to be extra careful as this was the night when we could be seen. We all made sure our clothes were dark and no one had anything showing that was white. No smiling. No talking.

We crept forward following our invisible path. Suddenly I tripped over something in the path and I sprawled out onto the ground. At the last minute I twisted so that I would land on my side and not on the home I was making for Nely. I groaned. Juan Pablo and Tomás turned and reached down for me.

"Rosita, are you hurt?" Juan Pablo grabbed me with his strong arm and pulled me to my feet.

"Check yourself, Rosita," Anselmo ordered, "you must make sure nothing is broken."

He walked over to the place where I had fallen to inspect the situation. He gasped and hurriedly began to move something from the path.

"What is it? What's there?" I asked. He continued to

drag and push something out of the way. I went over to him. "What is it?" I was scared. Why wasn't he answering me?

I saw now. It was a small child. Maybe six years old. A Mexican child. He seemed peacefully asleep except for the huge piece of his head that was not there. Something had blasted away the whole top of his skull. It left matted hair and dried blood. I ran a few steps away and vomited in the dirt.

"We must bury him, Anselmo," Tomás said.

"No time, Tomi. I'm sorry, but we have to leave him as a gift to the birds and other animals. We can try to cover him a little with some dirt. But we have to keep going. No time. No time."

"Anselmo," Juan Pablo said. "We must bury him." He said this with such finality, such authority. "We cannot leave him to terrify other people coming through. We must do it for us, for them, for him."

There was nothing more to be said. Using a small shovel they had brought and kitchen spoons and gloves and shoes and hats and rocks, we dug at the sand and formed a hole large enough for our small package. Tomás gingerly picked up the little boy and folded him into a protective ball with the missing part of his skull facing down. When we looked at him from above now he looked perfect: a small boy asleep in the desert. We bowed our heads, each saying his own prayer, and then we covered him with dirt. No gravestone marked the passing of our little angel. We moved on.

The days soon got lost one after the other. At night we walked, sticking to the underbrush, and dressed in dark clothing. During the days we slept in whatever shelter we could find. The brothers had a small machine with them that told them where we were, maybe some kind of GPS. They had mapped out a route using maps that they could see on the computer. The maps showed them where we could walk and they also had spoken with other *mojados* who had come back to Mexico to be with their families. With all of this information and the invisible trail left by our brothers and sisters, we were able to make progress. They told me we would eventually come out of the desert and there would be a diner where we could get some real food and there was a bus there also. Once we came to the diner we could go deeper and deeper into our own promised land.

I didn't even know how many days had passed now. Everything started blending together with the backwards life of staying awake at night and sleeping during the day. Several times as we were walking, I found myself straggling and the boys rested while I caught up. No one said anything. They consulted their little machine many times. I didn't think it would work in the middle of nowhere but we all gathered round it and talked. I just followed.

One early morning, we reached another place where we could sleep. I had a threadbare sock which I needed to fix. I soaked the sock in a small bit of water and added some salt from my pack.

"Why are you wasting water, Rosita? If you don't want it, we can use it." Tomás glared at me.

"I'm sorry, Tomás, but I must do this. My feet are full of blisters and I must try to heal them with salt water tonight before we go tomorrow."

"You don't really have to go with us, you know. We are

brothers. We go together, but you can go on your own. You were on your own when we met you."

"Oh, I didn't realize I was a burden to you. I thought we were *compadres* traveling together."

"A woman is always a burden. We have to watch what we say around you. We have to check for your comfort. We have to walk at your pace. You are a burden."

"Tomi!" Anselmo glared at his brother. "Pay no attention to him, Rosita. We are tired. We are irritable. He doesn't mean what he says." Anselmo began to wrap the salted water sock around my feet. The salt stung and I winced.

"That hurts? Good. That means it is healing your feet."

"You're not the boss, Anselmo," Tomás said.

"Please, Tomi, no squabbling." Juan Pablo was burying our trash. "We knew there would be others on the road. We knew we would travel together with our Mexican compatriots. We knew we would have to make efforts to accommodate each other. Breathe a deep breath. Breathe a deep breath."

Tomás did not look pleased. I smiled at Anselmo for helping me with my feet and I lay down on the ground with my feet on my backpack. The salt continued to sting but I knew that this would be the best solution for my blisters and my pain.

"I will try to walk faster tomorrow, Tomás," I said, right before falling asleep.

III

In the late afternoon, I woke to the sound of some animal running through the brush. I woke with a start, unsure where I was. There was no one around me. There was nothing. I was totally alone in the bush. The brothers were gone. I lay down for a moment and stared at the departing sun. I would never know the discussion that had prompted them to leave. Did Tomás argue for the burden I was causing them? Did Anselmo reply that we were compatriots? Did Juan Pablo stay out of the discussion, preferring to play the conciliator?

It didn't matter, did it? I never thought to travel with anyone else. I always thought it would just be Nely and me. Now it was. That was that. I had little to gather so I collected what I had and I set out. I had heard the brothers discussing the way and I followed the Mexican escape route. I knew that within the night I would come to a place where I could find some transportation. My feet felt fine. I would be OK.

I walked most of the night and, as they had promised, there was a little truck stop on the highway that was all lit up. It looked like an oasis in the desert; I walked into a brightly lit diner with no customers except for one old man who was asleep in a booth.

"*Buenas noches,*" I said to the waitress. I smiled.

"*Buenas noches, senorita,*" she said. Her name tag said

Dolores. She looked me in the eye and of course she knew. Why would a young girl be in the desert in the middle of the night by herself? Dolores spoke to me in Spanish, not even trying for English.

"Would you like something to drink?" she asked. "If you want something to eat, the menu's on the wall."

"Coffee, please." I looked at the menu and started translating it. "Two eggs and ham, please."

"Do you want potatoes or beans or tortillas or toast?"

"Thank you. Eggs and potatoes and beans and toast."

"Coming right up. I was getting a bit lonely tonight, nice to have the company."

She went to the back and returned without the little piece of paper where she had written the order. She sat down at the counter and lit a cigarette. I watched the smoke curl around her face.

"Don't worry. When no one's in here, I always have a smoke. I figured you wouldn't mind."

"No. It's OK, enjoy. Are you Mexican?" I asked.

"Honey, everyone here is Mexican. They were either born there or their parents were born there or they wish they were born there. We're all Mexicans."

I wish this were so. I watched Dolores smoke. I didn't really have much to say because I thought I had so much to hide. A little bell rang.

"That's your food, honey. I'll be back in a sec. I'll get you some catsup and some hot sauce too." She pushed herself up from the counter and shuffled back through the swinging doors.

"Here you go, sweetie." She put the steaming plate in front of me. The beans had run into the potatoes, but everything smelled great. "Here's some toast too. We put butter on it here in America so you better start learning the ways." *Was it so obvious?* I thought.

"How long you been moving, honey?" I was devouring the food like an animal at a watering hole.

"A while, I'm not really sure. Where am I?" I said, not even taking a breath.

"Hmm, you're in the middle of nowhere, honey, but not so far from Alice, Texas. Still, one day at a time, huh? What's your name?"

"Rositalia, but everyone calls me Rosita."

"That's a right pretty name. Mine's Dolores, but I guess you know that because it's written here on my chest. Let me take a look at you. You need to make some changes or you'll never fit in." She had turned me around in my chair with my fork still in my mouth. She eyed me up and down.

"Changes?" I didn't know what she meant.

"I seen a lot of girls like you. They come this far, which is really far, by the way. You made a lot of progress. But then, they get caught on account of the way they look. You're the right size, being small and all, and dark. There's a lot of Mexicans who are Americans now and they're all about your size and coloring. But you stick out. Like your clothes. No one from Texas would wear nylon gym pants like those. No one would wear a nylon t-shirt with 'Sexy Bitch' on it in English. You see what I mean, who's going to wear a shirt that says "*puta*"? I gotta do somethin' for you." She pulled herself up from the counter again and smashed the burning cigarette into the ashtray. "Be back in a minute." I looked down at my cheap market t-shirt and realized she was right, of course. No one would pay any attention to those English words in Mexico but here they all knew what *sexy bitch* meant. I didn't even think about that.

I continued to eat my food. Dolores had given me three eggs and a plate full of potatoes and beans, and I wasn't stopping. I had never eaten so much in my life. I had those little protein powders and the bread I had carried, but they were not enough. This was real food. I was sure it tasted terrible, but to me it was delicious. I focused on the plate and ate and ate. I heard the swinging door open after a while.

Dolores came through with an arm full of clothes. "Let's see now, these should fit you. They were my daughter's. She outgrew them. I keep planning to take them to Goodwill, but I never seem to find the time. Let's see now." She took the shirt and held it against my back while I ate. "Yeah, that looks like it'll fit just fine. The tricky ones'll be the jeans. Everyone in Texas wears jeans no matter how hot it gets. You'll have to get used to wearing jeans. But jeans're tough to fit. You'll have to try these on when you get finished."

"Thank you," I said in between bites. "You are very kind."

"Well, it just seems to me that things are tough down there in Mexico or wherever you come from. People is always comin' through here tryin' to get into the States and do somethin' with their lives. I think it's kinda brave. You're just a slip of a girl. It musta been hard for you to get this far."

I smiled at her. She understood; I didn't have to add any words. I ate. Finally I finished. The food was so good that it filled me with a spirit, like a holy ghost or something. Maybe Nely was really hungry, too, and I was getting her feeling of gratitude. I stood up smiling and looked around for the bathroom.

"Lawdy, child, you are pregnant." She had spied my bump.

"Yes, that's why I had to get to America, to give my baby a better life."

"Don't worry, I'll help you. The bathroom is at the other end. Wait a second."

I stood waiting, but I had to go to the bathroom real bad. I wished she would hurry up. She came back into the diner with an armload of something.

"Here, Sugar. Here's shampoo and soap and towels. You take a nice bath in the sink in there. There ain't no one there save the cook and he don't care about nothin'. Just wash yourself good. There's a hand dryer in there; you can put your head under it and use it for your hair. I'll help you to comb it out. You can't wear that long plait in the back. No Texas gal would wear that. In fact, I think I need to cut your hair. Sorry, but you need to be more modern here. You look like a *mojada*. Sorry, I didn't mean no harm. Here, take the shirts and the jeans, too. Try them on."

"Thank you."

I took the things she gave me and went into the bathroom. It was beautiful: clean and shiny with three stalls and four sinks. I had lots of room to spread out. I took off my dirty clothes and threw them into the bin. I undid my braid and put my head under the faucet and felt the luxury of warm water cascading down my hair. I used the wash cloth and scrubbed the deep dirt off of my legs and feet. I climbed up on the vanity and put my feet and legs across the sinks so that I could really clean them. The rinse water ran black with the grime of the trip. I took my time as I didn't know when I would get another chance to get so clean. I scrubbed and scrubbed trying to get every last bit of dirt off of me. Finally I bent over the dryer and dried my hair. I washed my dirty underwear in the sink and put it back in my backpack. I put on my new shirt and pulled the jeans up over my belly. They were too big.

"Let me see, here, don't you look great. Oh yes, yes, these jeans are a bit big but you are going to grow into them, if you know what I mean." She winked at me. "Hold on a sec."

She left again and I looked at my reflection in the mirror. I looked so different dressed in the clothes of a Texan. I could hardly recognize the girl from the village in Mexico. I turned sideways and examined the jeans against the bump of my belly. They were a little big.

"Here you go." She produced a belt and began circling my waist. "There, that should work." She backed up to survey her work. "Yep, that'll keep those jeans up until the baby grows."

"Nely," I said.

"Nely?"

"Her name's Nely. The baby."

"Oh, so you know it's a girl, do you?"

"Yes, she's Nely."

She smiled at me. "OK, Sugar, Nely it is." She sat down and lit another cigarette. We sat in silence while she smoked. I hoped she had forgotten about my hair.

"Come around back then." She stubbed the cigarette out and led the way through the swinging doors. The cook was asleep on some sacks of flour, snoring contentedly. We passed by him and went out a big door into the parking lot. "You sit there," she said, bringing around a chair, "under that light." She pointed to a light which illuminated the parking lot and I dutifully sat down. She went back through the door. In a minute she returned with big scissors. I started to cry.

"Now, now. This ain't no big deal. Hair is one of the most forgiving things on the planet. You can hack it off. You can burn it. You can bleach it or iron it or curl it or perm it and it still comes back. It still forgives you no matter what you do to it and it grows back. Yours will too. Just for now you need to look like a Texan. I wish I had some hair spray and mousse and all of that stuff so I could tease your hair up like a helmet. Then you would really be a Texan."

With that she started cutting and I felt the hair leave me and float to earth. I was really sad but I was also so astonished that a complete stranger would help me like this.

"Do you help everyone?" I asked.

"Nope. You're the very first. I think most people are damn idiots and I don't even want to give them the time of day. But you, honey, you are a person in need. And Jesus told us to help those who are in need. I am just doin' my Christian duty. And it feels real nice." She didn't stop cutting.

"There. You look like a Texas gal now. You got real pretty hair, honey. It's thick and wavy and now it looks real *chick*. I think that's what them French people call it: *chick*. Come on up. Let me look at you."

I stood up and she walked around me, appreciating the change. I stood silently, not knowing whether to smile or cry. I knew she was helping me. I knew what she was saying was true. But I felt my self, my Mexican self, disappearing, and I did not know who this new person was. I put my hand on my belly and protected Nely from the unknown. Dolores grabbed me then in a big hug and I buried myself in the bosom of a mother.

"Thank you," I croaked out. "I won't ever be able to repay you."

"Jesus didn't ask us for no repayment plan, honey. You just take care of Nely. Listen. I been thinkin'. I don't have much, but I have that little trailer yonder." She pointed to a small trailer at the edge of the parking lot. "It's only got one bedroom, but there's a bench that makes into a bed and a nice shower and a little kitchen. Well, we don't need the kitchen because we can always eat here at the diner. I was wondrin' if you might like to stay for a few days. We could use a real clean-up of the diner and you would help us a lot. We could feed you and you could stay in that little bed and keep me company. Might even be able to rustle up a few American dollars for your work. What do you think?"

I was overwhelmed by her offer and tears sprang to my eyes. "I don't know what to say. I am so thankful."

"You can just say 'yes.'" Dolores gave me a hug. "You remind me of my daughter and I don't get to see her enough. C'mon, let's go look at the trailer." She led me across the parking lot to the blue trailer. The door was tin and made a little squeak when she opened it. She walked in front of me up the steps and then moved aside when we were inside.

"It ain't much, but it's home sweet home." She walked over to the little table. "Looky here, the table goes down and these two benches go on top of it and you have a nice little bed." She went down the hall.

"This is the bathroom. It has a nice shower and even a

bathtub." I stuck my head inside and it was much bigger than I had expected. Dolores continued down the hallway.

"This here's my room. Not much, but it's fine for me now. I'm a widow and I don't ask much of people. I mind my own business, if you know what I mean. So what do you think?"

I put my arms around Dolores and hugged her. "Thank you so much," I said.

"Listen, honey. You're all clean now and I'm sure you're tuckered out. My shift goes for a few more hours so why don't you just lie down here on top of my bed. I'll get you some linens and you can just go to sleep. Would that be good?"

"That would be wonderful." I sat on the edge of the bed while she searched in the cupboard and brought me a pillow, blanket, and pillowcase. I helped her spread the blanket on top of the bed and I put the pillow into its case.

"Good night then, honey. I need to get back to the diner. Oh, by the way, we best be talkin' English now. You'll need the practice. You do speak some English, don't you?" She turned to go. I nodded.

"Thanks so much, Dolores," I said in English. I took off my shoes and lay down on the bed the moment I heard the front door close. I melted into its comfort. I had almost forgotten what it felt like to be comfortable. It was heaven.

I didn't realize it was so late in the day when I woke up. Dolores must have come in early because she was purring softly in the bed next to me. I looked at the clock on the sideboard and it was almost five o'clock in the afternoon. I wasn't sure when Dolores started work but I thought I'd better be quiet.

I snuck out of the room and tiptoed through the hallway until I got to the front door of the trailer. I carefully turned the handle and closed the door silently. The heat of the day was still strong and the wind was whipping up little dust bunnies. I crossed the parking lot and went toward the back door of the diner. I wasn't sure what to do, but I thought I'd best introduce myself as I was going to be hanging around this place anyway.

The cook, a big Mexican man, was sitting on an upside down white bucket smoking a cigarette. His lap served to hold several rolls of fat that were comfortably positioned there. His arm fat jiggled as he brought the cigarette up to his jowly face. He had deep dark hair that was just peeking out from under his hairnet and a white paper hat. He smiled broadly.

"Who you?" The smoke came out of his nose and mouth as he asked the question.

"I'm Rosita." I put out my hand to take his and he offered it after he transferred the cigarette to the other one. "I'm staying with Dolores for a little while."

"That's nice. I'm sure she could use the company. I'm Alberto. We immigrants gotta stay together." He winked at me. "You hungry? I could make you some eggs."

"I am a little hungry, but I don't want to put you to any trouble. Could I just make them myself?"

"Go ahead, honey. I'm fixin' to start work soon. This is my biggest break; the guys will be stopping by here on their way home. There's some guys drilling for oil in some godforsaken place near here and they stop by for steak and fries every night on their way home. We'll be busy. You go on and make some grub for yourself and I'll just set a spell."

"Thanks." I went through the back door and let the screen door slam. I made a mental note to catch it next time. The kitchen was set up for quick cooking with a grill and three burners. I found eggs and milk and cheese in the refrigerator. I threw some water on the grill and the beads shot up so I knew it was plenty hot. I found a bowl and scrambled the eggs into the bowl and added the milk. I threw in some salt and pepper and poured the concoction on the grill. The eggs started to cook in a flash and I had to scurry to find the spatula in time to turn them. I put two tortillas on the grill. Within minutes everything was ready and I sat on the sacks of flour which served as the cook's bed the night before, eating my eggs. In a few minutes, Alberto came in. He let the screen door slam behind him.

"I guess you found everything you needed." He walked across the kitchen to a big refrigerator and started taking things out of it and piling them on the counter.

"Yes. It was easy. Everything was where I expected it to be."

"That's the secret to short-order cooking. You gotta have everything in a place that makes sense and is easy to get to. I can't be wasting time rummaging around trying to find stuff." He talked to me with his head still stuck in the refrigerator and his arms coming out stacking things.

"Can I do something to help?" I carried my plate and fork and the spatula to the sink and washed them. I dried them on a towel and put them back where I found them.

"You know, there is something you can do. All of the condiments need to be filled on the tables. You know, the salt, pepper, hot sauce. The big containers are over there in the pantry." He pointed to a doorway across the room.

"OK. I can do that." I went into the pantry and the

condiments were all neatly stacked side-by-side. I got out huge catsup and hot sauce bottles and the salt and pepper containers. I brought them into the center of the diner and left them on a table. Back in the pantry, I found mustard, red sauce, and green sauce, and I carried these as well.

I went table to table filling each container with its condiment. I was really careful as I didn't want to skip any tables. It wasn't unpleasant work but I was pretty sure I didn't want to spend my life doing it. When I was finished, I took all of the big containers back and put them in their proper places in the pantry.

"I finished the condiments, Alberto. I think I'll just give the floor a quick sweep before the guys arrive." I found the broom in the same pantry and swept the floor. The dust was thick in there and it took me a long while to do the work.

"Come on in here, Rosita." Dolores was in the door, tying her apron. "I don't want you here when the guys come. We're never sure if a homeland security guy will turn up or not and you can't be around. Can you go on back to the trailer and find something to do? Do you have any clothes to wash? There's a washer and dryer in the trailer and you can wash your clothes. There's a TV in the living room. After these guys leave, I'll come have a smoke with you."

"OK, thanks." I waved to Alberto as I was leaving.

"Good idea to hide out." He winked again. "You never know."

I followed the advice of Dolores and washed out my clothes in the washing machine. It was easy to follow the instructions in the lid because there were pictures. I piled in all the dark clothes and set the washing machine to heavy soil. The desert was not kind to my stuff. I even threw in the backpack.

While the machine was chugging, I went outside and busied myself with the parking lot behind the building. I started by picking up all of the trash that had accumulated over time and putting it in the dumpster. I could hear the front screen slamming over and over and the clomping of the boots as the men came in on their way home from the rigs. The banging door and the booming male voices meant the level of noise rose and rose until it was a din. I could hear Alberto moving around the kitchen and the squeaking of Dolores's trainers. The men yelled out orders for more beers, but no one asked for hot sauce or salt or pepper so I felt I had done a good job.

After I picked up the trash I started sweeping the back lot. I didn't want to go inside because I wasn't sure there were no border police there. It might have been hard to explain the sudden appearance of a young Mexican girl. Even if I were introduced as the "niece" who had never been mentioned before, it might have been a stretch. Dolores and I looked enough alike to pass for family and most of the gringos probably couldn't tell that we weren't. But the cops whose families were Mexican would be able to tell. They would see the difference in skin color and texture of hair and face shape to know that Dolores and I shared heritage but not family. I put the broom away after I finished and went back to my washing. I found a clothesline behind the trailer. Even though it was getting towards nightfall, I knew the clothes would dry in the night time heat. I came around the front of the trailer to find Dolores and the cook sitting on upside down plastic buckets smoking cigarettes. They both looked tired.

"I heard a lot of noise in there. Must've been a lot of men." I walked over to them and squatted out of the path of the curling smoke.

"Many men." Alberto took a drag.

"But they're easy, you know." Dolores stubbed her cigarette out but picked it up and put it in the trash bag at her feet. "They've all had days of hard work and they want basic comfort food. Lots of them are away from their families. They work. They eat. They go to a bar and drink some beers and they go to sleep. They don't demand much. You can bet they're all going to have steaks—well done—and fries and beer. No greens for these guys. Not very demanding and very predictable, the waitress's dream customer."

"You cleaned up out here." Antonio motioned across the lot. "Good girl."

"I like that, honey. You just seen somethin' that needed to be done and you did it. I like that."

The screen door slammed then as the two of them got up and went back into the diner to return to work. I stayed in the lot staring at the stars in a place that had been so scary and dangerous just a day before and now seemed so sweet.

IV

I stayed on the schedule of the Full Moon diner with Alberto and Dolores. In truth it was like two diners. During the day, it was full of school kids dropping by for sodas and junk food and toward evening it was the workmen and the travelers that passed through on the highway. There was a day cook and a day waitress and there was Dolores and Alberto at night. I never saw the day people as Dolores thought it might be dangerous. We passed our time together as people living in the night. She worked and I used my time to clean everything. There were big jobs both in the kitchen and in the never-cleaned cupboards of Dolores's home.

"You certainly surprised Nanny." Dolores came into the trailer with two big plates full of ribs and cornbread for us. "She never seen the pantry so clean."

"Is she the day cook?" I took one of the plates from Dolores and put it on the table where I had already put our plastic placemats and napkins.

"Yeah, she's a sweet young thing from a trailer park down the road. She's closer to the age of the kids and parents who come during the day than me and Alberto. She couldn't figure out how I found the time to take everything out of the pantry and clean it all off and clean the shelves and put everything back. I told her I had a slow night. Just want you to know your work is appreciated."

She was shoving her bulk behind the little table across from me.

"It's nice to hear. I'm going to work on the shed tomorrow night." I cut into the steak which Alberto made for me with the blood still coming out. It tasted terrific. "So how'd you get yourself here, Dolores, were you born near here?"

"My story ain't a sad one, Rosita. My folks come from a small town near here and they was tenant farmers on the land of a rich man. But he was fair. He give us a nice house and he give us the land to use. My daddy told me that he only had to pay a percentage of the profits to Mr. Johnson and it weren't too much. I worked a bit too with the chores. There's always lots to do on the land."

"But what about your daughter?" I was munching a French fry while I talked.

"Oh, you know. I got married when I was about your age. Folks marry young on farms. He had him a little farm too. Nice man. Henry. We had us a daughter right away. Sharilee. She was the sweetest baby. Never cried. Smiled all the time. Now she's the sweetest grown-up woman with her own babies. She lives all the way over to the other side of the state so I don't see her much. I go to the library in town once a month and have a nice talk with her over that new Skype thing. It's great to see her and the grandbabies. But she's got her own life. She's nearly thirty-five now."

"And Henry?" I hesitated to ask.

"Oh, Henry died in a freak accident, honey. He was up on the tractor working and there was a rock blocking the way. Henry wasn't thinking. I guess he thought he could just jump down off the tractor and get that rock out of the way in a hurry. But the tractor had other ideas. It ran him down. They guessed it was the way he was bending over to pick up the rock or somethin' and it just killed him on the spot. I never asked for the explanation. Didn't care really. My Henry was gone and it didn't matter how." She was wiping the catsup off her plate with a piece of bread.

"But you never re-married?" I picked up her plate and utensils and carried them to the sink.

"Nah, honey, how was I goin' to have another man as good as Henry in my life? It wouldn'ta been fair to some other man. No one would've been as good as my Henry. He was one-of-a-kind. I'll give you an example. A neighbor woman lost her husband. They had a big yard and Henry knew it was gonna be hard for her to cut that grass every week. He never talked to her about it. He just went over there on the tractor when she went to church every Sunday and he cut the grass. She musta thought it was the good Lord doin' it. He never took credit. Never said a thing. That was my Henry." She stopped talking then and went inside her head and stayed there with Henry. She nodded to me and went outside to smoke a cigarette.

I did the dishes in the small sink and dried them with a clean towel. She made me wonder if I would ever find anyone as good as Guillermo. She was right. When you find a good man you can't believe you will ever be so lucky again. I understood her completely.

I stayed with Dolores and Alberto for two weeks and then I thought I had been there enough. You can only take advantage of people's hospitality for so long before it just gets to be too much. I knew it was going to be sad to go but I had to get on. Dolores knew it too because I was running out of jobs. We were eating dinner early in the morning like we did and I brought it up.

"I think I need to be going, Dolores," I said with my biscuit poised in mid-air. I thought I was very tough but when I said it tears sprang into my eyes.

"I know you do, honey. Makes me real sad too." She reached over and put her hand over mine. "I can't keep you livin' in a trailer in the middle of nowhere hidin' out from the law. It ain't right. I just wanted you to be safe for a spell. To get your bearings." She kept her hand over mine.

"I know. I know what you did for me and why you did it, and me and Nely will be forever grateful." I was happy to have her hand over mine.

"You're more than welcome, Rosita." The tears were running down her face now.

"I just want to tell you that there was a very good reason for my having to leave Mexico. I told you that Guillermo was shot in a hail of bullets from the cartels. What I didn't tell you was that I was there. I saw the man who shot him. *El Leon*. The Lion. I knew at the time that he didn't see me but someone else did. Cristina saw me running away from the shooting and she knew I must have seen it. Others saw someone running away but didn't know it was me. Cristina was a friend of mine. She swore she would never tell and for a long time she didn't. *El Leon* put out the word that he needed to find the witness and he was offering a big reward. Cristina is not a rich girl but she still didn't betray me. I knew it was just a matter of time.

"We live in an area of Mexico that is very poor. We have to buy all of the water we use in five gallon plastic bottles. Some people have cisterns and they can have a truck bring in their water. Cristina came from a family of five children. How did they find the money each week to pay for the plastic bottles of water? Imagine not being able to turn on the faucet whenever you like. Most of the people scratch out a living with little farms and we barter with each other for things. My mom and I can sew so we trade that service to others for repairing the house or fixing the stove. We have electricity but the cost is so high that we use kerosene lamps at night. No one can get sick because the nearest doctor is one hundred and seventy miles away and you better have money to pay for a bus to get there. So Cristina ignoring the reward to turn me in was really a strong thing to do.

"Suddenly the effort to identify me increased. I don't know why, never did really. *El Leon* offered two thousand dollars, enough to buy water for a year for the whole family. Still Cristina did not tell. Finally, in frustration he did what the Nazis used to do. He threatened to kill six people in the village until the witness came forward or someone told. Cristina was really scared then, and so was I and we had to do something. I decided to leave. I knew this would make me look guilty to *El Leon* but he would have no reason to harm her family—they had seen nothing. So I left."

"Oh Rosita, I am so sorry. So many terrible things you had to see in your life. So much pain for someone so young." She came around the table and pulled me to my feet and gave me a big hug. It felt so safe and warm in her arms. "I hope the rest of your story is a happy and a healthy one. Alberto and I have come to love you very much and to me you are one more of my grandbabies." She gave me a big kiss then. "How soon do you want to leave?"

"It will have to be tomorrow." I said it with such certainty that it was impossible to take it back.

"OK, honey. Let's get your bed fixed up so you can get some sleep. Tomorrow will be a long day for you." She gave me a final hug after helping me put the bed down and went into her room.

The next night I was ready. The place was spotless and my clothes were clean. I kissed Alberto good-bye and promised to write to him.

"Rosita honey, Jesse will be here at about five, so you need to eat somethin'." Dolores was talking to me through the screen door of the trailer.

"Who's Jesse?" I asked.

"Oh, he's the bus driver, honey. He's real nice. I'll talk with him about you and he can help you. He came over by himself on the river a long time ago and he knows what it's like. He'll watch out for you 'til Dallas." She handed me a big plate of food. "I needs to be goin' back now. For some reason, we got customers in the middle of the night." She ran back into the kitchen.

By the time the bus came I was ready. I had kissed Dolores and we had both cried and both made those promises to keep in touch. I knew I would never forget such kindness.

I talked to Jesse as he was waiting for people to begin showing up for the first bus of the day. He took me to the back of the bus and told me to pull a cap down over my face and go to sleep. I dug into my pocket for money.

"I gotta pay the bill for my ticket."

"No, Miss Dolores done paid for your ticket," Jesse said.

"Oh, I gotta go thank her." I stood up to go.

"She knows, Rosita," Jesse said. "You just go to sleep like I told you. You're on your way. She knows you're grateful." Jesse walked to the front of the bus and opened the door. He locked it when he left. He was right, of course she knew she had saved me. First the lady across the river on the bus, then the three brothers, and now Dolores. I was living under a lucky star.

I woke up hours later. The sun was nearly setting. I must've slept all day. The bus was loping along on a superhighway of some kind. Most of the people had on cowboy hats and they were connected to their little machines. Not too much talking was going on.

I was in the last seat of the bus and no one had sat next to me. I had a gravelly taste in my mouth so I dug into the bag and found the toothbrush and toothpaste. I gave my teeth a dry brush and swallowed the toothpaste. That felt better. I had a washcloth and used it to wash off my face. I went to grab my braid out of habit and forgot for a moment that it was gone. Chopped off in the back of the diner. I sighed. Hair forgives.

There wasn't much scenery. Just some scrub and some cactus. I knew we were going to a big city now. Somewhere where I could blend in. We all took lists of contacts with us. We *mojados*. We didn't know where we would end up so we tried to get addresses and phone numbers for places all through Arizona and Texas. I got out my list to find some contacts in Dallas. I had two: Maria Ofelia, the daughter of the owner of the tortilla shop in my town, and Cruz, the cousin of Antonio who had given me the money. I had phone numbers and addresses for both of these but, of course, they didn't know me and I didn't know them. I didn't even know if they had papers or if they were under the radar, like I was now.

The bus finally reached its destination and all of the people unfolded from their seats and started collecting their belongings. I tried to make myself small, pulled my cap down over my eyes, and tightened the belt on my jeans. I walked slowly down the aisle, the last person to leave.

"Good luck, Miss," Jesse said, winking at me.

"Thanks for everything," I said in English. It was my first attempt to mimic the words I had heard a million times in class and on TV and practiced with Dolores.

The Dallas bus station was very busy. People were waiting and walking around and eating and doing all of the things a big bus station would offer. There was an information booth at the end of the corridor. I knew that I had to act as if I was American now, I certainly looked like it. So I moved with confidence.

"*Señora*," I began. "Can you tell me how to take a bus here?" I pointed to the name of the street where Cruz lived. I hoped my English was close enough and she would not ask me any questions I couldn't understand or answer.

"Hmm, let's see here. Yeah. I have the street right here on my screen. Let me see the house number again." She took my piece of paper and typed the house number. She smiled at me.

"Yes, here it is. I'll print you out the directions. It says you only have to take two buses." She handed me a piece of paper that had just come out of the printer. "*Gracías*," I said, out of habit.

"*De nada*," she answered. I guess Spanish was so common here that even the *gringas* knew some words.

I had to get some money now and this would be my

first challenge. I had been living on the road with the brothers eking out my protein powder and Dolores made sure I never needed any money the whole time I was with her, so I hadn't had to get to the money. I had a little bit of glue with me and a tiny knife. I went into the bathroom and into the stalls. I locked it up tight and put my backpack far from the door so no one could reach over or under and steal it. I took off my shoe and made a little slit in the place where the sole meets the upper part and there was the money. I took out enough pesos to get me through for a while. I closed the sole back up after adding a bit of glue and then I hopped up and down to put enough pressure on the glue to attach again. It worked. I went to the change booth and changed the pesos into dollars. With the money I'd earned with Dolores and this money, I thought I would have enough for a while.

I could see the list of platforms and I found my bus and went to wait by the platform. There was a map of the bus route on the wall. I had plenty of time to study it. The paper in my hand listed the bus number for the first bus and told me the stop for the second bus and the name of the final stop at my destination. I found the first bus on the map and traced it with my finger until it came to the stop. I wrote down the stop before that one. Then I followed the second bus with my finger until it reached my final stop. I wrote down the stop before that one too. I had more time so I counted the number of stops before my transfer and the number of stops to my final stop. There were a lot. I knew I was going out to a barrio, West Dallas, and not to the center of town. I guess Cruz didn't become a millionaire after he got here. With all of the information about stops and transfers I felt confident to easily make my journey.

The bus was actually nice. It was modern and clean and people seemed to enjoy riding it. I was so focused on counting the stops that I didn't get to do much else. Dallas seemed like a huge city spread out all over the place. I knew it would be hard for me and Nely to live here. I had my arms folded protectively across my stomach. Everyone on the bus looked like me, they were even dressed like me. I was really glad that Dolores had changed me into a Texan so fast. I had to smile.

We got to my first stop. I had watched people when we got on the bus and I had done the same as they did— showed my ticket to the driver. Now I watched them push the buzzer in the back just like we do in Mexico and get off the bus. Many of them started walking but others waited. I waited for a while and didn't start any conversations in Spanish or English. The people didn't seem to want to talk anyway as most of them had earphones in their ears or were typing things into their phones. No one was connecting with anyone else. This made me a little sad. In Mexico we would have started chatting with strangers the minute we met them.

The bus came after about an hour. I saw the number on the front. I didn't want to be the first one on the bus because I wasn't sure what to do. I let an old lady go before me and she thought I was being very courteous. I smiled at her. When she got on the bus, she showed her ticket to the driver and so did I. No one talked so I didn't either.

As we moved along on this bus I got a sinking feeling as I watched us leaving nice houses with lawns and cars in the driveways. We moved over a bridge and I saw us move into an area that was not nearly as nice. The houses got smaller and smaller and the yards started filling up with old cars and old junk. People were sitting around on the front porches smoking or talking. No one seemed to be at work. These are my people, I thought.

The bus pulled beside the curb and I got off at my stop. No one else got off the bus and it sped away. I walked down the street following the numbers until I got to 235. It was a house like my house in Mexico. It looked run down and dusty and the yard was full of junk. There were two guys sitting on the steps.

"What you want, girl?" one asked me.

"I'm lookin' for someone." I didn't go inside the fence.

"Who dat?" One of the boys moved toward me, rubbing his stomach under his t-shirt. He had on a pair of long shorts and his baseball cap was at an angle on his head. He moved like a crab coming at me sideways.

"Cruz, I'm lookin' for Cruz." I didn't trust him.

"He be out. Why you want him?"

"I was sent by Antonio, the baker's son in my village. He's his cousin."

"Oh yeah, we know about him. We be Cruz's cousins too, but his mom's side. His mom and our mom are sisters." He had totally dropped the attitude when he realized I was family. "We know about him. C'mon in. Did you just get here from somewhere?" He looked at my backpack.

"I just got off the bus."

"Well, come on in. I'm Javier, well Javi, and this is my brother Alfonso. Call him Poncho." He pointed his hand at his brother like he was introducing a television star.

I came into the fence and followed him into the house. The floorboards creaked under my feet. The inside was a disaster. Clothes and dishes and takeout boxes were strewn all over the place going from sofa to coffee table to the floor. It didn't seem like these guys ever cleaned up. I looked for evidence of a woman. There was none.

"Sorry 'bout the mess but you know we are really busy." Poncho said this as he tried to move trash from one stack to another.

"Don't worry about it. It doesn't matter." It was easy to say the Mexican mantra, *no pasa nada*. But it really did matter. These guys lived in filth. Their Mexican mothers would be horrified. I put my hand over my stomach, shielding Nely from the sight of her *compadres* living like this.

"You wanna coke or somethin'?" Javi offered.

"That would be great," I said. "Do you know when Cruz will be home?"

"Let's see," he said. "It's Sunday today, you know, and he's out at a bar. I think maybe he'll be home soon." He seemed to feel comfortable with me now that I showed I didn't want anything.

"Is that right, Poncho?" He looked toward his brother as he led me into the kitchen that looked like it had been ransacked. He dug out a clean glass from the cupboard and put coke into it over the ice cubes he found deep in the freezer.

"Think so," Poncho said. "You hungry?" He looked at me.

"I am really," I said.

"OK, we can order pizza. All of the gringos order pizza. I'm thinkin' you haven't been in America long. Am I right?"

I smiled and shook my head. I didn't know anything

about the place. But people had helped me. I knew that. I knew Dolores and Alberto and Jesse had done something pretty special for a girl and her baby who they didn't know and would never see again. I knew that much about American people.

"OK, we're gonna order pizza now and you can wait. Do you need somethin'?"

"Do you think I could take a shower?"

"You stupid, Javi, course the girl needs a shower. Go get me a towel and take her to the bathroom. Stupid shit." Poncho moved into the living room and turned on the TV set. The show was in English.

"Come on here." Javi walked me through the house to a bathroom in the back. It was very clean compared to the rubble we had just walked through. I sighed with relief, at least the bathroom wouldn't kill me with germs.

"What's your name?" Javi handed me the towel.

"Cece," I answered. I had to use my real name because of my connection to Cruz's cousin in my pueblo. I walked into the bathroom and smiled at him as I closed the door behind me. I waited until I heard his steps walking away and then bolted the door. I didn't want to insult him but I wasn't taking any chances. I got undressed and got into a hot shower. It felt wonderful after the dusty bus ride. I let the soapy water drip down on my stomach and put my hand on my baby. Such a strange thing to all of a sudden be responsible for a whole 'nother life. So strange.

I heard voices outside in the yard and hurried up and finished. I guess Cruz was home. I dried my hair as best I could and put on clean clothes.

"Hi," I smiled, putting my hand out for Cruz.

"You here, girl! Antonio emailed me to maybe be

expecting you but I didn't really believe him. It's a real trip for girls to make it on their own. You done good. Let me look at you. You real pretty. Antonio said you was pretty. You a tiny thing, not much fat on you." He leered at me. Made me uncomfortable.

"I'm so glad to be here. I didn't really think I was goin' to make it but here I am." I tried to act like it was really light and easy. Like nothing was complicated. "Antonio said you might be able to put me up for a while."

"Sure thing, honey." Cruz put his arm around me and pulled me close to his side. My breasts were touching him. "We always got room for a sweet thing like you. We're practically cousins what with you knowing Antonio and all. We'll get along just fine."

"Hey Cruz, we ordered pizza." Poncho was standing in the doorway. Cruz moved away a tiny bit from holding me.

"Good move, man," Cruz said. "You was thinkin'."

Poncho smiled at the compliment. He walked back in the kitchen and started moving things around.

"I think I can help with this." I followed Poncho into the kitchen. "I'm great at organizing, do you mind?" I started picking up dishes and stacking them in a clean area of the table.

"Go ahead, sister. We need some help." He smiled then for the first time.

V

I couldn't pay them but I could work for my keep. The three boys went outside and I could tell they were smoking weed as the fumes floated into the kitchen. I didn't pay any attention. I found a trash bag and started scraping the food off the plates and throwing away the wrappers and the cellophane and the food cartons. I stacked the dishes on the table and got myself into an assembly line. I got a good sink of sudsy water and put the oldest stuck-on food dishes into that. Then I filled a big pan and washed the dishes that weren't so bad in that and stacked them up getting ready to dry. When the stack was pretty tall I took a break and dried the dishes and found places for them on the shelves. I could hear the boys talking outside. It went on for a while and seemed like an argument was brewing. I couldn't really hear it so well but I could hear Javi. I watched them through the window.

Cruz was by far the most handsome. He had a long lean body, not typical of Mexicans. He had piercing black eyes and a wide, white smile. His hair was cut in one of those modern styles that used gel or something. He wore a red plaid shirt open several buttons with a gold crucifix showing on his white t-shirt. Like all Texans, he wore cowboy boots over clean pressed jeans. I wondered who did the ironing. Everything about him showed high maintenance. He dressed for the ladies, that was for sure.

Poncho was at the other extreme—short, fat, with wispy hair that would be eternally in need of a comb. He had thick glasses stuck onto a round face with an equally scraggly beard. He was covered with stains and I imagined each time he ate there would be crumbs stuck in the beard, his hair, and all down his chubby chest.

Javi was not as tall as Cruz but he too was very handsome. His manner was not as cocky either; he was soft. I could tell from the first minutes that he was a gentleman. He was a darker color than Cruz; he probably had a long line of Indian blood in him. His features were stronger, flatter, broader, but the result was still handsome. He dressed more in a no-nonsense way. Definitely not a poseur. I listened as best I could to the conversation.

"I don't think she should stay in your room, Cruz. It ain't right," Javi said.

"She's like a sister to me, Javi, nothin' wrong with that. In Mexico we all share the same beds." Cruz was talking.

"Wait, wait a second. Let's think about this. We got your room with the double bed. We got our room with the two singles and we got a couch. We know that none of us guys are going to share the double bed, right? Yeah, that's what I thought. So it means that she can be on the couch cause she can't take the whole room with the single beds. But she ain't got no privacy there on the sofa. She can share a bed with you, like you say, Cruz. But that ain't right. You say nothin's gonna happen, but you don't give her no choice. She be stuck there with you, *pendejo*."

"She should be so lucky."

"What? Yeah. Oh, yeah, you right, she should be so lucky. Fuck. Dog. She ain't got no choice. I say there's another way. You stay on the couch. She take your bed and your room. She have privacy and you can put your hairy snoring ass out there in the living room and sleep on the couch. Everybody wins."

"I think a better idea is for you to sleep on the couch, *culero*."

"What? Hey, no, no, no, I can be like I am now, in my own bed," Javi retorted.

"I pay the rent." Cruz scoffed at the others.

"OK. You do pay the rent. OK. OK. I'll take on the couch. You take a single bed and she takes yours," Javi summed up.

It seemed like I was going to be OK. I would be in a bed. In a room. With a door that closed. I was in heaven. I finished cleaning up just as the doorbell rang. I guessed the pizza was here.

"Hey girl, come get some pizza," Cruz walked into the kitchen flashing me a big smile. "Chica, this looks like a new place. It actually looks good. Nice work." He winked this time but not the kind of wink I got from the cook Alberto at the diner. There was something in that wink that was not right.

I smiled too. I felt like I was already doing something, making a contribution of some kind. It felt good. I followed him outside to the front porch carrying napkins while he brought the beer: *Corona,* the most popular beer in Mexico. I felt right at home. He opened a beer and handed it to me.

"Don't be shy, girl. We ordered two pizzas 'cause we figured you'd be pretty hungry." Cruz hung a slice over his mouth and ate it like a seal taking a fish. I reached over and took a slice, too, careful to put it on my napkin and not drop it in the dirt. The other two guys were eating rapidly.

"This the best pizza, Rosita. Remember the name: Pizza Hut. They deliver it right to your door. It's great." Poncho made this statement like it was a law in America which I must remember.

"How do they keep it hot?" I asked between bites.

"They got some special bags that keep it hot. I think there're like the bags that keep things cool only these bags keep things hot. It's pretty great." Poncho was obviously a fan of all food.

"I'll have to remember that. I'll be going to Los Angeles. Do they have Pizza Hut there?"

"I'm sure they do, don't they?" Poncho searched the faces of the other two guys. "Oh, yeah, I'm sure they do. LA is even bigger than Dallas, so they gotta have Pizza Hut."

I smiled at him. The thought of trying to get to LA made my heart beat a little faster. But I was here now. I was here and there were cars and buses and trains and no borders to cross or coyotes to pay. I was here.

"So, Cece, how you get here? You bein' a girl by yourself and all?" Javi asked. He couldn't look me in the eye. He looked at my forehead or my lips but for some reason he couldn't look me right in the eye. I was surprised how shy he actually was considering how he had greeted me at the gate when I arrived.

"I am sure that you guys had a hard time getting here too and so did I. The coyotes were mean and they asked for more money before we barely started. I got caught and sent back right away. I had to try again so I swam across the river with three brothers. We walked through the desert. Saw a little kid with his head blown off." I stopped then. I started to cry.

"Oh, I'm sorry. Don't cry." Javi stood near me but didn't reach for me. Cruz came around him and wrapped me in his arms.

"Don't cry, little girl. You safe now. You safe." He stroked my hair. I cried a little more.

"It's just that I saw that kid in my mind. Such a little kid. So small when we buried him."

"Wow, you buried him. That's sweet. You took the time." Poncho nodded his head like he was listening to music. "Sweet."

"The three brothers had a discussion about it but the quiet one, Juan Pablo, said we had to do it. We had to bury him for himself and for Mexicans who would be passing him. So we all buried him and said some prayers and we walked on. It was sad."

No one talked for a few minutes. We were all thinking about the little dead boy. I ate my pizza in silence too. Cruz went into the house and let the screen door slam behind him. I heard him walking around and then some music came blasting out into the yard. It was Latin rap, something I had barely heard on the radio in Mexico but something I knew the young people in the United States listened to all the time. I preferred Mexican music, but I guess I'd better get used to this. After we ate, the guys smoked some more weed and I just listened to the music. It finally got dark and we needed to get ready for bed.

"Listen, Cece." Cruz got up and put his arm around me. "I decided that the right thing to do would be to give you my bed." I started to protest. "No, no, I already decided. It is the gentlemanly thing to do. You will have your own bed and some privacy. The boys and I will stay in the other room and on the couch. It'll be fine." I glanced at the other two to see their reaction to Cruz taking credit for the magnanimous decision.

I was grateful even with the lie. "I won't be here long, just a couple of days to get ready for the big trip. I won't be in the way. I am so grateful. Thank you so much."

"Respect," Poncho said. So many American terms that didn't make any sense to me but I was sure they would. I needed to go to sleep.

"If you don't mind, I really need to get some sleep," I said.

"You go on then. Go to sleep, Cece. Sweet dreams." They all sent me off in their own ways. I turned and smiled and waved at them at the door to the house and went in. I brushed my teeth and washed my face and headed for the sanctuary of the bedroom. Cruz had a big double bed and I lay down on it like it was a cloud. After the tiny bed made from the kitchen benches at Dolores's trailer and the bus, it was heaven. I covered up with the quilt and was asleep in seconds, dreaming of a road to a better life with Latin rap playing in the background.

I woke confused, in a strange house, with voices all around me. I quickly remembered where I was and got up and dressed. I went into the kitchen where the boys were congregating, having coffee.

"Can I make you some breakfast? *Huevos divorciados* and *chilaquiles?*" They smiled broadly at the names of Mexican breakfasts which their moms probably made for them every day. "Do you have *salsa verde*? Green sauce? Eggs? Tortillas?"

"Well since you are going to be so useful, Cece, just look in the cupboards and the refrigerator and find what you need." Cruz went to a high cupboard and brought down some *salsa verde* for me. "I'm sure you wouldn't be able to reach this green sauce so here it is." He presented his find like a treasured gift.

"OK, this should be ready soon." I started to work fixing the breakfast that would probably remind them of home. Poncho and Cruz went out into the yard and the smell of weed floated into the kitchen. Javi sat at the small table

"Does this remind you of home?" I asked Javi while I cut up the tortillas.

"It's like home and not like home." He leaned on the table. "We're kind of in the middle here. What's home and what isn't home? We are Mexicans but we don't live in Mexico. We live in America but we're not Americans. What are we? It's kind of like being lost at sea or somethin'. We don't belong here and we don't belong there. The government can't agree about what to do with us and so we are just tryin' to get by without being noticed or seen. But that means we can't really do as good as we could do if we were free. See what I mean?"

I understood the words but I didn't really understand everything Javi was saying. It sounded sad and I realized that this is what I would be too. I would be stuck in the middle, not Mexican and not American. I just put those thoughts into the back of my mind and continued to make breakfast.

"Sounds sad," I said. I looked in the refrigerator for cream for the *chilaquiles*. I had already found the tortillas and the cheese so I was nearly ready to make them.

"Yeah, it is." Javi looked away and was quiet. I finished making breakfast, got out four plates, and served up the food.

"Here, I'll take some of those. It smells great." He took three plates like a practiced waiter and carried them out to the porch. Poncho joined him there.

"Wow, we are gonna be spoiled," Cruz said coming into the kitchen. He smelled like weed.

"I might have to give Cece a kiss," I heard Poncho say.

"I don't think so," Javi said. "You never kiss girls."

"I know, but I'd like to." I didn't see Poncho's face when he said this, but I bet it was disappointed.

"I'll be right out with more tortillas," I called from the kitchen. I watched the tortillas warm up on the stove on the *comal*. I was surprised these boys had the flat skillet we use to heat the tortillas. They must have done some cooking in their lives. I could hear them mumbling words of appreciation. When the tortillas were hot, I put them on a plate and took my plate out to join them.

"Thanks, Cece, these are great." Cruz was smiling. "This will keep us going all day."

"Mmm. Great, Cece. Like Mom used to make." Poncho smiled, too.

"Me too," Javi said, shoveling in the food.

"I'm glad you like it." I smiled. At least I could do a little to pay them back. "What are you going to do today?" Javi took another tortilla.

"We all go to work and we will get back at about four," Cruz said. "You know I work in the garage with Javi. Poncho works at the Ford assembly plant. He's the rich one. He's got a green card." He poked Poncho on his arm.

"Yeah, very rich, be careful with my gold Rolex." He shoved more eggs into his mouth.

"Do you need somethin' today?" Javi asked.

"No, I don't think so. I'll just hang around here."

The boys took their dishes to the sink and started moving faster as the time approached when they all had to leave for work. I just got out of the way and let them get their teeth brushed and gathered their stuff. Javi started to fold the sheets that were on the couch.

"I'll do it," I said. I took the sheets away from him.

"Bye bye," they waved as they sailed out the door and were gone.

"*Que les vaya bien,*" I said and they called "*igualmente*" as they moved across the lawn to the rusty cars each called his. I guess I would have to start saying the American words: "Have a good day" and "You too."

I waved to them from the door. Home. What was home anyway? I went back into the kitchen to wash the dishes. As the dishes dried, I explored the house for things I needed. I found the broom and the bucket and the mop, at least they had these. I found some liquids that I could use for cleaning and they all had labels in English and Spanish. I studied the English words, hoping that I could figure out how to pronounce them. English was tricky. In Spanish, words were pronounced just like they were written but English was a mess. I remembered a time when one of my friends was practicing with me in English. We were looking at some words that all had the letters *o-u-g-h* in them. We later learned they were pronounced completely differently: *thought, enough, though, through*. How was I going to learn this language? I guess I would be watching a lot of television.

It was easy to clean the house once all of the stuff was moved out of the way. I found where most things were stored like the CDs and the DVDs and the backpacks and the hats. I made piles of things I didn't know, like whose shoes were whose and which jacket went to which room. I thought the boys could sort those things out when they got home. I had so much time that I was able to polish all of the furniture and mop the floors and clean all of the mirrors and the glass. While I was cleaning, I was making the *pozole*. They had plenty of chicken already in the refrigerator for this wonderful stew and the smell of the cooking filled the house.

They had a map of the United States and I had a chance to look at how far away Los Angeles actually was. It looked like it would take me forever to get there. I found a phone book and I looked up the name *Greyhound* because a friend had told me that this was the bus I would have to take to get around America. I called up the company and there was a mechanical voice which told me to press *two* for Spanish. After that, all of the choices were in Spanish and I was able to find an agent.

"Where do you want to go?" a sweet female voice asked me in Spanish.

The question was so abrupt. We would never do this in Mexico. We would always be polite first so this is what I did.

"*Bueños días,*" I began. Always be courteous. "Good morning."

"*Bueños días.* Where do you want to go?" she asked again in Spanish.

"Los Angeles."

"From where?" She was abrupt again so I guess the courtesy was over.

"Dallas."

"When?"

"A few days or a week from today."

"How many travelers?"

"One."

"Time of day?"

Such an efficient system but so cold? So distant. I felt a shudder. I answered all of her questions and I wrote down the information. I could leave very early in the morning in a few days and I would be in Los Angeles in three more days. I would have to pay a lot of money, but I would be there.

Javi was the first one home. He went right into the bathroom and took a shower. He was going out with his girlfriend for dinner and told me he wouldn't be home until tomorrow. He gave me a kiss on the cheek and I could smell his aftershave. I heard about it in the movies but had never smelled it before. My family didn't have money for such things. I hugged him.

"Have a good time." I smiled at him.

"I always do with Angelina." He walked out and into his old rusty car looking like a prince going to pick up his princess.

Poncho and Cruz arrived at the same time. They came bustling into the house and Poncho headed for the bathroom.

"I need the first shower. It smells great in here," he yelled as he was already in the bathroom.

"How you doin', Cece?" Cruz smiled at me. "Wow, the whole house looks like it's shining. What did you make us for dinner? It smells so good."

"*Pozole.*" If there was one thing all Mexicans loved, it was this chicken stew.

"Boy, I haven't had that in so long. It seems like

forever." He hugged me and held me close. Too close. I moved back out of his embrace. "Yeah, I thought you might be missing it."

"You know just what a man likes." He reached for me, but I turned away from him.

"I have to check on it. Don't want it to stick, do I?" I escaped into the kitchen.

"OK, Cruz. I'm done in the bathroom." Poncho walked through the kitchen wrapped in a towel. "Thank for you making dinner, Cece." His hair was plastered down onto his head and he looked like a totally different person. The towel was barely large enough to get around his big stomach.

"It should be ready in about two hours. Is that too early?" I stirred the pot.

"No. We need to watch Monday Night Football, so that's perfect." Cruz blew me a kiss from the bathroom door. I looked down at the bubbling pot of *pozole*.

The boys ate dinner with great enthusiasm. I was proud of making them something they obviously liked so much. We talked a lot about the football game that was coming on and we naturally slipped into English. The words were football words and I think many were the names of players. It's hard to know about American names. In Mexico, all the names are Spanish. But in America there are names from all over the world so you never know if the people are Americans or players from other countries. I wonder if Americans ever realize that these people, like me, started somewhere else. Do they appreciate what they have? Everything was new to me.

I watched the game with the boys and they were jumping up and down and yelling *hijo de puta*—son of a bitch—at the television screen and giving it the middle finger. I really wanted to laugh but I knew this was very serious to the boys so I didn't say anything. When the game was over, I asked them for directions to walk to town to buy a few things I needed for the trip to LA. Poncho drew me a little map and he gave me his key to the house. I was tired so I said good night and had another wonderful sleep in a real bed.

VI

The days passed and I regained my strength from my trip across the desert. I got up and fixed them a big breakfast every morning and spent the day cleaning or doing the laundry. They all came home to Mexican cooking. After a few days, I ran out of things to clean and started working outside. I started in the backyard, which was luckily quite empty of trash. I worked on the plants and pulled the weeds and cut the grass. Three days later, the backyard looked like a park.

The front yard was more of a challenge. Everything was cast aside like the living room was when I first came. I didn't recognize the parts but I knew they went into cars or trucks or motorcycles. I began with the small pieces that looked like they went together like screws and bolts. I found some old plastic containers and stored all the little bits in these. The bigger pieces were harder to categorize. I figured just getting them off the ground would be an improvement. I asked the boys to move a big wooden table under the tree so I could work from there. I put the pieces in plastic milk crates that I found in the side yard. After several days, it looked like there was some possibility that the front yard would be presentable. Not a paradise, but presentable.

The backyard, however, became a new hang out. The boys sat there smoking and drinking beer every day. It was a very pleasant place to be now that it was cleaned up. They were very appreciative.

I needed to start making preparations to leave. I got up one day and this time I made a frittata and they were really happy to have such nice food. I put a pot on the stove to make Aztec soup and later some enchiladas for dinner.

"I need to buy some provisions for the road."

"Are you really thinking of going? We were getting used to having you around. And the food is so wonderful." Poncho looked at me with his big brown cow eyes.

"Oh thanks but I've got to get started with my life. So I have to go."

I waved to them as they went off to work. I got myself together then for the trip to the store. I had enough money from the money I changed at the bus station. All the time I had been at the house the three boys paid for everything. They felt I did enough with the cooking and the cleaning and the working for them.

I followed the map that Poncho gave me and walked to the center of this area where they lived. I passed many houses that looked old and broken down, like a mouth with teeth missing. The yards were full of rusted junk and the weeds fought for space with the trash. I walked faster.

In the center of the town, there were a few small shops like a hardware store and an auto parts store. There was also the big supermarket named Walmart that Poncho had told me about. I had only seen these stores in the movies. I entered the store and got paralyzed immediately by the sheer number of things. There were aisles and aisles and aisles piled high with things. I was stopped dead in the doorway and people had to walk around me. I didn't know where to start.

I walked down the cereal aisle. There must have been 100 different types of cereals. How can anyone decide what cereal they like? I was in the shampoo aisle and there were so many colors of shampoo bottles, so many things calling for my attention. I found myself spinning around in the aisle like a top. I felt dizzy. I moved out of this aisle and made a sharp turn to the right. There was a big box there and before I knew it, I felt myself slipping and down I went.

"Miss, Miss, can you hear me?" a man was asking me. He had on a blue and white uniform with a stethoscope around his neck. He was touching my face.

"Miss, Miss. I think she's actually all right." He didn't sound sure of this.

"I hope she doesn't sue me. I don't have time to work through a long court case." This was a second voice. Not a friendly, caring voice.

"Nice of you to worry about her. She's pregnant," said the doctor man.

"Oh my God, she will sue. I'll be in court forever," the uncaring voice answered.

"Your concern is touching. Miss, miss, can you hear me?" The doctor man was touching my face again.

I realized they were talking about me. A circle of people were all standing around looking down at me. I appeared to be on the floor of the store. I wanted to disappear and float away from all of these people.

"I'm fine. I'm fine. I just tripped. There was a big box in the way."

There were two men in uniforms who were wearing stethoscopes and taking my blood pressure like they did in the mobile clinic when it came to my village. I struggled to get up thinking that all of these people would disappear when I was OK.

"Hold on, Miss, get up slowly. You still had a bad fall." The doctor man was so kind.

"We are so happy you are OK," said the uncaring voice which belonged to a man who had on a suit and wore a badge with his name on it. He seemed important. He also seemed insincere, nothing like the man in the uniform. He didn't really care about me at all.

"Walmart wants you to know that all of your shopping will be free today. Fill up two shopping carts with anything you want," said the man with the badge.

I looked at the man. Something was going on inside his mind that I didn't understand. Maybe this was something about America. I didn't know what it was but I knew that I did not have to pay today and I thought it had something to do with the fall. When he said that I didn't have to pay, the crowd standing around me applauded. Why were they applauding? I was so embarrassed.

"Is everything OK?" I asked the nicer man with the uniform.

"We can't be sure, Miss. You should go to see your doctor and make sure everything is OK. In your condition and all." He paused and looked at me shyly. "Right now you seem fine but doesn't hurt to be sure."

I had actually been distracted. Distracted by all of the stuff. I was overcome by all of the choices. Who in the world could possibly use all of this stuff? Aisle after aisle, packed from the floor to the ceiling, with stuff. In my village, you had a choice of three cereals. You could choose one of two shampoos. People bought bread at the *panadería* and we bought meat at the *carnicería*. All of this stuff meant wrappers and boxes and bags. No wonder the house of Cruz and Javi and Poncho had so much stuff everywhere. No wonder all of the houses had lawns full of trash. We would be swimming in trash here. Everyone should fall on the floor.

"This is Paula, Miss. She is going to help you to do your shopping today." The man with the badge smiled at me. The smile was fake. He was pointing to another woman who had a similar badge on her shirt but it said *Paula*. The people around us applauded again like we had just sung a great song for them. The men in the uniforms were packing their things.

"Thank you so much." I put my arms around the man with the uniform and hugged him. He was a very, very white man with freckles and red hair. This was the first time I had ever seen anyone with freckles and they were like red dots all over his face. When I hugged him, his face turned a very dark shade of red and the people laughed, which made his face turn even darker red.

"You're welcome, Miss. Go to see your doctor." He waved as he and his partner walked away. The people in the circle started moving off.

"OK, Miss, what is your name?" Paula was talking to me now.

"Rosita," I lied.

"Well, Rosita, let's go to the front of the store and get a cart. We can fill up two carts for you today as everything is free." This is exactly what we did, Paula and me. We went everywhere in that huge store. I put things in the cart that I had only seen in the movies. There was champagne and caviar, beers, wine, lobster, steak, several pounds of flour and sugar and laundry soap, light bulbs, and toilet paper. I put everything in that cart that would not rot or get wasted once it was opened. I chose only the most expensive things for the precious space in the refrigerator and the freezer. I wish I could have put a new car in the cart. By the time I was finished, I had loaded the carts with all of my treasures. I was careful to buy some very practical things for the trip to LA like fruit juices and nuts and cheese. When we were finished loading the carts, we went through the checkout line.

"Why are we going through the line?" I was panicked. "Do I have to pay?"

"No, Rosita, this is just so we can take the items out of the inventory. You know, the list we keep of what is in the store so we know when to order more."

"You're going to make a list of all of these things?" I would be here forever.

"No, the machines do it all. It's all electronic now." America was very different from my Mexico.

The store manager asked someone from the back of the store with a truck to drive me home. I gave him the map. I had $6,457.65 worth of food and stuff in the back of that truck. I was smiling.

For the rest of the day I made dinner: Aztec soup and all of the makings for the inside of the *fajitas*. I had tried to find a place for all of the things I bought and finally I had to stack some of the staples on the back porch. There wasn't enough room in the cupboards. I was going to wait until all three of the boys were together but they came home separately and started noticing things: new towels, soap, shampoos, some special body cream for men, some special men's cologne.

"Wow, you must have spent a fortune on all of this,

Cece. We thought we were helping you." Javi smiled. "Can I use some of this body wash?" He was pointing to something called *Hugo Boss*.

"Of course, this is all for you three for being so nice to me."

"I hate to ask you a personal question but how did you afford all of this?" He was walking toward the bathroom through the kitchen. "By the way, that food smells wonderful!"

"Let's wait until we're all together and I will tell you the story." I grated the cheese into a big pile on the plate on the counter.

"Can't wait to hear it." He closed the bathroom door behind him and I heard the shower start.

Poncho and Cruz came in shortly and they too noticed things right away. Maybe it was the big box with the skinny television that gave it away.

"Oh my god, a 50-inch flat screen TV. Did you steal this, Cece?" Even before they took their showers they ripped the box apart and began to pull plugs from the wall and out of the old TV. They moved things aside to put the monster into the center of their world. They sat down immediately and turned on a sports channel and amidst whoops and yells and arms pumping in the air they were as happy as anyone on this whole planet.

Now they were eating and I insisted that we turn off the TV and sit outside and talk as this was our last night together. I told them the story.

"The rat bastard!" Javi said.

"What a dick," Cruz said.

"No, no, no," Poncho said.

"What? What?" I was very confused. I thought this was

all a good thing. I had told the whole story about what happened at Walmart except for the part about being pregnant. "Didn't I do good?"

"Yes, Cece, it isn't you. Did you sign anything?" Javi asked.

"Yes, they gave me a piece of paper to sign about the stuff I got. Why? What's wrong?"

"Cece, this is just something that happens in America. When anyone gets hurt somewhere they sue the place. Like we sue someone in Mexico for telling lies about us. You fell down in Walmart, the biggest store in America, and the store manager was afraid you would sue him. He gave you all this stuff to look like a good guy but actually he's just covering his ass. That's why he made you sign something. You probably signed something that said you wouldn't sue him."

"Well I signed Rosita anyway." I smiled at that.

"Who's Rosita?" Javi asked.

"I don't know," Poncho said. "Who's Rosita?"

"She's my *mojada* self."

They all laughed at this. I guess there was something interesting about a signature on a piece of paper in Walmart that was a fake name. I laughed too. The gods were smiling down on us. The night made for a big party. The boys found the tequila and the champagne and they mixed it up. We were like the kids on the feast of Three Kings, running around the house finding stuff everywhere. I was getting tired.

"Come on, Cece, give us a little kiss." Cruz came ambling up to me.

"No, Cruz, you're drunk." I moved away.

"So what? Drunk is good. Drunk sex is the best sex."

"Only for the drunk," I said. I'd never had any experience with drunk sex but I knew that men could be selfish and I didn't want to find out what smelly drunk sex was like, that was for sure. I pushed him away and got up to go into the kitchen to wash the dishes. He followed me.

"Come on there, girl. This is your last night. Last chance for us. You know you want it."

"OK, Cruz, you've had too much to drink. Go watch TV with the boys, I think there's a Mexican football match on tonight. Javi, isn't there a Mexican football match on TV tonight?" I screamed into the living room. I prayed there was. Mexico had about twenty football teams and I hoped that one of them would have a match. I needed to protect Nely from drunk sex.

"Yeah, Veracruz vs. Morelia. This'll be a good match. Let's find it. Yeah! It's like we're at the stadium. It's so big!"

"There you go, Cruz. Go watch the game." I walked around him, putting the dishes away.

"You're a fuckin' ungrateful bitch, Cece. You women are all alike. Take, take, take and never give back. I know you bitches. I know you bitches." He suddenly turned me around and grabbed my jaw in his hands. He held it tight and made me look at him. He reeked of alcohol.

"Fuckin' bitches!" He stared into my eyes with deep anger. He shoved my face then and turned and abruptly left. I leaned back on the counter and tried to calm my beating heart. He was dangerous, that was for sure. I could hear him yelling with the boys and I made a note to be thankful I was only staying this last night.

I had plenty of time to do the dishes while the boys watched the match. I moved slowly to avoid having to go into the living room and see Cruz. The other two came in periodically to get beers and were oblivious to the drama unfolding between Cruz and me. I decided to dry the dishes and put them away and this dragged out the time. I finally couldn't wait any longer so I went to talk to them.

"I'm saying good night now." They could barely hear me over the din of the match. "I'll be leaving before you get up in the morning, so I just want to say thanks for everything."

"Cece, we should be thanking you. It's like an angel came down and brought us all of this great stuff." Poncho got up and hugged me. "Take care of yourself, girl." He kissed me on the forehead.

Javi got slowly off the couch and gave me a tentative hug. "You are a sweet girl, Cece, take care of yourself." He looked down at the ground.

"Yeah, take care." Cruz hugged me with one arm. He didn't look me in the eye.

I waved to them from the doorway and went through the kitchen to the bathroom. I brushed my teeth and got ready for bed. When I got to the bedroom, I was careful to lock the door. I thought about moving the dresser in front of the door but I felt foolish for being so paranoid. It would be fine, I thought. I'll be gone in the morning.

VII

Of course it wasn't fine. Of course he had a key. I didn't hear the key in the lock. I didn't hear him sneak in. I didn't hear him get into the bed. The first I knew I was catapulted from a deep sleep into a living nightmare. Someone was shoving my face into the pillow. His hand was on my head. His other hand was fumbling around looking for his prize. His whole weight was on top of me and I was suffocating. I moaned into the pillow and struggled with my hands trying to break his grip on my head when he rammed himself inside me. The pain shot through me like a harpoon. I couldn't move for the weight and the power. I started to cry but my sobs were muffled by the pillow. He drove himself into me like a battering ram, harder and harder, deeper and deeper. I was helpless under the force and the weight. I tried to shake him off but my struggles only resulted in his doubling his efforts to hold down my head and drive himself into me. And there were the words.

"Yeah, you fuckin' bitch. You come here, you bitch, and you take and you take and you think, what? You don't owe us nothin'? You can just take, you cunt, take and take. You're just like all the rest of the bitches. How does it feel to have someone take somethin' from you, huh? How does it feel? It don't feel good, does it? You don't like it, do you? Well, fuck you bitch, you deserve everything you're gettin'. I only asked for a little attention, bitch. Fuck you. Fuck you."

I tried to pull myself away mentally from the experience I was having. I wanted to cast myself high above the fray. I did this and looked down on the bed. But I couldn't escape, even in my mind. I was the center of the action. I couldn't get away. His words pounded into my head like his dick. His weight and his power and his words ambushed me. He was trying to pulverize me, to break me into little pieces. I couldn't move my legs. I couldn't hit him with my hands. I was trapped under him with his alcohol stink and his beastly grunting. Then. Nely. Oh my god, would he hurt Nely?

I struggled to turn my head. Under all of the attack, the driving, the dripping words, the booze, I tried to turn my head. I stopped fighting with my arms and tried to turn my head. "Pregnant," I whispered hoarsely.

"Pregnant," I said it again, barely audible above the pounding of his prick. "Pregnant," I said again.

"What? What'd you say, bitch?" He grabbed me by my hair and lifted my head. "What did you say?"

"Pregnant," I said.

"What the fuck?" He jumped off of me, his hard cock dripping. He pulled up his sweatpants. "You bitch. Pregnant? You didn't tell us you was pregnant. We didn't know you was pregnant."

I turned over on my side and he could see the baby bump. I looked at him like the weasel slime ball that he was. "Pregnant, you fucking bastard. Get the fuck out of here."

He looked at my belly and like the coward that he was, he turned and walked away. It was all over in a matter of minutes. I was breathing heavily and my vagina throbbed.

I hoped he hadn't hurt the baby. I got out of bed slowly and everything ached. My neck and shoulders felt sprained. The pain between my legs caused me to hobble. I put on a big t-shirt and limped to the bathroom. There was no blood. No blood meant Nely was OK, didn't it? I got into the bathtub and washed warm water around my vagina. I found a little mirror and put it between my legs to look. Everything was red and swollen and bruises were starting to appear. I let out a little moan of pain. I held the warm washcloth there and sat in the tub resting everything. There were bruises on my neck and my arms where he must've held me down. I hung my head between my legs and tried to get some calmness back. I breathed deeply.

I stayed that way for a while trying to avoid what I had to do. Finally, I pulled myself up and dried myself off. I brushed my teeth and collected my stuff and limped back to the bedroom. I put on the little lamp and by its soft light I packed. There wasn't much to take so the time to get ready was short. I stuffed everything into the bag. I took it and went into the kitchen to collect some supplies for the trip. I could see Cruz smoking weed in the back garden. He was mumbling to himself. What could I possibly say to such a *pendejo*? No, not even *asshole* was a bad enough word for him after what he did. He was so much more than that.

Ready to go now, I walked out the front door and closed it behind me forever and went into the night. The streets were deserted and so quiet. It was actually beautiful because the darkness hid all the rusty junk in people's front yards. Even the dogs were asleep. The walk was easy as I had passed the bus station on my journey to Walmart. What a funny turn of events that had been? I would be early for my bus but it would be safer for me in the downtown Dallas bus station than in the home of Cruz. Who knew what he would do next? He felt tricked about the pregnancy. Maybe guilty to have raped a pregnant sister. Mexican brothers. I had such hope for them, and then this.

I wondered if he had hurt the baby but there was little pain now and no blood. I was sore, that's for sure, but no blood. I thought I was all right; Nely was all right. I came to the bus station and it was lit up like an oasis in the desert. Even in the very early morning there were people there. The ticket seller windows weren't open yet so I sat in the center of the lobby and waited. There were about ten people in the lobby and they were all attached to their little tablets and phones. No one paid any attention to me. I put my backpack in my lap and threaded my belt around it so that if anyone tried to grab it, they wouldn't get away with it.

I felt so dirty. My mind swirled with impressions of him. His hot, boozy breath on my face. His hand on my head. His weight. The pain of his ramming inside of me. I raced around my memory looking for things I had said or done that might have led him on. Why do women always do this? Why do we think it's our fault that men use their power against us? I felt so damn helpless. I had gotten to America on my own for chrissakes and then a man, a damn man, had used me like I had no more substance than a rag doll. My heartbeat quickened. I felt utterly helpless at a time when I needed all of my strength to get by. To keep going. To win. I wished my Mami was here. She would know just what to say and just what to do. She would soothe me and make it better. I knew men. I knew

Mexican men. I had been in love with one of the good ones. Damn man! I wished I could cry and scream at this injustice. In the middle of the bus station in Dallas, Texas, I wanted to wail. Instead, I silenced the voices howling inside my head and pulled my things closer around me. There would be time for my screams but not tonight. He would not beat me. I went to sleep.

A hand was shaking my shoulder.

"Miss, Miss." It was a woman's voice. I woke up.

"Umm, hello," I said it in Spanish. Force of habit. The woman had a large braid down her back and was wearing clothes like a Texan but she was Mexican. I sat up and rubbed my eyes.

"*Señorita*, do you need a ride somewhere?" She spoke Spanish, of course.

I thought it was a strange request so early in the morning. The woman gestured to where a young mother and her two small children had lined up near the door where a Mexican man waited.

"Yes, I am waiting for the bus."

"Where are you going?"

"I'm going to Los Angeles." Why was she asking me these questions?

"Oh, that is a very long way. But we are going to the other side of Texas, all the way to Arizona and we could drive you. We make money this way and it is so much better for the travelers. We stop for food and we have a very comfortable car. They even call it a *people carrier* and it has air conditioning and radio and we can all have a nice conversation. That lady over there with the two little ones will be coming with us. We are much, much cheaper than the bus. We are leaving right now."

Leaving right now was very tempting. I knew the bus would be safe and of course I wasn't sure about this couple. The woman seemed nice and the other woman with the children was trusting her. I knew I had to start trusting my instincts with people. I also knew that Mexican people would have to be creative to make money in the USA. We didn't have the connections or the language or the education. This is how I would have to live. I would have to be creative and resourceful too.

"Can you wait a minute while I go to the bathroom?" I asked.

She smiled at me. I waved to the woman with the children and the man at the door. They went outside, the woman gathering her things and the man helping her by carrying two sleeping children. He would be very helpful, I thought.

When I got out of the bathroom she was waiting for me at the door of the bus station. A few of the people waiting shifted in their seats but most didn't even wake up as we left. She led me across the street to a big van with lots of seats in it. The woman and her kids were in the third seat with the heads of the little kids resting in her lap. She looked to be falling asleep any minute herself. I settled in the second seat and spread out. The couple sat in the front.

"I am Raquel," the woman whispered. "This is my husband, Jose Cruz."

"Nice to meet you. I am Rosita," I whispered back. I knew we had to travel in silence now because it was so late and the woman and the children were sleeping. I had decided to take a chance and trust that this was safe and so I closed my eyes.

I woke to the gentle movement of the car. Jose Cruz was sleeping in the passenger seat and Raquel was driving this big van. For a second, I was proud of her. In my village, you seldom saw the woman driving, but this was America and I knew that I would have to learn to drive as well.

"Can we stop for the children to go to the bathroom?" the woman in the back seat asked. She didn't seem to mind that Jose Cruz was sleeping.

"Of course, I will watch for a filling station." Raquel smiled into the rearview mirror.

"I'm Rosita." I turned to the woman.

"Ann Marie." She pointed to herself. "Her name is Brenda and this little rascal is Homer." She pointed to each child as she introduced us. Homer might be a rascal but she was smiling when she said it.

"Hello, lady." Homer had a twinkle in his eye. He was definitely a rascal. "Are you from Mexico?" he asked.

"Yes, I am." I smiled at him.

"You look like a Texan," Brenda said. "You don't look like a *Mexicana*." Brenda made a challenging face at me.

"Well, what do *Mexicanas* look like?"

"Everybody knows that silly. They wear big hats and big dresses with big skirts. They are red. The dresses are red."

"I guess you're right then. I don't have a big hat and I don't have a red dress, so I must not be a Mexican. I must be a Texan."

"Yes, I thought so. You are a Texan."

"Is she bothering you?" Ann Marie put her arm around her daughter.

"No, she's adorable." I smiled at Brenda. Homer was reading a book and was totally uninterested in the silly conversation of women and girls.

We rode around in silence for a while, appreciating the scruffy view. Homer stayed inside his book and Ann Marie chatted with Brenda. I didn't want to ask too many questions yet because the drivers were intent on finding a rest stop or a filling station. Besides, Mexicans didn't usually ask each other a lot of questions.

"We will stop at this filling station to get some gas and to go to the toilet." Raquel pulled into the filling station. It was really the first one I had noticed. Like the Walmart, it was oversized. There must have been room for sixteen cars at the pumps. I got out and helped Ann Marie to take out Brenda and Homer. I pried the book from Homer's hands and gave him over to Ann Marie to walk them into the store. Meanwhile, Raquel stuck a credit card in a slot, punched in some information, put the nozzle in the car, and started pumping gas. Jose Cruz was still sleeping. I watched other people come and use their credit cards to get gas. This was a new thing in Mexico. Our Pemex station had people who came and pumped your gas for you and cleaned off your windshields. I heard that they cheated you. I don't know. I went inside the store.

Like everything else in America that I had seen so far, the store was huge. It had about ten rows of potato chips and row after row of cold drinks inside glass cases. There was a lot of Coca-Cola; Mexicans love Coca-Cola. There were no tortillas in sight but many bags of snacks. The rest of the shelves had items for cars like plastic lenses and lights and rubber hoses. I didn't know what any of that stuff was but I was sure it was necessary for the cars. It reminded me of all the stuff in the front yard of the boys in Dallas. I was so happy to be gone from there.

One whole side of the store had coffee machines with lots of tiny creams and sugars and artificial sweeteners. There were about twenty kinds of coffee with all kinds of flavors I had never heard of like macadamia roast and hazelnut. There was a vanilla flavor, too, but it wasn't Mexican vanilla; it was French vanilla. I didn't know that the French grew vanilla beans. I walked among the coffees just trying to read the labels and guess how I might pronounce the words. I was glad of the English classes in school; at least we learned to read even if our pronunciation was terrible. I hurried to the bathroom.

When I got back outside, Ann Marie was drying the faces of Brenda and Homer with a paper towel and throwing it in the bin. She sent the children to the back seat and climbed in beside them. I followed in the middle seat and Raquel took the front passenger seat while Jose Cruz took over the driving.

"Everybody ready?" She said this in Spanish and I felt right at home. I put my hand on my stomach to comfort Nely. Jose Cruz pulled back onto the highway and we were gone. Raquel broke the silence.

"Why are you going to Roscoe, Ann Marie?" She turned around to look at the mother in the back seat.

"My husband has a new job there. He took our things and moved about a month ago and we are coming now. It is a good opportunity working on the wind farms. He can fix anything."

"That sounds fantastic for your family. He must have papers," Raquel said.

This was the second time a Mexican mentioned

papers. I think this means that we are legal. We have immigration papers, the Green Card. I knew this was what everyone wanted. Without the Green Card you couldn't ever go back to visit your family. You were hiding all the time like I was now. I had just gotten here, and already I was worried that someone would ask me something, and I would be sent back to the deportation center and would have to try again.

"Yes. We came before everything got crazy here. The Americans needed us and they wanted us and now they don't want anyone else to come. I think they are being silly because they really need us. Who will do the dirty work for them?"

"What do you mean?" I asked. I turned sideways so I could see both women talking.

"She means who will do the laundry and the house cleaning and the gardening and the roofing and the fruit picking? We Mexicans do all of the dirty work. You know that, think, girl. You see our sisters and brothers every day doing the dirty work. Who will do it? They don't even take care of their own children. We do it." She did not have bitterness in her voice, just facts.

"All of my sisters work as nannies. We take care of the kids of women who have to work. Everyone works here. It is so expensive to live, don't you think?" Ann Marie braided Brenda's hair as she spoke.

"Yes, it is expensive," Raquel said. "But there are jobs. There is work. Your kids can go to school and they learn. Our kids are in the community college. The boy is learning to fix computers and the girl is learning how to keep track of the books for businesses. They will have good jobs when they are finished."

"Do you have papers?" I asked.

"Yes, we too came when times were more welcoming for immigrants. The children were born in the United States. They are legals and they both have part-time jobs. In the beginning it was very hard for us but, little by little, it got easier. When we came here we had to wait for a while for papers but you could still get a driver's license even though you did not have papers so we could find work driving places. Jose Cruz is a carpenter so there was work for him. They say I am a wonderful cook and rich people are always willing to have me prepare their meals. Together we made a much better life here than we could have done in Mexico. It was worth the danger. What do you think, Jose Cruz? Was it worth it?"

"Yes. It is harder now for people trying to come." He spoke for the first time and then lapsed back into silence. Raquel had more to say.

"Ahh, I don't know. Many years ago it was worth it. The people were nice, they helped you. Now they are cold. They turn their backs on immigrants like something is wrong with us. Like we are dirty or criminals or something. I watch the news and I learn that things have changed. I notice it in the little ways that people look down on us or insult us or make life hard for us. My husband has very good work and we are the lucky ones. But I see the new *mojados* and life is very difficult. If no one is sponsoring them and they have no education or money, then what are they going to do? If they are rich or they have a special talent then they are OK but if not, I don't know. It seems that life here might not be better. Just being away from your family makes life more difficult, I think.

"Americans don't understand how important family is to us Mexicans. They think they are as close to their families as we are. I have never had a babysitter for my children but Americans have them all the time. We went out always as a family and they do that sometimes but you don't see a whole family out together on New Year's Eve, do you? You don't see the grandmother living with the family. It's just different. What do you think, Rosita?"

"I just got here recently so I have no opinion yet. I am being sponsored by my sister so I guess I will have papers." It was so easy for me to lie about this and to keep up my false identity of Rosita. I was getting good at this.

"Ah, you will be one of the lucky ones." Jose Cruz smiled at me in the mirror.

We got quiet then. America was a confusing place already. Raquel thought I could have a better life here and Ann Marie did not think so. Everyone at home was so sure that life was better here. Now I wonder. And what could I do? I couldn't fix anything like Ann Marie's husband or Raquel's son. I couldn't cook like Raquel or keep the books like her daughter. But I could take care of children. I had taken care of my little brothers all my life and watched as my aunts and neighbors took care of their children. I could definitely take care of children. So I would be a nanny. I put my hand on my belly and thought about my own child. Wasn't this why I was going to LA because I thought there were lots of rich women there who wanted someone else to take care of their children. Didn't the priest in my village promise this would happen for me?

VIII

"Yes, we are on the way now but we will be in Roscoe at the end of the day." Ann Marie spoke into her cell phone.

"I am excited too. The children have been wonderful. Yes, they're nice. The van is beautiful and they drive very carefully. We didn't take the highways; we took the smaller roads. For us, it is much better than the bus because we can sit together in the back seat. On the bus, we would have to separate. It's easier. We won't be bored waiting for you. The couple that is driving us likes to go and see strange things in America. Yes, I know, it is strange itself. Today we are going to see some of those strange things, the kids are looking forward to it. OK, we will meet you there, Papi."

"Mami, Mami, let me talk to Papi." Homer pulled himself out of his book. He took the phone.

"Hello, Papi." Homer's smile was very wide and he cradled the phone like a treasured object. "Yes, we are being very good. I am reading about airplanes. It is a very interesting book and there are a lot of new vocabulary words about airplanes. Yes, yes, I know you like them too. Today we are going to see the World's Largest Paper Airplane and a big pig and a big bull skull and something else. I can't remember. Listen, Papi, I am so happy to be seeing you soon. I miss you. I am sorry I was upset about leaving Dallas but—yes—my friends. I can see them on

Skype. Yes. Yes. I love you too, Papi. Bye." Homer ended the call.

"Your Papi was disappointed that you were so upset to be leaving Dallas. We have to go to Roscoe. It is best for the family. We must do what's best for all of us." Ann Marie stroked his hair.

"I know, Mami, but my friends..."

"No, no, we will talk about this later. We will discuss this when we have some time in private." She looked at him like they were spies trying to keep their secrets. I know that Mexicans are very private so I didn't care. I turned farther from them to give them a bubble of privacy. We drove on.

This is the first I heard about the diversions we would be taking to see all of these strange things, but I was happy for the company and, besides, I wanted to see these strange things too. I was curious why we were going there but I didn't want to be rude and ask a lot of questions. I thought looking at these things would tell me more about what it meant to be American.

"Pay attention, Raquel, we need to find the park with the sculptures." Jose Cruz was talking to her with his eyes on the road.

"I will. I will. Just keep driving and I will lead you." She was following a set of directions on her lap. "Rosita, this won't take long. Are you in a hurry to get to Los Angeles?" She turned around and faced me waiting for my answer.

"No. I am enjoying my introduction to America."

"OK then. We have the whole day to spend here, and Jose Cruz and I love to see all the things that Americans think are interesting. We do this all the time, it's our hobby. For example, today we will see the pig, the skull, the airplane, Dr. Seuss Park, and Dino Bob. Those are the things on my list. But if we find something else interesting, the list might change."

"They do sound interesting. I'd like to get some food sometime today from the grocery store. I can't afford to go to restaurants. Would that be OK?"

"OK, no problem." Raquel turned back around and studied the directions in her lap.

I didn't know if I was in a hurry or not. All of a sudden, I was here in the United States. My goal had been to get here and I hadn't really thought a lot about what would happen after that. So now there was no goal and I was with nice people and I was seeing some of the country. I had money. Experiencing America was the goal itself and strange for me too.

"Look! Look!" Homer had pulled his face out of the book and was pointing. We all followed his arm to its destination: a large metal pig on wheels. This must have been the first stop. We were all laughing.

Jose Cruz pulled into a parking space and we gathered our belongings. It was just like being on a family outing at the little park in my village. All of a sudden, I was surrounded by my new parents, Raquel and Jose Cruz, and Ann Marie was like my sister, and Brenda and Homer were like my niece and nephew. We were going to see something interesting together and we were all anticipating the experience. Is this what people felt like when they traveled? Is this how you went along the road and met people and just formed these immediate families? I felt like I had known these people my whole life.

"Let me take Brenda." I took her little hand in mine as we entered the tiny Everman Park. I could barely control her as she wanted so desperately to run up to the pig. It was fun, this piggy. He seemed to be smiling and he was like a pig and a bicycle combined or he was riding a bicycle. He must have been ten feet tall. He didn't have any feet because his legs came down and they became bicycle wheels. He was made of some kind of metal.

"Can we climb up on him, Mami?" Homer whined and was already climbing onto the pig before Ann Marie could even answer. She turned, looking for Raquel and Jose Cruz, but they were busy across the park looking at other sculptures.

"I suppose so, *hijo*. If we can't, I'm sure someone will tell us." Homer scaled the pig.

I walked around the pig, inspecting him from every angle. He seemed to be such a happy fellow. The kids loved him. They hung onto the bicycle wheels and made the whole thing into a makeshift playground for themselves. Since the kids were having a wonderful time playing on him, I walked back the other way a little to inspect something that had caught my eye.

There was a beautiful pink flamingo. He was brightly colored and twisted around bending down to take something off his leg. He looked so real that I expected him to just fly away. I had seen real flamingoes sometimes because they like to come to the tropics near us.

I kept an eye on Jose Cruz and Raquel who were checking on me too, so I waved. I walked back past the pig where the kids were still having a ball. I ambled along then and saw these odd-shaped white blobs in the grass. They looked like little robot bodies or like hats. They were made up of three levels of balls put on top of each other. I went over to touch them and they were some kind of stone.

They looked very cozy sitting on the grass like any family come here for a party. I loved them because they weren't as real as the other sculptures; they were more abstract so you could create a story about them in your mind.

Since everyone was busy I kept walking and came to a very realistic sculpture. It was a canoe that seemed to be flying over the waves. There were three children in the canoe and one of them was pointing forward. What did he see? Was it something fun or something scary? I walked around it and it was so lifelike even the fingernails were perfect.

"It's wonderful, isn't it?" A lady in jeans and a cowboy hat was pointing at the statue.

"Yes, it's so realistic." I hoped that was the right word.

"Yes. I love it but I love the abstract ones too."

"Oh, there are more?" She was smiling at me like we were sharing a magic moment together.

"I guess you're not from here. Abilene is full of sculptures. Wait, let me see. I know I have it here." She was rummaging in a big tote bag she had on her shoulder. She pulled out a crumpled piece of paper and put it on her leg to try to smooth it out. "Here, take this. It's a good guide."

I took the brochure. It said *Outdoor Sculpture Tour* along the top and had a map with numbers and pictures and descriptions of the sculptures.

"Thanks so much. This is very good. I could use a guide." I held the brochure tenderly, not wanting to wrinkle it any more than it already was.

"You're welcome, sweetie. You go on and look at those sculptures, ya' hear. Have a good day." She traipsed off and waved to me as she went.

"Thanks again," I said.

The map showed more sculptures. I walked over to Raquel holding my new treasure.

"I'm just going to walk down a little way and look at these." I showed her the map.

"Where'd you get that?" She looked at the map in my hand.

"A lady gave it to me near *The Hats;* that's what they call those white things over there." I pointed to the robot blobs. "Do you want the map?"

"No honey, you take it. I can download it when I get home and we can come back here some time. Are you enjoying it? Should we move on?"

"No, no, it's great. The kids seem to be having a great time and I am too."

"OK then, we'll come by and fetch you when we're ready to leave."

I went back to *The Hats* and walked past them to other sculptures. The first one I passed was a huge skull of a bull with giant horns. He seemed so real because he was white like a bull's skull would be after it had been bleached by the desert sun. He was such a symbol for these people in Texas, wasn't he? All of the movies showed the cattle drives and the bad guys and the gun fights. It was all about the cattle.

I kept walking and passed by *Abilene Piers*. This one was kind of weird to me. It was a series of blocks made up of bricks piled on top of each other. I didn't get the significance of the blocks but there they were.

If I thought *Abilene Piers* was weird I sure wasn't prepared for *Biomorphic Form*. This was like some kind of portal into another dimension. It reminded me of the TV shows that took people into other places through time or space by walking into some kind of strange doorway. I walked all the way around this sculpture and even went inside it to get the feeling of walking into another place. It was kind of eerie but I liked the feeling. I decided to go back and find the others before my exploring got us separated.

The kids were running around in the sculptures, laughing and playing. Since we were there in the middle of the day, there were no other kids playing so Brenda and Homer had the space to themselves and were taking full advantage of it. I was amazed how clean the park was. No trash. No litter. Even the plants were beautiful.

"Get off of that, Homer." Ann Marie pointed to him playing on the giant skull. I didn't know if it was for play or just to look at, but Homer had obviously decided it was something to play on. Homer dutifully got off the skull.

"Homer, Homer come, come, it's the Lorax. Come! Come!" Brenda took off running at top speed with Homer and Ann Marie trailing behind.

"Where are you going, Brenda? Stop. Where are you going?" Her voice betrayed worry.

"Mami, Mami, look it's the Lorax." She pointed to a sculpture that was of an animal I had never seen.

"And Horton!" Homer was screaming with excitement. The kids had led us to a small sculpture garden filled with strange creatures. Horton was an elephant. There were more. As the kids identified them, they spun around and excitedly ran up to us. They had seen their idols all in one place at one time and were beyond happiness.

"Look, look it's *Grinch. Grinch. The Cat in the Hat.* And

mira, mira, Yertle the Turtle. And that one, that one, *Green Eggs and Ham.*" The excitement was infectious. I found myself totally emotional about characters I didn't even know. I got tired with all of this energy and just sat on a bench. Beaming, Ann Marie came and sat by me.

"Who are all of these?" I asked. "The children are so excited."

"Ah yes, we love to read and there is a writer called Dr. Seuss who was really fun for them. He created all of these characters that you see here and his books all rhymed. So the kids loved them. They read them all dozens and dozens of times. The stories had some very good lessons about fairness and sharing and taking care of the planet. Very good. The books are all in Spanish too but we never read them in Mexico. The kids can read them in both languages here. I want them to read in English so they learned the books in English."

We sat and watched the children getting so excited about something that educated them. It gave me great hope for Nely that there were writers here that could excite children about learning. I was just starting to learn myself in university when I had to leave. Now I was coming somewhere that Nely would have a chance to have a dream and follow it. I breathed a sigh.

We sat for a while then while Raquel and Jose Cruz walked around and read all of the little plaques explaining the sculptures. This was obviously something they loved to do. I felt embraced by this family.

What a treasure these sculptures were. In Mexico there are sculptures all over Mexico City and the big cities too, I guess. But a small town of this size would not have many sculptures. The money would have to go for roads and telephone wire and water pipes. There wouldn't be extra money for something like this.

"Can we go now?" Raquel was asking. "We need to see the world's largest paper airplane."

I laughed out loud. What a strange thing to say. I knew it was supposedly true but who would be saying that to another person? Did America think everything it had was the "world's biggest"? Ann Marie gathered the kids and took them into the bathroom. I followed her and helped her with them. We had a drink at a machine that shot water into the air. It was delicious. They told me you could drink the water here right out of the tap. I had already learned you could flush the paper down the toilet. America had a lot to teach me. I wondered if the people here realized that so many of us in this world could not even get fresh water in our own homes?

We got back in the van then and Raquel was making a phone call.

"Yes ma'am, that's right, four adults and two children. Yes, we are very well behaved. The little boy loves airplanes."

"Is she talking about me, Mami? I love airplanes." Homer seemed agitated.

"I don't know, Homer, but I'm sure it's OK. Just relax, son."

"Yes in about five minutes. We won't stay long." Raquel put down the phone.

"Just keep going on this street, Jose Cruz, and we will see it from the road. It's on the lawn in front of a B&B. She said we could come in." She turned to us then. "We are going to see something special for Homer now because you two children were so good in the car."

"What is it?" Homer was suddenly thrilled, his nose out of a book for a change.

"I can't tell you because that would spoil the surprise, wouldn't it?" Raquel winked at Ann Marie.

We drove a very short distance before the surprise loomed into our sight. It was behind the fence of a big house with a sign that said *Bed and Breakfast* and it was magnificent. It was a gigantic paper airplane. I guessed it couldn't be made of paper or it would dry up or get soaked in the rain. Homer was bouncing in his seat.

"*Mira! Mira!* Mami, it's a giant paper plane. It must be 100 feet long. *Look! Look!* Can we go see it?"

"I think this is the surprise that Señora Raquel was preparing for us. Thank you so much." She looked at Raquel with gratitude.

Raquel got out of the car at the gate and spoke into an intercom. The gates opened like magic. I had seen this in movies but it was much more impressive to see it in person. We drove through and a worker pointed to a space where we could park. "Please don't climb on the plane," he said.

Homer had a hard time holding in his excitement as we all got out of the van. He ran ahead of us and whooped and hollered as he darted around the plane. It was strange to see such a shy little boy being so animated. He circled it over and over, noting everything about it.

"Mami, look, it's made just like a paper airplane. You can see the folds like you would in a piece of paper. "

"That's great, Homer. Enjoy yourself." Ann Marie was sitting on a bench with Brenda. As usual, Raquel and Jose Cruz were walking around reading brochures and looking for plaques or anything that explained the plane.

"Homer seems so happy." I sat on the bench with her.

"He's such a good boy. He loves to read but planes are his passion. He is going to be so excited in Roscoe about the wind farm. He doesn't realize that it will be like living among propeller planes. It will be good."

"Do you mind me asking how you and your husband got here, I mean, got to America?"

"Just like you, *Señorita*. We swam the *Rio Bravo* or like the Americans call it the *Rio Grande*. In those days, you could apply for a Green Card if you could show that you had been living in America and you were a good person and a good citizen. By then, the kids had come along and my husband had worked for a long time fixing things. He saved his money and saved a portion for taxes. It turned out to be a good idea. When he went for his interview, he had a check made out to what we call the Department of Revenue. That's the agency that collects taxes. He basically had his tax payment for all the money he had earned on the black market since we got here. The man at Homeland Security did not take the check but I think he was impressed. He knew that my husband would be a good citizen. So he got his papers and life has been sweet since then. We can take the kids to visit our families in Mexico. Without those papers, we could not leave. You know the family can't come and see us anymore. Homeland Security makes it impossible for families to visit each other in the States if they are illegal. I have many friends who came here and can't get papers and they have never been able to see their families again."

"You can see them on Skype or FaceTime."

"Can you hug someone on Skype or FaceTime?" She looked at me.

We walked back together to the car. Ann Marie settled the kids in the back and made a quick call to her husband. Meanwhile, Jose Cruz had put us back on the road after our lovely diversion.

"Excuse me." Ann Marie was calling from the back seat. "We need to stop at the Valero gas station in Roscoe. My husband says it's on the main street. Can we do that?"

"Yes, Ann Marie. We will be coming into Roscoe soon. Can you find Main Street, Jose Cruz?"

"*Sí*. No problem."

"Pick up your things, children." Ann Marie was putting things into bags in the back seat.

"Can I help?" I asked. "Maybe one of the kids can come up here with me and you will have more space to gather your things."

"Yes, thank you. Brenda, go up there with Rosita. Give her your book. Leave your jacket here."

"But the seat belt," Brenda whined.

"Just go fast and Rosita will put the seat belt on you. Go! Go!" She pushed her daughter up to the center seat beside me. I strapped her in with me.

"There you go, Brenda, all safe and sound." I smiled at her. "Are you excited about your new home?"

"It's in Roscoe," she said.

"Yes, I heard that. It will be fun to live in a town called Roscoe." I couldn't think of anything else to say so I just looked at her pink plastic purse and her pink plastic shoes. "Very nice," I said.

"I like pink," she said.

"Me too. I think all Mexicans like pink, it's one of our favorite colors." I smiled. She was doing exactly as I was doing: going somewhere for a better life. None of us were

JULIA REID GALOSY

so different after all.

"I think this is Main Street." Raquel was pointing to the big important building in a plaza. "I'll watch for the Valero station." She peered out of the front of the van.

"I'm going to see my Papi." Brenda smiled at me shyly.

"Yes, you must be very excited," I answered.

"We're going to live in Roscoe." She twined her hair in her fingers and sucked on the end of a braid.

"Yes, I heard that. I'm sure you will have a great time and make a lot of new friends."

"I like dolls," she said as if it were an answer.

"Me too." I smiled at her.

"*Mira*! There it is!" Raquel pointed at the Valero gas station up ahead. It was as if she was announcing a big ship spotted on the sea. The kids started bouncing in their seats.

"Papi, Papi!" They were shouting at a small, dark man standing outside of a pickup truck. He could have been anyone with his cowboy boots and jeans and straw cowboy hat. Jose Cruz pulled the van beside the truck and got out. He shook the man's hand. They went around the side and he opened the sliding door of the van and Brenda popped out.

"Papi, Papi!" she cried as he caught her up in his arms. She buried her face in his neck and wrapped her legs around him. Homer came out more shyly, manfully shaking his dad's hand until his dad grabbed him in a big hug. Ann Marie came out last over-burdened with the stuff of traveling with kids. Jose Cruz grabbed her bags from her and walked them over to the truck, giving the couple privacy. Ann Marie put her arms around her husband's neck and hugged him, kissing him on the cheek. He was

110

beaming. The family was back together. I watched this little family drama with fascination. I wondered who would be the Papi for Nely. I hoped we would be as happy as this family.

The family moved now to the pickup truck. Ann Marie opened the doors and the kids got in the back. Jose Cruz moved around to put the suitcase in the bed of the truck and clapped his hands together like he had dust on them.

Ann Marie's husband shook the hand of Jose Cruz. "Thanks for taking care of my family." He said it in Spanish. So much Spanish here. He looked serious as he said this, no smiles. Many times Mexican men did not smile when I thought they should. He fumbled around in his wallet and came up with money. He handed the money to Jose Cruz.

"Thank you and take care of the family," Jose Cruz said. He walked back toward the van. The husband got into the driver's seat. He turned around and said something to the kids. They both showed that their seat belts were on. Ann Marie smiled at him and I could see her put her hand on his shoulder. He smiled at her, looked into the rearview mirror, and drove away. He made a little wave as he passed us in the van.

"We'll take you as far as we're going in Arizona." Jose Cruz was at last speaking to me.

"That would be good. It's very nice to be with you." I smiled at him in the mirror.

"So what are you doing, *Señorita*? You seem lost," Raquel said without any criticism in her voice.

I don't know why I trusted her, maybe because she reminded me of my mother. I found myself telling her the whole story about my brothers and Guillermo, the first try to cross the border, the second try, the three *mojados* with me in the desert, the dead child, and the three men in Dallas. I didn't tell her about the rape. I was still wrapped up in the horror of it. I didn't tell her about Nely.

"Ah, *niña*, you have had a very hard time." Her compassion sounded deep in her voice.

"Now, what are you doing going to Los Angeles?" She frowned between her eyebrows.

"I can take care of children and I know there are a lot of Mexicans in Los Angeles. I got the name of a cousin of the priest in my village. Father Bustamante told me that he will help me to get a job as a nanny. I would be a very good nanny."

"I am sure you would but Los Angeles is a very great distance. It is a big city with thousands of cars and huge highways piled one on top of the other. It might be a difficult place for a young girl."

"I don't have a lot of options, Raquel." I looked at her directly so she could see the truth in my eyes.

"Hmm, we have some time now. We will think on this. I have to rest now. Jose Cruz, are you good driving?"

"Yes, *mi amor*." He looked at me in the rearview mirror. I felt safe with this man.

The view from the side window was changing rapidly. The whole trip up from Mexico was desert and then trees. Trees from the bus. Now the space between towns was widening. The trees were disappearing. Dust replaced the trees and it looked like Mexico. There were even tumbleweeds along the roads. Fewer and fewer cars passed by and miles upon miles had only telephone lines as company. Still we drove easily and happily together.

"Do you want to stay in a hotel with us?" Raquel was

asking me. "We're a bit tired of driving now."

"I don't really have the money," I said. I had to be careful because the supply of money was not endless.

"We have to get a room anyway. You can stay in a bed with me, and Jose Cruz can sleep in the other bed. We need to get real rest." I thought about the Mexican custom of putting four or five people in a bed and, of course, Raquel would know this. She was straightening her clothes as she turned back around to face the front. "Let's stop at a Mexican restaurant and then we can get a room, Jose."

Jose Cruz was driving slowly looking for something like a small Mexican restaurant. There were many restaurants but most of them were restaurants from American movies like McDonald's and Wendy's. I didn't see anything else.

"There, there," Raquel called out to him and pointed to the street we had just passed. He turned the car around and drove to this small restaurant with a sign advertising that it was Mexican. It felt good to get out of the car. I unfolded myself from the back and took my backpack with me. Raquel and Jose Cruz came around the front of the car to meet me and we all walked into the restaurant.

It was so much like home that I gasped. There were small tables painted beautiful colors and covered with tablecloths that were woven in all the patterns of Mexico. We pulled out our chairs and Raquel went away to go to the bathroom. There were wild murals on the walls showing scenes of our country. You could see the San Miguel parish church, the *Parroquia*, the Cathedral in Mexico City and, of course, the Virgin of Guadalupe. It made me homesick for a minute. I put my hand protectively on my belly to take care of Nely.

"Welcome to *La Hacienda,*" a waiter was smiling at us. "Do you know what you want to drink?" He said all of this in Spanish. With the colors and the name and the language I felt right at home.

"Corona," Jose Cruz answered.

"Coca light," I said.

"Corona," Raquel added as she sat down at the table with us.

"Nice place. Is it expensive?" I asked Jose Cruz.

He shook his head. I counted out my money and I knew I had plenty because it would only be about ten dollars for the enchiladas that I was going to order.

"This is a nice place. Look at the cooks in the kitchen. Look at the waiters. Everyone is Mexican like so many people in America. These are our people."

"I am beginning to understand that." I looked at the faces of the people working here and she was right. If we were American you couldn't tell it. I wasn't sure what an American looked like anyway. What was an American?

Raquel and Jose Cruz started talking in English to each other then and it was too fast for me to follow at all. There were some other strange things they wanted to see at a place called Lubbock, Texas, and they spent some time talking about that place. We were destined to see more strange American sights.

IX

The room in the motel was huge. We could have put my whole family into the two big beds. There was a TV on a dresser and a small refrigerator that was underneath a cabinet. The sink was outside the bathroom. Jose Cruz went to the bed closest to the bathroom and Raquel and I put our things on the bed near the window. There was even an air conditioner. It made a humming sound. I wondered how people slept with that sound.

We were all pretty tired from our long day together and we took turns taking a shower. It was lovely using a shower that never ran out of hot water. Raquel and Jose Cruz had little discussions and they hugged each other and kissed before she crawled into bed with me. He spread out on his bed and instantly fell asleep. He snored loudly. My dad had died long ago so I didn't remember if he snored. My brothers snored so I heard it a lot. I never had the opportunity to sleep with Guillermo. I wonder if he snored. I would never get a chance to find out. I soon fell into a deep sleep and I suppose I might have snored as well.

The shouts came like cannons in the night: shrieks and screams. I woke in terror, unaware of where I was. I flipped over in bed and made out the figure of a woman trying to soothe a hysterical man on the other bed. It was Raquel caressing Jose Cruz. His shouts were deep rumblings of horror screamed at the top of his lungs. They bounced off of the walls and hit us like bullets. I couldn't understand the words. He lunged out at her screaming, shouting, cursing. His words were spit out of his mouth like pellets. His arms punched the air and his whole body twisted. He struggled like this in her arms: screaming, shouting, cursing, fighting her off. Great whooping cries with no meaning came from deep inside of him. Spit and tears mingled on his contorted face. I shrunk below the covers, horrified at the sights I was witnessing. Just as suddenly as it began, it stopped. He collapsed like a rag doll. She continued to hold him until his breathing deepened and his snores began again. She sighed and put him gently back onto the bed. She tiptoed to the bathroom. I heard the door close and the toilet flush. She washed her hands in the sink and returned to bed.

"What is it? Is he all right?" I whispered into the silence.

"He will never be all right, *joven*. He was in one of those wars in one of those deserts and forever he will have something they call post-traumatic stress. He will never be all right."

"Does this happen all the time?" I was still terrified by the sudden entrance of this drama into our quiet trip.

"Don't worry, *hija*, this is not a problem for you. You have enough with your life and your baby. Go to sleep now." It felt good to be called *daughter*. She knew. Always other mothers knew; I was now one of them. I turned over and faced the air conditioner. The hum was amazingly soothing. "Good night, Raquel," I said into the wall.

"Good night, Rosita," she whispered in the other direction.

In the morning we didn't say anything about what had happened. We got up and I followed them into the little lobby. It is a good thing that there are television shows in the world or I would not know what to do as I encountered life here in the USA. I had never been to a motel. I had watched all of those American television shows to practice my English and I knew that this food here was for everyone staying at the motel. These pieces of bread and buns and muffins and cereals and eggs and bacon and milk and coffee and juices were all for us. There were people taking food and passing plates around to each other along a huge table piled with all kinds of wonders. We were saying sorry when we found ourselves in the way. The TV was blaring out the morning news and the weather and the people pretended to watch it. Most seemed dazed or asleep.

Raquel and Jose Cruz made their way around the buffet and piled food on their plates. I took pieces of fruit and yogurt and stored them in my backpack. I didn't know what today would bring and I wanted a little extra food in case I had to part from this couple. I piled eggs and bacon and beans onto my plate and added two big pieces of bread. No tortillas.

"We'll be taking a small detour today to Lubbock, Texas." Raquel clipped her seat belt. "Is that OK with you, Rosita?"

"Yes, I am really enjoying seeing my new country." I thought about the money I might have to spend on food. So far I had shared a meal with Raquel and had stored lots of supplies from this morning's breakfast. I thought I was doing fine. Meandering around the countryside looking at strange things had not been the plan. Now I was in a van with a Mexican couple who were obsessed with the strange sights of America. But I had promised myself that I would take whatever came my way on this trip and I was sticking to that promise. Anyway it was giving me an opportunity to see some sights in America and understand the American mentality a bit better.

"How long have you been visiting strange sights?" I shifted in my seat and put my legs up.

"A long time. We talked about it as a family when the kids were young. We were looking for some family outings that we could do that would also take us for drives around our new country. If the kids had been raised in Mexico we would have taken them to see Teotihuacan and Chichen Itza, and the other Aztec and Mayan ruins. Those are the sources of the Mexican culture. But what do you take them to see in America? The Liberty Bell and Boston are the historical sites but what do you do to help them to understand the culture? We thought that the fun side of the culture, what they call *wacky* would give the kids some insight into America and also would be fun for the kids. We made them watch the History Channel and the Discovery Channel on TV so that they would learn. Of course we learned too. I feel like an expert on the culture of America, maybe even more than Americans."

"How many places have you visited?"

"Oh, hundreds. Would you say hundreds, Jose?"

"Hmm, yes I think so. We have been doing this for about, let's see, twelve, thirteen years. We did it every summer when the kids were young. A long time. And there're new sights all the time."

"How do you find the sights?"

"We use the internet like everyone. And from other

people. When you visit the sights you get to talking to people who are visiting and they make recommendations to you. Americans like to be the most—the fastest, the smartest, the richest, the biggest—sometimes we would be talking to four or five people visiting a sight and they would get into a competition about who had been to the most sights. They would start asking each other leading questions like 'Have you been to...?' It was a contest. We never got involved in the contest but we listened and found out about sights that seemed like they would be fun or interesting." Raquel pulled the visor down and used the mirror there to put on her red lipstick.

"Where did you find the time? As a carpenter and as a cook, those are very demanding, time-consuming jobs."

"Well actually, Rosita, life has been kinder to us than this. We have businesses. I own a catering business and Jose Cruz owns a furniture making shop. We do fine."

"Why don't you tell that to people like me when you meet them?" I brought my feet down to the floor and shifted my backpack to the other seat.

"So many Mexicans ask each other if they have papers and it usually means they need something. At first, when we got our papers, we told people and then everyone was coming out of the woodwork asking us to be the long lost cousin of our mother or grandmother. It happened so much that we just got used to lying. It's sad really. It was much easier before 9/11 to become an American citizen. Now the whole country is paranoid and everyone is closing in rather than opening up."

"So did you go to school?" I faced her in the mirror, which she had left down to shield her from the morning sun.

"Yes, of course. Education is so easy here. As you know, education is free in Mexico but families like ours have to pay for books and uniforms and transportation. It's still too much money for Mexican families. But here it's different. There are junior colleges all over the country and you can take all of the courses you need. I took bookkeeping and tax preparation so that I could keep our books and we could be legal. Everything is here in America, you just have to be resourceful and take advantage of it." She gazed directly at me in the mirror.

"I will be doing that, I'm sure. But why do you go to the bus stations and ask people if they need rides? You don't seem to need the money."

"Ah, we started doing that a few years ago. When we take our little trips to see our strange attractions we always stop at the bus station to see if we can help some Mexicans to get where they want to go. Usually we can convince them to go along with us to see a bit of America. We charge them so little that they usually agree to come and then we bring them with us to the sights. You saw what happened today. I call it 'delight.' Do you know that word in English? It's like giving them a gift of laughter and delight. If there are kids, then it's even more fun because they are thrilled. Usually everyone laughs when they see the attractions. They're so unexpected that you have to laugh." She smiled at me in the mirror.

I suspected that this couple was more than they seemed. They were so smart and knew so much about all of these places to go. Poor Mexicans would never be looking for things like this to see and do. They would be going down to the cantinas having beer. Those Mexicans would not even be visiting the ruins in our own country.

They wouldn't be able to afford to go there so why learn about it? It would be just one more of life's disappointments.

I was beginning to believe that my plan to go along with whatever happens to me was working. So far my structured plans—to go with the coyotes and to stay at Antonio's cousin's house—had been disasters. The successes had been to trust in life and go. There I met the woman on the bus at the border, the three brothers, Dolores and Jesse, and now Raquel and Jose Cruz. It was chance that showed me a better way. I felt like I had learned more from these connections then anything I would have learned from Cruz, the Dallas boy I had trusted. Now my plan was to go to L.A. and find the priest's cousin. I wondered if I should just abandon that plan and see where life in America was going to take Nely and me.

Texas was dry and dusty and reminded me so much of Mexico. We drove on the *blue highways,* that's what Raquel called them. There wasn't much traffic but there was a lot of dust. We listened to Mexican music on the radio.

"Lubbock is a big town with a university called Texas A&M," Raquel was explaining to me. "What do the letters mean, Jose, do you know?"

"No, *amor,* I think something to do with agriculture."

"Americans love competitions, like I said, and this university has a lot of competitions with the other universities in Texas."

"Are there a lot of universities here?" I asked, thinking how we just had one university hours away from us in Mexico.

"There are many universities in America. Every state

has more than one university and then there are junior colleges and technical colleges and private colleges: hundreds of places to go to school. It seems they all compete with each other in a lot of ways. Mostly to get some sports trophies and to get some money for research and things like that. Anyway it's a big town and it has several strange sights. Today we are going to see, let's see, let me look at my list: *Jesus in a Box, A Giant Arrow, Barnyard Space Ship.* So many things are the world's biggest or the world's largest or whatever. Americans always think they have the biggest. Texas, especially." She laughed at that.

"Why's that?" Texas was getting complicated.

"I'm not sure. For a long time Texas was the biggest state until they made Alaska a state and then it wasn't the biggest anymore. I think they make up for it by having a lot of the world's biggest things. Just relax for a while; we will be there soon." She sat back in her seat and faced the road.

I sat back, too, and looked out the window. I pulled myself from the van and sent my consciousness up into space so I could look down and observe myself traveling in Texas. I wondered how a girl from Mexico got here. How did I get to this place? I knew how I traveled physically but how did I travel in my mind and my emotions to be here now? It didn't seem possible that I could be here in a van with two Mexican-Americans and not in a poor village in Mexico. My mind could hardly believe that it was real. I thought I would wake up from my dream in a minute. Now it was even more absurd since I was in a van traveling to look at strange attractions beside the little roads of America. How was that even something people did and how was it something that I did? I breathed a sigh. I breathed deeply and let the experience flow over me like a cool stream in the hot sun. It felt free and joyful to be experiencing this connection in the middle of Texas. It felt spontaneous and fun to be with these two interesting people who had been through what I had to go through and had come out the other side just to be finding strange places to go and visit. How wonderful that this was what took up our time now and not the day-to-day grind of digging in the dirt or living in poverty. How liberating to spend the day just searching for things that made you laugh. I couldn't even believe it.

I pulled my cowboy hat down over my eyes. Even the hat, a last minute parting gift from Ann Marie, was an unexpected pleasure. Something so small, but so useful, and so symbolic of belonging. Would I actually belong someday? Would I walk out of the door of a house or an apartment and be an American? Would my new country actually be my own country then? I thought about that possibility and on this day, at this time, at this exact moment, that possibility seemed as remote as landing on Mars. In a way, I was on Mars: a stranger in a totally strange land. I looked at the backs of Raquel and Jose Cruz and was thankful that, at least for a little while, I had some guidance.

"We can't miss it, Jose Cruz, it's 21 feet high." Raquel was talking to Jose. "We're going to see a huge arrow." Everything was huge, I thought.

It turned out the arrow really was huge: a giant arrow sticking out of the ground. We pulled in to take a look and I went to sit on a bench while Jose Cruz and Raquel searched out the history. So strange to me that Americans revere the people they slaughtered. Here was a shrine to Indians and the first immigrants to America who just killed them. Maybe that's why Americans were so afraid of immigrants now. I wondered how all of this worked anyway. It had been so simple from Mexico but each day it gets more and more complicated. I didn't see much to appreciate about the arrow. It was more of a symbol I guess.

"Did you learn something interesting?" I asked, more out of politeness.

"Yes we did. We have seen some more of these markers. This is part of the Quanah Parker Trail so it's more historical than strange. The Trail is something set up to show where the last Comanche chief, Quanah Parker, was. His mother was a captured white woman who became a Comanche. His father was a Comanche warrior, but I can't remember his name. Jose Cruz and I might make a list of the sights on this Trail and find them some time in the future. They don't seem strange enough for us, though. What do you think, Jose Cruz?"

"I think the United States has many more strange sights to see, but I think you should make your list. It's important to learn about this trail, I think. Besides, one more list in the house won't even be noticed." He smiled at that. "We are going to a really strange one now, Rosita. The *Jesus in a Box.*"

I didn't even want to ask what that meant. I watched the giant arrow get smaller and smaller as we drove away. I wondered if the Americans ever felt guilty for making money off of those they exploited. We did the same in Mexico. The Aztec and Mayan pyramids make a fortune for the Mexican government. I wonder if anyone ever thinks about what was done to those people? I guess we did at least think about it because we learned all about it in our history classes. I was always so busy working at home and now I've had all of this time to think. I've never had so much time to think before, to be inside my own head. But then, I've never been an immigrant. Here, I was like the boys had told me: I am between. Neither Mexican nor American. I felt like I was an empty bin that needed to be filled up on all things American. I thought watching movies about America would prepare me for living here. Now I felt like I knew nothing.

You could see the glass box from the highway. It was like one of those greenhouses or botanical gardens under glass that you see in the movies. I expected it to be full of plants. But instead it was filled with a Jesus on the cross. He was life-size with very realistic features like blood dripping from his wounds. He looked like a person in terrible pain. My heart felt so sorry for him.

Jose Cruz and Raquel nearly leapt out of the van and stood with all of the people who were crowded around the Jesus. Many were holding rosaries and praying quietly. Others were drinking beer and laughing, posing for selfies with the statue. They thought it was a big joke. I didn't know what to think. Was this a tribute to faith or something that made fun of it? I watched the two types of people.

The selfie-takers were loud. They ran around the glass box, laughing and pointing. They drank their beer. They took turns posing with Jesus like he was a candidate in an election. They were mostly white boys. The faithful on the other hand were taking this very seriously. They were quiet and reverential and they bowed their heads in the presence of the Lord. They prayed. It must have been difficult for them to ignore the shouts and whoops of the young men. Yet they persevered; they continued their praying. I guess that is what faith is anyway. It's staying the course, going with it even when it was really difficult to believe.

I had seen this faith over and over in Mexico. Heads are put on the top of fence posts and the families go to church and talk to God. People in the government take the money from the poor and everyone goes to church and prays. So many people don't even get to finish grade school and the people go to church and pray. I found it amazing. With so many distractions and so many temptations and so much corruption, the people go to church and pray. I know these boys with their beer and their camera phones thought that the people praying were out of touch, old fashioned or maybe even delusional. But I found them admirable. It is easy to be a person of faith in good times. It's when they are really being challenged that it is so hard to keep the faith. But they do, and I am amazed. I wanted to tell these boys to shut up and stop their stupid drinking and pictures and to have some respect. But, of course, I had to hold back and fade into the background.

Jose Cruz got to the van first. He had tears welled up in his eyes and I saw him put a rosary back into his pocket. Raquel was quiet when she came in and we rode in silence for a while. I wondered if we were going to talk about it. I waited. Nothing came. Perhaps this was not such a strange sight after all. I began to think that the sights were becoming serious rather than strange. The arrow was a sad reminder of a time that should not have made Americans proud. And the Jesus. The Jesus was people's faith. I did not see anything strange about that. I hoped the next attraction would be odder, not so sad.

"Do you have a favorite attraction?" I needed to break the silence.

"What do you think, Jose?" Raquel put her hand on her husband's shoulder.

"We've seen so many. I would have to think about that. And then, there will be so many more. How can we decide?" He kept his eyes on the road.

"I have to think too. Some of them were historic like the arrow so I don't think they're strange. Some are strange like the pig. Hmm. I will think about that. The one we see now will be strange, I'm sure. It's a spaceship with aliens." Jose Cruz said this so seriously that I had to laugh. *We're all aliens*, I thought.

It was a spaceship with aliens. It looked like everything we thought of as aliens when we were children. It had little green creatures all around it and they had big black circles for eyes and their heads were a strange shape. The spaceship was a big aluminum disc.

"I'm a bit tired." I didn't really want to get out and look at the spaceship. "I'll just rest here, if you don't mind. Please don't hurry."

"OK, here're the keys in case you need to go to the bathroom or something." Raquel handed me the keys. They both trudged over to the spaceship dutifully looking for brochures or plaques to learn about it. They were so passionate and happy in their hobby. These were people who were at home in America. They weren't Mexicans anymore, they had made the transition, over the real border, not the river, between the two cultures. I hoped that Nely would do that, that she would be an American and feel at home in her new culture. What would she do about the old culture? How would she love the Mexican culture too? I didn't know the answer to that question.

X

Jose Cruz, Raquel, and I passed our time together just like this for many weeks. We drove around Texas doubling back and going up and down, all in the pursuit of strange sights. I couldn't even keep up with all of the sights we saw. I had to agree with the Texans; Texas was huge! Sometimes people would tell us about sights that weren't on the web yet or that we had overlooked. This information would send us off in different directions entirely.

At night we went to small motels, Raquel and I sharing one bed and Jose Cruz the other. Sometimes Jose Cruz would have his night terrors and Raquel would hug and soothe him until he calmed down. They would stay like that for the rest of the night. I tried to pay several times but they wouldn't have it. They were going to take the room anyway so why should I pay? Every day we ate a huge breakfast and took sufficient food for lunch. We only had to pay for dinner. By the time the nighttime meal came around, we were often not too hungry, especially if we had loaded up on meat earlier in the day.

So the days flowed by and I was able to conserve my money and get stronger and stronger. For some reason, I was no longer in a hurry to get to L.A. The journey itself, not the destination, had become my goal. I was learning so much about America and my English was improving so much that I hesitated to abandon this experience.

"Rosita, we have a suggestion for you." Raquel and Jose Cruz were back in the van and woke me up. "We have a friend who we think can help you. She is in New Mexico, very close to here, and she owns a small ranch. She has a lot of animals and we're sure you could stay with her for a while before you continue your journey. Her people are Mexican. You could learn a lot from her."

"Are you tired of me already?" I asked, only half kidding.

"No, *Cariña,* we just thought that you seem relaxed now and you don't have to be in a hurry. She could find you little jobs around the ranch to make some money and you could get used to America while staying with her. She could teach you some things and you would be safe. And, although we haven't talked about it, we know there is a baby on the way. You would be safe with her."

"Oh thank you so much. It would be wonderful to be safe for me and the baby. I have been having such a good time with you that I was not really moving on, was I? I was avoiding the hard times by just flowing with you. I do need to get going now and find my way. Please take me to her place." I smiled at her sadly, fully aware of the bittersweet aspect of this step.

"She has been a friend of ours for years. We'll take you. We should be at her place in a few hours. Here's a sandwich for you and a coke. We'll head right there."

I took the sandwich, unwrapped it, and started eating it in the car. Suddenly, the reality of my situation hit me between the eyes. I had been lulled into a kind of dream, just meandering around the countryside with Raquel and Jose Cruz. Now I had to face that I was an illegal immigrant in a country hostile to my kind, with a baby coming. I felt a quickening of my heart as I thought about a future so unknown. Why did I leave Mexico for this?

Breathe. Breathe. I took deep breaths and started to feel myself relax. I knew that I would have moments like this all the time until I found that future that awaited me somewhere. In the meantime, I needed to just keep going. I needed to find that better life that I still hoped was out there. Cruz's attack on me and the negativism Ann Marie felt toward America had side-tracked my optimism but I had to get it back and keep going. For me. For Nely. I fell asleep until we came up to the farm, my new home.

The farm was a combination of dust and green. It had a fence all the way around as far as we could see with barbed wire and posts. We drove along a road following the fence line for a few miles. At the end, there was an open space with a couple of old pickup trucks parked there. Inside the fence were four horses, a mule, three sheep, and I counted four dogs. All of the animals were in and out of each other's legs. Across from the field was a small two-story house made of wood with a tire hanging from the giant tree outside. A screen door banged shut as the woman approached our truck.

"Well, look what the cat dragged in." The woman walked across the space in big steps. She had wispy curls coming from under her cowboy hat. Her skirt was hitched up in a belt and several underskirts floated around her boots. She took big loping steps that demonstrated her energy but her face was a roadmap of wrinkles. It was impossible to tell how old she was. I didn't see any cat so I didn't understand what she meant about the cat dragging something in.

"Angela!" Raquel screamed the name across the dirt road and bounded out of the van before Jose Cruz had barely stopped. The two women ran to each other and blended into one. They just seemed like a two-headed being. Jose Cruz and I climbed out of the van. I didn't know if I should take my backpack because I didn't want to assume that I would be staying here.

"Get your stuff, *Joven*," Angela called to me from behind the embrace of Raquel.

Jose Cruz walked shyly toward her. I thought her energy would consume him. If his relationship with Raquel was any indication, he was one of those men who were attracted to energetic women but they nearly ate him up. He put out his hand to shake Angela's. She grabbed it and pulled him into a hug.

"C'here, you old goat. So good to see you two." She kissed him on both cheeks before he was able to make his escape. "Let's go have some coffee. I got some good biscuits that Cook just made and they'll be a real treat." She was somehow capable of gathering both of them in her arms and moved them into the house through the old screen door. I followed, suddenly shy in the face of all of this power.

The house was just like you see in the American movies. It had homemade furniture covered with cushions. Books were stuffed into all of the shelves and even piled up on the television and the refrigerator and at the top of the cabinets in the kitchen. The floors were wooden boards. All of the cupboards were rough, bulky and probably very heavy. For the first time since I was in America there didn't seem to be too much stuff, except for the books.

In the kitchen she had several pots suspended over the stove and all of her food was in mason jars. The dishes and glassware were neatly stacked on shelves. A few pictures without their frames were around the walls. In fact, everything about the house said "simple." It seemed the perfect place for Nely and me to stay for a while. There was a big pot of coffee percolating on the stove.

"Sit down, sit down." Angela went to get the cream from the refrigerator and gathered the sugar on her way back to the table. She was doing a great job of putting everything out. For some reason, I got up and started to help her. Everything was visible so I got the cups and the small plates for the biscuits that were sitting on the stove cooling. I put them on the table and put the butter there while I searched for cutlery. I found spoons and knives and forks and put these out too. I was amazed at myself because I would never do this in Mexico at another person's house. But the infectious warmth of Angela made it the most natural thing in the world to just help her.

She was keeping up a steady stream of conversation with Raquel and Jose Cruz. I just listened to the two women sort out my life. Raquel was explaining my situation as if we had known each other for years. She told my story in detail, remembering all of the things that had happened at the border and with the three men and Dolores and Jesse and the three guys in Dallas. She didn't leave out anything that I had told her.

"Well, child, you have had quite a time, quite a time." Angela pushed the hair back off of her face that had curled around her eyes. She reached across the table and squeezed my hand. "You're welcome to stay here as long as you need to. We've all been through tough times. If we don't help each other, who will help us?"

We passed a short time talking about the trip and the strange sights we had seen. Most of the time Angela just listened and she laughed at the descriptions of the sights. I helped her clear the table after our snacks and she poured more coffee for Raquel.

"Why don't you go visit the animals with Jose Cruz so Raquel and I can gossip?" she said to me. Jose Cruz got up immediately. I guessed he was happy he didn't have to hear this stuff. I followed him out of the screen door and across the road to the animals. He hung on the fence and watched the dogs and sheep play together. The sheep didn't seem too interested.

"They've been friends for about twenty years." The effort to start a conversation was hard for him.

"They seem like sisters," I offered. I was sitting on the top rung of the fence looking out at the animals too. "They have so much energy together."

"It wears me out when we're together. I need to escape."

"This is a nice escape. Do you want to take a walk along the field?" I was pointing to a field that ran outside of the fenced area. I thought it might be fun to explore anyway. We had been cooped up in the car for days now. In response to my question, he turned away from the fence and in the direction of the field without answering me. I came off the fence and came alongside of him.

"Do you think it's impossible to live as an illegal here?" I was walking around the fence with him now, heading for the open field and the woods beyond.

"I don't think it's impossible; it's difficult. The atmosphere is different. The laws have changed.

Immigration is a political issue now. The politicians in this country don't agree on anything and they fight all the time and nothing really gets done. As immigrants, you just wait for the next change. It keeps everyone insecure." This was the most Jose Cruz had spoken since I had met him. I was amazed that, without Raquel to talk for him, he did have something to say.

"So what advice would you give me?" I tried to catch his eye but he kept looking down at the path as we circled the fence.

"Be careful who you trust." He flicked his eye toward me for a second. "You will want to trust Mexicans because in Mexico we could trust each other. But when Mexicans come to the United States they get caught up in the American way: every man for himself. This country is proud of its spirit of independence, individualism. It likes the fact that it has all of these people who think they are strong. We would just see them as bullies. You will be really surprised to see some Mexican mayors and congressmen and senators talking on the television. They will be talking about keeping immigrants out of the country. They will not be talking about helping their brothers and sisters to have a better life."

We walked along in silence while I thought about this. What did I expect, really? Really. Really. I expected to be helped at every turn by Mexicans. I expected the cousin of Antonio to help me, not to rape me. I didn't expect, but I hoped, that the coyotes would do no harm. I still expected the cousin of the priest to help me. I even expected Raquel and Jose Cruz to help me just because we had Mexican blood in us. Who had really helped me so far? Three Mexican brothers who had abandoned me in the end. An

American waitress. An American bus driver. So far no American had done me harm. But Mexicans had. Now the in-between people—the Americans who came from Mexico—had helped me.

Jose Cruz didn't really want to talk anymore so we walked along, enjoying the natural beauty of the place. Behind the pasture, the hills in the distance were a soft blue color nearly blending with the sky. Jose Cruz walked with his hands in his pockets and his head down. We walked for a long time until we came to the end of the fence on the other side of the road by which we had entered

"Maybe we should be getting back." He turned abruptly and headed back in the direction by which we had come. I turned too. "The girls should've had enough time to talk by now."

I wasn't sure of that. It seemed to me, as girls, we never ran out of things to talk about. I got a stab in my heart then, missing my mom and my aunts. Where would I find girls here to talk to? I didn't want to think about that now. I needed to take each day as it came, not to make a plan. Not get anxious. I took a deep breath. Jose Cruz had picked up the pace and I did too to keep up with him. When we came into the kitchen, Angela and Raquel were washing the dishes.

"What did you two find to talk about?" Raquel dried the plate and put it in the stack on the shelves. "I don't think he's been alone with another woman for that long since we got married." She gave her husband an affectionate look. I looked at him to answer the question but nothing came from him.

"Trust," I said.

"That's a lot heavier than the local town gossip." Angela and Raquel laughed at this. I guess they're right. Trust can be a heavy topic.

"Well, we better be going," Raquel said. She linked arms with Angela and they walked out into the yard. Jose Cruz was kicking the dirt off of the tires of the van.

"Bye, sister." Angela wrapped Raquel into a big bear hug. "I'll see you when I see you. I love you loads."

Jose Cruz came around the van then and gave Angela a stiff hug. He did the same to me and then climbed into the driver's seat and busied himself with getting settled.

"Wait, wait, I must pay for the ride. Give me a minute to get the money." I turned to go and get my backpack.

"No Rosita, you don't need to pay us anything. We were happy to have you with us." She smiled at me.

"But no, how will I ever repay you?" I implored her.

"Americans have a great saying: *pay it forward*. It means that you need to do something for someone else in the future now to pay us back. It's a way of growing acts of kindness between all of us. I really like it." She turned to go into the truck.

"Raquel, I love you and Jose Cruz so much. Thank you for taking care of me. I will do something wonderful for someone in your name." I looked after her.

Raquel turned to me then. "Good bye, Rosita, my little angel, take care of yourself and the baby. God will be with you." I buried myself in her arms.

"Cece." I croaked through tears.

"Cece?"

"My name is Cece."

"Why do you call yourself Rosita?"

"It's a story. The coyotes told us to disguise ourselves.

I know it sounds stupid."

"It's trust now, Cece. You don't have to lie to others. Trust others and trust yourself. Angela is a very wise woman. Learn from her."

I started full-blown crying then. I couldn't stop. Why were these two people so important to me? No one tried to stop me or soothe me. It was like letting a dog get on with it. I stood crying, waving good-bye to the van with Angela's arm around my shoulder. She tightened her grip when the van pulled away.

XI

"Come on then. I'll show you the palace grounds."
Angela let go of me and started walking toward the barn.
I sniffled and the crying stopped.

The barn was a big old-fashioned one like you see in
the Wild West. There were four stalls for horses, and all
kinds of bridles and reins were hung up neatly along the
walls. At the far end was a big pile of hay bales and a ladder
that led up to a loft which looked to be full of hay too. As
we walked through it, Angela pointed out the stalls and
names over them where the horses would go at night.

We walked through the barn and came to a chicken
coop with about a dozen chickens. There was one rooster
strutting around like he was the king and his harem of
ladies and chicks ran around scratching at the dirt and
pecking at treasures. The little chicks were so cute
following their mothers.

On the other side of the chicken coop there was a
pigsty, which we could smell before we got to it. Pigs really
were stinky. There were six fat pigs. Five of them were
sound asleep stretched out on the ground, but the sixth
one was actively rolling in the mud. He looked blissful. He
snorted as we walked by. Neither one of us talked. I don't
know why, but I didn't feel like it. We walked back to the
house and up the stairs.

"This will be your room, Ros—er, Cece." She led me

into a small room with a metal bed and a small dresser. It was on the second floor so the windows looked out at the valley. I could see the dogs playing with the horses. "Here's a little closet and the bathroom is in the hall. You'll find some towels in there and there are some sheets here on the top of the wardrobe."

"I don't really know what I'm doing here." I just said out loud what I was thinking.

"Me neither. I just think it's one of those times that we have to trust in life. Sometimes life sends us in a direction that we didn't expect, and we needed to go there even though we didn't know it at the time. For something. For an experience or for some lesson or for a connection with a person who will be important. I don't question it. What brought my husband and me here to this place? It was a twist of fate and it worked out well. What brought you here to this place?" She spread out her arms, gesturing out the window, taking in the whole landscape.

"Fate?"

"Right. I think there's some reason you're here and maybe we'll find that out and maybe we won't, but the process of finding out will be fun. Don't you think?"

"I do think so." How could I not benefit from being around a person who was so positive and so upbeat?

"I'll leave you to it," Angela said. "Let me know if there's something you need. Farms have a little bit of everything." She turned to watch me unpack.

I started taking my things out of my backpack and hanging them up for the very first time in their new home.

"Hmm, you'd best put those in the washing machine and out on the line before you hang them up in the closet. They have seen a lot of the road, I expect." She said this kindly with no hint of criticism in her words or her eyes. "Follow me to the laundry area and we'll get those washed."

We went downstairs and she showed me where the washing machine was. It was a bit older than the one in the Dallas boys' house but it was the same principle. Not so different from the ones in Mexico either. I put in the clothes and the soap and went into the kitchen to follow her.

"What can I do to help you?" I asked.

"Cece, I think you need to explore on your own. I don't really need any help. There's two people you'll need to meet here. Cook and Efrahim. They're part of our family here too. You need to understand the place to see how you might add some contribution. We eat at six. You'll find your place here but you have to understand us first. I need to work on the books this afternoon so I'll be at my desk if you need anything. Go explore." She walked out of the room then, leaving me standing in the kitchen on my own. I felt a bit lost.

I went outside and walked over to the corral where the horses were. Four dogs came running up to me: a brown one, a black and white one, a golden one, and a black one. I patted the dogs and walked toward the corral with them at my heels. What was I going to do now?

I walked to the other side of the corral and came to a big vegetable garden. There were rows of crops coming up with weeds sprouting all along the furrows. Here was my first job. There was a little lean-to with a tin roof at the other end of the garden. I walked over there and rummaged through it until I found a trowel and some gloves. Just like the barn, everything you needed was here.

I put on the gloves, took the trowel and a hoe, and moved back into the garden.

After all of those days in cars and buses it felt wonderful to be back outside doing work. I was amazed at how much I had missed just working in the garden. I recognized most of the plants from the ones we had in Mexico. There were beans, peppers, tomatoes, cucumber, eggplant, lettuce, onions, cantaloupe, and various fruit trees as well. I worked methodically from row to row, hoeing and digging to get out all of the weeds. It was very hot but it felt wonderful to be outside and doing something. I started to feel my body un-kinking. The dogs came by and sniffed periodically as I worked but, mostly, I was alone with myself and my thoughts.

I finished weeding the garden and looked around for a compost bin where I could throw the weeds. I found one, of course, at the edge of the garden and piled the weeds into it. I washed the trowel and the hoe with the garden hose and hung them back on their spaces in the shed. I brushed the dirt from my jeans and walked back toward the house. I had been so lost in my work that I didn't notice the time, and hours must have gone by because the sun was way past midday.

Cook was in the kitchen and the lovely smell of onions frying in the pan greeted me at the screen door when I opened it.

"I am Cece. Nice to meet you," I said in English, not knowing if Cook spoke Spanish. Besides, I needed to practice.

"Everyone calls me *Cook,* short for *Cookie,*" the chubby lady spoke to me. "Angela said you might like to take a shower. I think you know the bathroom is upstairs and the towels are there too. Dinner won't be ready for about three hours."

"Can I help you?"

"You can help me whenever you like. There's always jobs for another pair of hands in a kitchen."

"Well, let me help you now, and then I'll take a shower before dinner. Where's Angela?"

"Believe it or not, there's actually a town here and she went there to get some supplies. She'll be back soon. Start by peeling those potatoes there." Her head bobbed in the direction of a stack of potatoes on the counter. She was elbow-deep in bread dough and was having a bit of a problem getting her arms around her big bosom. She was managing in spite of the challenge.

"The peeler is hanging on the rack over there." Her head bobbed again in the direction of a rod over the sink.

I washed the potatoes in the sink and started peeling them into a big bowl I found under the counter. The peels flipped into the bowl but many escaped and landed on the countertop and on the floor. I continued to peel anyway, knowing I would pick them up later.

"Do you live here at the ranch, Cook?" I kept peeling, wondering if she had a room out back or some other arrangement.

"No, I live in town with my three kids and my no-good husband. There's Rafael, he's nineteen and is studying computers. Maria is seventeen and is taking classes at a beauty school and little Elena, she's only eleven but she's really the smart one. Straight A's that one. She'll go far. Rafael is pretty athletic. He plays soccer or, as I think you all call it, football. He has a girlfriend and I hope they're not serious because they are too young. Her name is Emily.

Her dad owns the car dealership so that makes them rich. She has long blonde hair too and that makes her special in this town. Everyone here looks like you. No offense, it's just that most people come from Mexican stock.

"Maria, my second one, spends all day fixing herself. She's always changing her hairstyle and putting stuff on her face and fixing her nails. She puts these sticker things on her nails so sometimes they're covered with stars or strange colors or little faces. Her nails are useless to her anyway because they're made of plastic. The other day it took her three hours to get ready for a friend's party. Three hours! Who has that kind of time?" Cook didn't stop for a breath as she continued the description of her children.

"Little Elena is the total opposite. She plays softball and runs track at school. She's always out of the house doing something, you know, athletic. She's a great swimmer and she wants to learn to play tennis too. Her PE teacher, oh, PE that means *Physical Education,* I'm not really sure that's what it's called anymore but it has to do with athletics. Anyway, her PE teacher thinks she can get a scholarship to college for either track or softball. She's that good. But you know, she's smart too, she gets really good grades and she works hard. Kind of the opposite of Maria, I guess. But kids are all different. My three seem to come from three different fathers. They didn't, of course. They all came from the no-count. He's a no-count because he would rather have a few beers than a few hours of work. He can't seem to take himself away from those Mexican cantinas. He loves those places. I don't know why. He ain't Mexican. No offense."

She paused and took a breath. Her round face was

covered with a thin film of sweat as she worked over the dough. Her arms were like sausages caught in a white sheath. Even her hands were chubby. I guessed she liked her own cooking. She had laid the dough out on the table and was rolling it with a rolling pin. I saw now that it was going to be a pie. The fruit was already prepared in a bowl waiting to be scooped into the crust when she finished it. I had never had a pie before. Mexicans eat a lot of cakes and pastries but this would be my first pie.

"My God, girl, I been talking so much you ain't had a chance to get a word in. Do you wanna say somethin' now?" She kept rolling.

"Oh, I was enjoying your description of your family. I'm finished peeling. Do you want me to cut up the potatoes?"

"No, I think we'll rice them, you know, make fluffy mashed potatoes so we want the potatoes to be big so they are easier to rice. Do you know how to do that? Mostly your people eat tortillas so I guess you don't rice potatoes very much. Am I right?"

"No, we don't rice potatoes. I don't even know what ricing is. Why do you rice potatoes anyway?"

"To make hash browns, silly, or to get your mashed potatoes real fluffy. Why else would you rice them?" She gave me a big smile like I was just being foolish. "Let's just go ahead and put them in a big pot and boil them. The pot's under the counter, down there." She bobbed her head again toward a big pile of pots under the counter.

"Where do you keep the bottled water?" I asked, looking for the big five-liter bottles we have in Mexico.

"We don't use bottled water, honey. Right there in the sink. You just turn on the faucet."

"Oh, of course, I think it's amazing here that you can drink water from the faucet."

"Yep, clean water right there in your house. You tellin' me you can't do that in Mexico?"

"No. You have to buy your water in five-liter bottles from a truck that comes around and delivers it or walk to a store and buy it and carry it home."

"I never heard of such a thing. That's just plain loco. That's one of your words."

I smiled at that comment. I always wondered where all of those big jugs of plastic ended up anyway; in piles of rubbish all over Mexico, I guessed. I filled the big pot with water and put it on the stove. I put in the potatoes and then searched around for a match to light the stove.

"I'm sorry to keep bothering you, but where are the matches to light the stove?" I felt stupid asking these continuous questions but the Dallas house was electric. This was my first gas stove.

"Oh dear, honey, you really are a newcomer, ain't ya? We don't light the stoves here unless you're out in the country in some kind of cabin or somethin'. Just push in the button on the stove, the one on the far right, yeah that one, and turn the burner you want to the right. See, the flame just starts up when that little clicking noise comes on. That's the electric starter. We all have electric starters these days to light the fire.

"Now, good job. Would you go under that counter again and get out the ricer? It looks like a metal cup with holes and a long handle. Yep, that's it." She nodded at the contraption I had in my hand. It didn't look like anything I had seen in Mexico or on American TV or movies either. It was just like she said, a metal cup with holes. It had a lid that came down into it and at the other side it became a handle. I knew I was going to get to use it today and I looked forward to using something else that was new to me.

"What next?" I was enjoying myself. I was being part of a family now; not going on the road and facing the unknown. At least for now, I had jobs and I could do them well.

"Can you make a salad?"

"Yes, I can. Should I just find things in the refrigerator?"

"Good girl. Rummage around in there. There are some carrots and onions in the larder, through that door on the other side of the kitchen. Wash everything good under the tap and set it out to dry while you're cutting things up. There's some beets in the larder too. You can put them on the stove to boil so we can add them later, now that you are such an expert at using the stove, that is." She gave me a big grin, very pleased with her own humor.

The larder was full of great things that were probably from the garden. There were turnips, carrots, onions, beets, and some things I didn't recognize. In the refrigerator I found tomatoes, lettuce, celery, and cucumbers. I got out a big bowl and started to tear the lettuce.

"There will only be three of you so don't make too much."

"I didn't realize anyone else lived here." I was washing the lettuce under the tap.

"No one does but Ms. Angela will have her beau with her tonight."

"What's a beau?" I asked. I thought maybe it was a

word I didn't know for a friend or something.

"A beau is kind of an old-fashioned word. It means boyfriend but it's hard to see anyone over forty calling a grown man a boyfriend. If you see what I mean?" I did.

"What's he like?" I was cutting the tomatoes on a small cutting board I found hanging on the counter.

"You'll see. It's quite a change when he comes around. Miss Angela turns into a girl." She was laying the dough inside the pie tin now, carefully lapping it over the edges.

"Isn't she always a girl?" I cut up the cucumber into little bits.

"She's a tough cookie. She runs this ranch all by herself. She ropes. She drives the tractor and the plow. She's tough. With him, with Richard, she's a softie. You'll see it. Tell me tomorrow what you think. Anyway, to answer your question, he's a real nice man. Very quiet. She told me he is very interesting because he reads a lot. He's a teacher in the town here and the kids love him. Sometimes he brings the kids out here to spend a day on the farm. A lot of them are from the city. Well, if you can call it a city. I think a lot of them are those wetback kids. No offense. They have a great time taking tractor rides and watching the people ride the horses and do lariat tricks and stuff. Sometimes they are very useful and they fix things around the place. 'Course those days are really busy for me what with all the extra food I have to make for 'em. Are you following my English, honey?"

"I watched a lot of Western movies so I am following you, most of it anyway." My eyes were tearing because I was cutting up the onion now.

"Oh, those damn onions, there's a clean towel over there, honey." She bobbed her head toward another wall.

She was carefully cutting around the edge of the dough now. I found some clean dish towels folded up under the counter and used one of these to wipe my eyes. I came back and resumed my cutting.

"Oh, he's real handsome too, did I tell you that? He looks like a movie star. All of those little girls are in love with him. He's not too tall. Not much taller than she is. But he's lean. He has a beard. A really fluffy beard and he wears glasses. He's nice. You'll like him. He won't talk much."

I thought I had made enough salad.

"What do you think, Cook?"

"Oh sure, honey, that's plenty. You all will have roast beef, mashed potatoes and gravy, of course, corn on the cob from the garden, a big salad, and fresh peach pie. How does that sound?"

"I will think I am in heaven." I didn't know what roast beef was and I had never had mashed potatoes, but Cook listed the ingredients with so much enthusiasm that I knew I was supposed to think I had a great treat waiting for me. I was actually looking forward to my first real American meal. I hoped it was American. I had eaten in restaurants with Raquel and Jose Cruz but they were Mexican restaurants. We had eaten breakfasts on the road but they were like Mexican breakfasts. I had cooked Mexican food for the Dallas boys and of course, I had eaten at the diner, but not a real American meal.

Even on the road with Raquel and Jose Cruz, we never really stopped at any restaurants for dinner. We just had sandwiches which we made from supplies from the grocery stores. There was no doubt that Cook was an American so I hoped she was preparing just that kind of

American meal.

"You go on and take a break now. I'll finish this." She was expertly attaching the top crust to the pie.

"Thanks. Can you call me when you're using the ricer? I want to see how that works."

"Sure honey. I'll give you a shout. Go on now."

I went up the stairs to my room. I had totally forgotten about my laundry in the washing machine. Luckily it was still there. I would've felt guilty if someone had put it on the line for me. I took some hangers out of the closet for the shirts and went outside to put everything on the line. It didn't take long and I came back in after that.

Upstairs, I sat on the bed and looked out at the beautiful hills again. I moved closer and looked down at the barn. Angela was there with a big pitchfork and she was putting bales of hay into the back of the truck. She must be really strong as those hay bales can be very heavy. She worked at a steady pace and didn't even seem to be struggling.

When the back of the truck was full, she drove it around the front to the fence. She opened the fence, making sure that the horses were behind the gate and her truck was blocking their exit. She drove through the gate and jumped quickly out of the truck to close the gate. The horses were already crowded around the truck. She shooed them away and drove the truck to the back of the corral. She got out and the whole process started again with her lifting the bales and stacking them at the back of the field. Finally, she took out a tarp and tied it down to cover the hay. She never stopped working and didn't even seem tired.

She was covered with dust from the field and she used

the back of a grimy hand to wipe the hair out of her eyes. The curls got plastered down on her face with the sweat. She looked about forty, I guessed, with delicate features and soft curly hair. She held it back from her face in a ponytail but some of the tendrils escaped. She had the blue-black hair of a Mexican but besides that she didn't look Mexican at all. I wondered if she was from somewhere near the border which would have had a lot of mixed-race babies. She climbed back into the truck now and repeated the process driving through the gate and parking the car alongside the house.

"Cook, have you got slops for the pigs yet?" she yelled through the screen door. Maybe she didn't want to track dirt into the house, although it seemed impossible to stop it, but still she waited at the door. Cook came out holding a bucket with garbage in it. She held it at her chest with two hands.

"Here you go."

Cook struggled with it and Angela took it from Cook's two hands with her one hand and swung it down by her legs. She took loping steps across the dirt to the pigsty. The pigs lined up along the fence sticking their snouts through the railings in an effort to get at the food and making a huge racket. Angela opened the gate with her free hand and carried the bucket full of food across the sty with the pigs at her heels. She threw the contents into the trough and the pigs pushed each other out of the way to be first to eat. We never had pigs in Mexico, and I can see how they might have been highly entertaining.

Angela still wasn't finished. I guessed I should have helped her but I was paralyzed with admiration. Then, she pulled down four huge food bowls and arranged them in the dirt. She dragged a big bag into the center of the four bowls and started shoveling food into each bowl with a big scoop. As the first bit of food hit the first bowl the four dogs came running across the dirt track.

"Psssh." She kept shoveling food even after she made this sound. The dogs stopped in their tracks. each in front of a bowl of food, sitting and waiting. She continued to shovel until the bowls were full. The dogs just sat waiting.

"OK," she said and each dog tore into a bowl and started eating like they hadn't eaten in days. I doubted this, as I could already tell that not much was left to chance here. How I would fit in, I didn't know, but I knew that I could do nothing but benefit by being here.

Now covered with hay and slops and dog food, Angela finally turned toward the house. She moved with those same lumbering strides to the screen door and I could hear her boots clomping across the kitchen and the conversation she had with Cook.

"Wow, that pie smells mighty good, Cook." She loped across the floor. "Did Cece help?"

"Yes she was a great help."

"Good. Did you ask or did she volunteer?"

"I didn't make a big deal of it. I just acted like she assumed she was going to help and she helped. She's a good girl."

"She did the same thing in the garden. When I went there to get to work, I saw that she had already done it and she washed the tools and put them away. I think she'll be fine."

"Are we going to turn her into an American?"

"Sure, whatever that means, Cook. I'll be upstairs in the bathroom if you need me."

"I'll take a break and come back in about a half an hour after a little nap, if that's OK. I just need to whip the potatoes and put the finishing touches on the roast."

"That'll be fine. Many thanks, Cook."

I heard Cook go out to the porch and I heard the porch chaise creak under her weight.

XII

I heard this conversation and stayed in my room with the door closed so that Angela could have some privacy. I heard the bath going. I had never actually had a bath. Wasn't that funny? I saw it in a lot of movies, but in Mexico only the rich can afford the luxury of a bath. I wondered if this place out in the middle of nowhere would have enough water for a really hot bath.

I lay down on the bed and fell asleep. My dreams were disturbed by mad gun men running after me down dusty alleys and cobblestoned streets. Every time I turned another corner I ended up in a dead end and had to double back and find another way. I woke up with a start, feeling very scared and frustrated. The clock showed five. I had had a good nap.

I heard Cook and Angela talking in the kitchen. I went down to join them. The transformation was incredible. Instead of the rough and tumble cowgirl, there was a sophisticated lady in the kitchen. Angela had on a long skirt of hundreds of colors and beautiful red boots. Her hair was pulled back in a soft ribbon and floated down her back in ripples of curls. She had on a white peasant blouse with a turquoise necklace and earrings. She even had on lipstick. When she saw me appraising her, she blushed.

"Do you think I can take a bath now?" Cook was working at the stove and Angela was putting the dishes away from the drainer. When she moved, her skirt swooshed around her.

"Sure, Cece. You'll find everything you need in the bathroom. There's even some bubble bath in the blue bottle on the bath rim if you want bubbles."

"Thanks, I guess I do want bubbles. I've never had them."

"Don't get used to such extravagance, Cece girl. We don't want to spoil you your first day here." Cook smiled at me.

The bathtub was in a special place in the bathroom. There was a skylight overhead in an alcove where the tub was up two steps and surrounded by windows. It was the most beautiful setting I could think of for a bath. You were completely in nature.

I turned on the taps and added a small amount of bubble bath to the water. I wasn't sure how much it would bubble up. I went outside then and got my laundry. Everything was dry and smelled wonderfully fresh from the clothes line. Dolores had given me some skirts with elastic waists so I chose one and a long blouse. I could use the belt she gave me to make a dressy outfit. I didn't really have much choice.

I took off my clothes in the bathroom. The mirror gave me a fright. My breasts had swelled up and were now round and a bit droopy. My stomach had grown to about four times its size. It was no longer a baby bump; it was huge. Not really, of course, but it seemed like it to me. I hoped that Nely liked a bath.

I sank down into the bath and let the bubbles play around my chest and arms. The water felt wonderful and hot and it let off steam that floated up around the windows and fogged. I sat there looking out at the wide expanse of green around the house, feeling like I was in the middle of the forest. I didn't know if Angela designed this bathroom or not but whoever did was a genius. I laid back and looked up at the sky. After the bath, I joined Cook in the kitchen.

"Come and look at the ricer before I whip up the potatoes," Cook said. "You look very nice, dear. Here, watch this. You put a piece of the potato in the ricer and just squeeze the two handles together and the potatoes come out just like that, like strings. Here you try it."

I took the ricer from her and did exactly as she had done. The big fat potato came out as a set of strings now. "But why do this? Why not just mash up the potatoes?"

"It makes the mashed potatoes fluffier. Don't ask me why. My mother did it so I do it Isn't that always the way?" She took the ricer away from me and quickly riced all of the potatoes. She flew around the kitchen, getting the mixer and butter and milk and mashing the potatoes.

"Hurry up then. They're waiting for you in the living room," she said over the noise of the mixer.

"Oh my God, I didn't know. Am I late?" I turned toward the dining room.

"No, dear, you're fine. They're talking." She continued to mash the potatoes.

If they were talking, I couldn't hear them. The farm had so many noises with the animals and the machines. Now it was quiet and so were Angela and her friend. I couldn't remember his name.

"Can I carry something in to the table?" I turned back toward the kitchen.

"Yes, dear, you can really help. I got myself overextended with the potatoes and the pie, I'm afraid. I got fancy. Take the salad and the roast there and the bread and put it all on the table. Take a look there and see if there's anything else they need."

I did as she asked me, carrying the food in several trips to the table. Angela and her friend were already there, talking quietly. They were in their own world so they didn't notice me at first.

"Ah, yes, here is Cece. We were just talking about you." Angela let go of the man's hand when she focused on me. "This is Richard."

The man stood up as if he were meeting someone important. He put his hand out. I guessed that I was going to shake his hand, not give him a small hug like we would have in Mexico. I stared at his hand for some seconds, not really knowing what to do.

"Oh, I'm sorry," he said. "Should I give you a little hug or would you like to shake hands? In America, we usually shake hands. I'm afraid we're not as warm as the Mexicans." He had a big smile on his face.

"I'd better learn to shake hands then." I shook his hand and it felt soft and warm. I remembered the hands of my brothers, which were calloused and rough. I hadn't really touched the hands of the boys in Dallas. We had hugged like Mexicans do.

"Wow, I'm glad we survived that." Angela was laughing and Richard and I laughed too.

As I made the trips to and from the kitchen, I thought about what else we might need. We got meat about six times a year in Mexico and there was a huge roast simmering in the pot with its own gravy right now in the kitchen. We never had fresh bread. There was a loaf just taken from the oven. I had never even seen mashed potatoes. There was a bowl just prepared with butter, salt, and milk. How would I know if we needed anything else? To me this was a feast, not the usual soup and tortillas that I would be eating at home.

Cook came into the room with the mashed potatoes steaming in a bowl. "You'd better eat these before they get cold." She put the bowl on the table. "I think that's everything, Angela. I'll just be going then. Good night. Enjoy your supper." She smiled and waved and was on the way out the door with everyone's 'thank yous' floating in the air.

We spent the first few minutes of our supper just passing around plates and getting helpings of everything on the table. We made appreciative comments about the food. I was just about to start when everything stopped and Richard reached for my hand while Angela took the other one. With heads bowed, Richard led us in saying grace. Even in Mexico we don't say grace anymore. I was surprised.

"How do you like it here, Cece? There was a lot to take in for the first day," he asked.

"It's beautiful, isn't it? I thought taking the bath was like magic. It's like you are in the middle of the woods. I never thought I would take a bath surrounded by windows."

"Yes, that was Barry, my husband," Angela said. "He had a lot of good ideas for this place. The reason it's so organized and works so smoothly is because of him. He had a very practical mind and he made plans logically and now we are all enjoying his ideas."

"I'm sorry. I hope I didn't make you sad." I didn't really know what to say. I thought I had put my foot in my mouth.

"No, Cece, it's fine. He died a long time ago. It actually brings up nice memories of one of his good qualities."

Richard reached for Angela's hand and squeezed it. He smiled at her.

"Barry and I built this house together piece by piece," Angela went on. "He was a carpenter, an amateur inventor. He really could do anything. We didn't have to hire anyone to help us and so we could build a nice place for very little money. He could do the plumbing and the electrics too. I don't know how we became farmers but somehow that just worked out. Now we get our hay free for renting out the field to another farmer. The pigs and the chickens are easy and we make a deal for the butchering and the curing so that we don't have to pay for it. We board two horses for pay. It all works."

Richard didn't seem bothered by her talking about her dead husband. He really didn't talk much. He listened to her and he ate his meal and the atmosphere was relaxed and easy.

"What was it like for you in Mexico?" Angela asked. I knew from her time with Raquel that she knew my story since I was surprised anyone would be interested in my life in Mexico.

"Life was hard. My father died a while ago and left my mother with five children. Two of my brothers came to the US several years ago and we never heard from them again."

"Oh that's terrible, your mother must be devastated," Richard remarked.

"I really don't know. It's so common for this to happen in Mexican families that we think it's part of life. We hope they are alive and, for some reason, just don't want to get in contact with their old life. We hope." I watched her reaction and saw sadness in her face.

"Go on then, I didn't mean to interrupt you." She passed the butter to Richard for his mashed potatoes.

"Well, that left two brothers and me. We didn't have much money so we basically did what we could to survive. Sometimes we grew vegetables. Sometimes we took in sewing. Sometimes the boys would do construction work or take odd jobs at the gas station or the little restaurants. Sometimes we would be cleaners. There is an effort by the government now to try to put in some factories in our area or maybe some greenhouses. We're not too far from the beach so maybe we could put in something connected with tourism or fishing. There are some ideas but nothing has come of it. One of my brothers just got a job as a cook in a taco restaurant nearer to the beach. He has to ride his bike about an hour to get there but the money really helps. It is steady. I had a boyfriend but he was killed in a gun battle with *narcotraficantes*."

"He was involved with the cartels?" Angela asked. I was surprised that she knew the name we called the drug traffickers.

"No, he was just in the way. He was collateral damage." Tears leapt into my eyes. Angela got up and put her arms around me from above.

"I'm sorry, Cece, I didn't mean to upset you." She hugged me.

"It's OK. I have to get used to it. It's just hard."

"Is that what made you decide to leave?" Richard asked.

"It was worse for me after he was killed. The cartels

knew there was a witness to the murders. I'm not even sure the police would have done anything if I came forward. But in Mexico if you tell the police you are likely to be killed and they will kill your whole family, even the children. I knew I had to get out to save myself and my family."

"Well, we are going to try to make it easier for you." Angela went back to her seat, putting a hand on Richard's shoulder when she passed him. "Now let's have some of that pie. I'll cut it but we need coffee. Can you just go in the kitchen and turn on the burner under the coffee pot, Cece?"

I got up and went into the kitchen to do as she asked. It gave me a chance to find a tissue and dry my eyes. I was surprised that the memory of Guillermo's death was still so raw. I found the small plates under the counter and got the coffee started. It started making gurgling sounds right away. I carried the plates back into the dining room.

"Do you want me to pour the coffee in here?" I put the plates down on the table next to Angela, who was cutting the pie. I paused, waiting for her to decide before I sat down again.

"That would be a good idea in a few minutes when it stops percolating. Can you bring the cream and sugar too? Richard has a sweet tooth." She pointed the knife at him.

"Everyone should drink coffee with cream and sugar." Richard was eyeing the pie.

I got the cups and made another trip bringing the cream and sugar. The coffee continued its gurgling sounds.

"What do you teach, Richard?" I was happy to move the conversation away from me.

"I teach Shop," he answered.

"What's that?" We didn't have any subject like that in Mexico. "Is it about buying things at a store?"

"That's very logical, Cece." He laughed. "It's a subject that's very practical. The students learn metal working and carpentry and even a bit of auto mechanics. These days, they also learn to repair electronic equipment." He began the shoveling of the pie into his mouth.

"Oh, for boys."

"Yah!" Angela screamed. "Cece, what are you saying?"

"Oh my God!" Richard was laughing. Their reaction surprised me. I was completely confused.

"Cece, did you really mean that?" Angela asked.

"What did I say that was wrong?" I was embarrassed.

"You didn't say anything wrong, Cece." Richard was gentle. "It's just that in America, the boys and girls both take classes that are practical as well as academic subjects. It's a new world."

"So you have girls in your class who learn to fix cars?"

"Yes, and make furniture and weld metal. The girls do as well as the boys and some of them are better. If physical strength isn't the criteria, then they do very well, easily as well as the boys."

"Cece, how do you think we keep the farm working so well? We give Richard's class some great practice fixing everything around here. The kids come out all the time and fix something. You'll see young people around here a lot. Not much younger than you are, really. It's great for us and it's great for them. We pay them money or we pay them in pork chops or horseback riding or in a great meal together. The girls are very talented."

"They're so lucky," I said.

"That's the truth and they don't even know they're lucky. They think their life is just normal, that everyone in the world has these opportunities. No matter what their parents tell them, it isn't real to them. They experience their parents' words like a story someone made up. In their experience, everyone has a house and a car and TVs and Xboxes and smart phones and everyone gets to go to school and even to college." Richard put three teaspoons of sugar into his coffee cup.

"They have no idea," I said. "None of us even had computers except at school where there is an internet connection."

"That's right. They have no idea. Let me get the coffee." Angela got up.

"I'll help." I got up too.

"Shall I help?" Richard got up.

"Nice try, Richard, you know it doesn't take more than two of us to get coffee." We laughed at that.

Angela brought back the coffee and she added some wonderful treats to it. Richard added whiskey to his and Angela and I added something called Bailey's Irish Cream to ours. It tasted like warm ice cream. I only had a little bit because of Nely but it was a great treat. The pie was a gift from heaven. There was a top layer of pastry and the inside was full of juicy peaches and some gooey stuff that tasted like sugar jelly. I believed as long as I lived in America I would be eating pie. After the coffee and the pie, I was stuffed. I stood up to gather the dishes.

"No, that's my job." Richard got up and began stacking the plates on top of each other and carrying them into the kitchen. "I guess a man would never do this in Mexico," he called back over his shoulder.

"He wouldn't," I said to Angela.

"We expected that, Cece. Richard's just teasing you."

Richard came back several times to get some more dishes and Angela and I didn't get up to help him. I felt myself itching to jump in and help, but I knew that this was how you shared work. I didn't understand it. I didn't really know how to do it yet but I would learn. This would be the life Nely would lead. Finally, all of the dishes were in the kitchen and Richard brought back a wet towel to clean off the table.

"Please tell Cook she outdid herself tonight." Richard scooped the crumbs into his hand. He went back to the kitchen and washed the dishes, setting them in the drying rack. "I'll give her a treat and wash the dishes for her tonight. She'll get a surprise in the morning." He hung the dish towel on the rack and faced Angela.

"Cece, we're going to go for a drive so we'll be leaving. You might have one or another of the dogs come in and sleep on the floor of your room tonight. They might want to keep you company." She got up and stood in the doorway with Richard. He was easily a foot taller than she was. He had his arm around her and was nuzzling her with his beard in her hair.

"Good night then, Cece. I'm sure I will be seeing a lot more of you." Richard talked to me over Angela's head.

"Good night, Richard, it was nice to see you. Good night, Angela, thanks for everything."

"Welcome to the family, Cece. Good night." Angela waved to me as they left. They walked out arm in arm and got into Richard's old Jeep. I heard it rumble away.

I went around the house turning out the lights. I didn't know if I should lock the front door or not. We were so far out in the country and we had four dogs so I decided against it. I went upstairs and put away my clothes and went to bed. I had been tempted to put the dishes away but it was Cook's job and I didn't want to upset the balance of this well-run home.

The stars flickered out along the horizon and I felt in paradise. There was no danger here. No predatory men. No vigilantes. No rapists. I sunk down into the bed and fell into a deep, restful sleep. Just before I dropped off, I heard the clicking of nails across the floor and two of the dogs came and curled up in balls at the foot of my bed. My protectors were on duty.

XIII

The farm came alive at dawn. Roosters were crowing. Pigs were snorting. The dogs still slept but everything else was restless. I heard clanging in the kitchen as Cook was putting away the dishes. I got up quickly, dressed, washed my face and brushed my teeth. I came bounding down the steps.

"Oh, Cece, you gave me such a fright. I forgot you were in the house," Cook shrieked.

"Good morning. Oh sorry, Cook, I am just so excited to be here. How are you this morning?" I didn't want to forget my Mexican manners.

"I'm fine, dear. Breakfast will be ready soon." She was making scrambled eggs.

"Where's Angela? Should I be doing some chores?" I asked, still standing in the doorway. Was I supposed to sit down?

"Cece, she's with her beau. Angela would have spent the night with Mr. Richard, didn't you know?" She was putting away the dishes that Richard had washed last night. "Mr. Richard must have washed the dishes. Such a nice man." She sighed. I helped her stack the dishes in the space under the counter. Of course, that's what *we're going for a drive* must have meant. It was some kind of secret signal for *we're going to spend the night together.* Was I supposed to know that signal? We never got the chance to say that to anyone, Guillermo and me. We had to sneak out somewhere and make love, in fields and in churches. It was amazing we never were discovered during the day in the church pews. No one found out that we were there. I felt stupid not knowing what Angela meant. But it wouldn't be the last time I would feel stupid in America.

"Doesn't she know what?" Angela was coming in the door dressed in the same clothes she'd had on last night at dinner.

"That you'll likely be home any minute, dearie." Cook covered very fast. "Coffee's ready in the pot." Cook kept handing the dishes to me to be put away.

"I'll be down in a minute. Best have a big breakfast, Cece, we have some hard work to do today." She clomped up the stairs.

"Whew, that was close. Angela doesn't like anyone talking about her private life. I don't really blame her. This can be a gossipy town. If you know what I mean?" I was working on the pots now, scrubbing them out.

Gossip. Maybe things weren't so different in America, after all. I thought that there wasn't a place on earth that was immune to gossip. I had seen it destroy people.

"So, I'll make you some bacon and eggs then. Would that be good, Cece?"

"That would be wonderful. Do you make *huevos divorciados*?" I asked Cook directly.

"Divorced eggs? I don't think so. This is America, Cece. We make scrambled, fried, poached, over easy, and sunny side up eggs, not *huevos divorci*—whatever that is." She was not speaking unkindly.

"So, I know scrambled, and I know fried and I know

poached, but what is over easy and sunny side up?" I pictured a smiling egg in my mind.

"You know how everyone has their preferences? God knows I do, being a cook. So sunny side up just means that the eggs are fried and they are cooked just like they land in the frying pan. No turning. And over easy means that just before they are finished being cooked, they are flipped over for about thirty seconds so they're not so runny. Simple really. The description fits the label completely. So how would you like your eggs?"

"*Divorciados,* please!"

Cook laughed.

"Just kidding." I was happy that she laughed at my joke, it meant I could tease her. "Two eggs sunny side up, please."

"Oh so you're a bit mischievous, are you? I'll have to watch out for you. Angela likes her eggs like that too. I see you had some mashed potatoes left over from last night so I'll make you a special, one-time-only treat: potato pancakes. I'll bet you never had those before, did you?"

"I never had any kind of pancake. And all treats are appreciated." I felt so happy to be with such a warm person.

I had a hard time deciding whether to help Cook. I knew it was her job and I knew that she liked it and was proud of it but what was my role? How was I to fit into this family? It wasn't a real family, was it? No mother. No father. No children. Yet it felt like a family. Cook, Angela, and Richard. Even the animals were part of the family. The dogs had their jobs. And Efrahim, where was he?

"Shall I get the frying pan for you?" Cook was scooping out the mashed potatoes and adding flour to them. She had flour all over her apron already. She began shaping the floured potatoes into balls.

"I'll need two frying pans today, one for the eggs and another for the potato pancakes and the bacon." She put the bacon into the first frying pan and let it cook slowly. She turned on the oven.

"You can go ahead and set the table, Cece, if you'd like."

I carried the plates and cutlery into the dining room. Cook had a nice rhythm to her work. She was rushed and yet things progressed at a steady pace. By the time I was finished putting everything on the table including the bread and butter and cream and sugar for coffee, everything was ready. Angela came down, dressed in jeans and an old shirt.

"We've got some tough work to do today, Cece. I hope you're up for it." I was carrying the coffee into the dining room and pouring it into our cups.

"Sure, I want to learn everything. I don't want to be a burden. I want to do my share. I want to earn my keep." I had my pride too.

"Oh, don't worry about that. You will surely earn your keep."

Cook came in then with platters of eggs and bacon and steaming potato pancakes. Everything looked delicious. On my way back, I picked up the third plate and cutlery.

"I'll just take these," I said, circling the coffee cup with my crooked finger.

"Cook never eats with us." Angela was slathering butter on to her bread. "She likes to keep our relationship professional."

"She seems like such a part of the family." I was testing

the potato pancakes, which had been fried in the bacon grease.

"Oh, she is. She is very much a part of the family but she likes that little distance, you know? It's fine with me either way. She is a wonderful woman, has three kids and a useless husband. Always has interesting stories to tell about her home life. But, she likes her little distance. Don't ever try to re-arrange the kitchen or take over. She gives the orders there." She put cream into her coffee.

"Yeah, I was trying to find out how I should help her." I added cream to mine too.

"Don't bother. She'll ask you if she wants help. She never asks me for help even when I see she is struggling with something. It's her kingdom. We are mere visitors."

We ate in silence for a little while, savoring the great tastes of the bread fresh from the oven, the bacon from our own pigs, and the eggs fresh from the chickens. To me, it was another feast. With the way I was eating you would think I was taking it in for more than two. But everything was so good and fresh that it was hard to resist.

"We'll be mending the fences today, you and me." Angela broke the silence. "Last night Richard and I talked and we decided that you needed to stay here with us until the baby is born, at least. I know you want to get to L.A. and find work and everything, but there really isn't time. The baby will be coming: how will you get there, find a job, and then keep a job as a pregnant woman?"

"But I don't want to be a bur—" she stopped me with her hand raised.

"You will have to work here. Don't worry, you won't be a burden. There is always something to do on the farm and you will have to do your share. But it's important for you to get stable and find your feet. After the baby, you can go wherever you want. But, for now, we feel this is for the best. We would love to have you."

"How could you decide this so fast? You don't even know me."

"Well, I will get to know you. For now, I like you and I trust you and I felt that way from the first minute I met you."

"But why?"

"Raquel and Jose Cruz brought you here. That was enough for me."

"But they don't know me either."

"Cece, you are a young girl. But you know already from what you have been through in life that even though we are really alone, we can't make it on our own. There are times in life when you need help. And there are times in life when you need to be the helper. I have had incredible helpers in my life. When Barry and I came here, there were people who welcomed us into their homes and into their lives. I was the granddaughter of poor people from Mexico and Americans opened their hearts to them. Strangers helped them.

"This country gave their children and their grandchildren a good education and the possibility, something they did not have in Mexico at that time, the possibility, the chance, for a better life. My parents took that chance and made something of themselves. All four of us children went to college. We learned how to learn and that was the best gift of all. Since then, I have had a wonderful husband and a wonderful marriage. Since the first day of our marriage, we have given back to the universe what it gave to us: help. People who didn't know my family helped us anyway. Now we help people whom we don't know. Don't get me wrong. There were a few times when we gave our help to the wrong people. There are liars and cheats and thieves everywhere. But for the most part, for 99% of the time we took a chance on the right people. We saw people blossom before our eyes. That's what I expect from you. In fact, I have a little present for you." She fished around in her top shirt pocket and produced a little package in a bag. She handed it to me.

"For me? Please, I can't take it. You have done too much already."

"Take it. I'll explain it to you." She waved at the little bag in my hand. It was in one of those gift bags we have in Mexico. It gave me a little stab of pain, missing my mother.

"It's a little notebook with a pen. Thank you so much." It was a beautiful little notebook with a picture of a sunset on the front and a pen attached.

"It's a special present, Cece. It is your learning book. I gave it to you because, as you go through your days, there will be little things that will confuse you. Little things we say or do in America that you don't do in Mexico and you will wonder about us for a second and the thoughts will flit out of your mind. This little notebook allows you to write them down. At the end of the day we will go over these thoughts and I will try my best to explain the American ways to you. Any questions that pop into your head should be written down. To become an American, you have to fold yourself into the culture. Hold onto your Mexican heritage but embrace the American culture."

"Oh, this is a wonderful present. I wish I had already had it as there is so much that's new here and that I really don't understand. I'll do this."

"There's something else you should do as well." She got up and went to a desk in the corner of the dining room. She opened the center drawer of the heavy desk and pulled out a piece of paper and an envelope.

"Before we go to work this morning, I want you to sit down and write to your mother. Tell her you are safe. Tell her about your future here so she knows you will be safe. Tell her anything else you want to tell her. Give her this address here." She took an envelope from the desk and showed me the address to use for her farm. "You have to write to your mother. She must think you are lost like her two sons. You can't do that to her."

I knew what she was saying was the truth. It made me ashamed that I had taken so long to write to my mother. I was afraid to talk to her about my plan to leave because I knew she would try to talk me out of it. I couldn't tell her the real reason—that I was being hunted because I witnessed the killings. This information would terrify her more. What would have happened to me and to Nely in Mexico? I would have been found dead by the side of the road. Or worse, my mother would have found my severed head on a stake in the front yard. I had to go.

"I'll do that at the end of the day."

"Please do it now. We can put a stamp on it and put it in the mailbox before we go out to work. Do it now."

Cook came in and started taking the dishes. Angela thanked her as she walked out the door and climbed up the stairs. I took the paper and went to a clean corner of the dining room table.

"Writing a letter?" Cook was stacking the dishes on top of each other.

"To my mother." I had my pen poised over the page.

"Good thing too. Tell her I think you're a good girl." Cook took the dishes away and winked at me on her way out the door. I heard her running the water to fill the sink. She crashed the dishes into the water.

The blank paper looked like it was ten feet long. It was so very, very blank. I stared at it. How would I start such a letter? How could I tell her I had really abandoned her? I just had to start:

Dear Mami, I miss you so much. I hope you are well. I know you are sad. I should start by telling you that I am so sorry to have abandoned you. I am sure that is how you feel right now. But, Mami, I had to go. Everything you warned me about was coming true. You didn't know it but I have Guillermo's baby inside of me. You warned me that I would have a baby as a girl myself and I should finish my education first. But you know how it is, you did the same with Papi. You warned me that I would be a girl with a baby and no husband. You were right about that too but for different reasons.

So I had to go. You know there is no future for the young people of our village. So few jobs to keep us working. So little to give us respect for ourselves. I am not sure that America will be any better but I hope it will. I know you are shocked now. I am in America. I did it on my own.

Someday I will tell you the whole story. For now I just want you to know that I was in grave danger after the killing of Guillermo. I had to leave. Now I am safe. I am really safe. A wonderful woman named Angela has taken me in and is giving me a place to live and food and everything until the baby is born. I am living in somewhere called New Mexico. Isn't that funny? I ended up from old Mexico with a new life in New Mexico.

Please write to me at Angela's address. You write on the envelope just like it says here. I am not putting this address on the outside of the envelope because it is important that no one knows where I am. No one can know. This must be a secret.

I love you, Mami. I will write to you again and tell you how I am doing. I hope you can find the time to write to me. I love you, your daughter, Cece

I wrote Angela's address just like she showed me on the water bill. I went outside and put the letter in the mailbox. I went upstairs to get my things and joined Angela in the kitchen. Cook was just finishing the dishes. I followed Angela out the door and got into the passenger side of the truck.

"The things we need are in the back of the truck." Angela was backing out of the driveway and turning the truck back toward the road. "In the future, I think you'll know what we need when we go to do a job and you can get our supplies ready for us. That's a big help on a farm. A lot of time is spent getting things out and using them and cleaning them and putting them back. Are you neat?"

"What do you mean?"

"You know, are you neat, are you tidy? Do you put things where you found them?"

I thought about this for a minute. I had my uniforms

and my shirts and shorts. Did I put them away? I thought so. I didn't really think about it. I had so few things.

"Yes, I guess so."

"Well, that's really important here. I guess you saw that everything has a place. We have a lot of jobs with the horses and the pigs and the chickens and the garden. All of those jobs have tools attached to them and all of those tools have a place. If we didn't clean up after ourselves and put everything back we would live in chaos. A farm in chaos is really a mess. So please, please rule number one: always clean up your tools and put them back where they belong, OK?"

"Yes, I will be very careful."

"I noticed you did this with the tools for the garden. By the way, thanks for weeding the garden; especially since no one asked you to do it. It makes me think I did a good thing betting on you. Anyway, you put the tools away and that was great. They were clean too."

She stopped the truck on the side of the road near the fence. "Here's our job today." She pointed to a piece of the fence that had been pulled down. The barbed wire was all twisted. "We'll be fixing that today and it won't be pretty." She smiled at me.

We worked on that fence all day together. It was like a surgeon and her nurse. She would pull the wire up and then ask for a nail or a hammer or a tack or something. I would hand it to her. After a while, I could anticipate her needs and have things ready in my hand so that when she asked for them I had them immediately. We worked like a dance team, moving together as one. Angela wore heavy leather gloves to protect her hands from the barbed wire. Sometimes I had to put on a pair too because when the wire was particularly twisted it took both of us working together to get it untangled. She made fun of herself the whole time she did it because she didn't really know how to fix a barbed wire fence. She just smashed away at it with nails and tacks and the hammer until it was more or less back in place. She didn't seem too disturbed that it wasn't perfect. I was enthralled by the whole thing. It was wonderful to see our work change the fence so dramatically in just a few hours' time. In the middle of the day, we took a break.

"I hope you like salami sandwiches." She was pulling a crate out of the back of the truck and starting to walk by the fence. "Let's go through the gate there and under the tree."

I moved by her side and took the small cooler from the crate to lighten the load. She nodded thanks and we went through the gate, careful to close and lock it. Maybe the horses would come down this far and we didn't want them to escape.

She put the crate down and started unpacking its contents. She spread a blanket on the ground, and I helped as she piled plastic containers on the blanket. Cutlery followed the plastic containers as she produced two plates and two cups and a thermos of coffee. We sat down and she passed me a sandwich wrapped in plastic wrap.

"This is delicious," I said, biting into the sandwich.

"Yeah, that's Cook. She always surprises. Just when you think mayonnaise and mustard are your only choices in life she comes up with something like this."

"What is it?"

"Beats me. I think she mixes up secret concoctions in her house in the middle of the night just to surprise me. I never know what's in the crate when I go out to do a job but I'm always surprised. I think it's the spices or she adds yogurt. I don't really know. But no sandwich ever tastes like you think it will. And look at all of this other stuff. All these containers. What's in them? Take a look. Those are called deviled eggs. I don't think you have them in Mexico." She pointed to the box I was opening.

"This one has celery with cream cheese in it. Here're some carrots and cucumber slices. Here's some of that great pie from last night." She was opening the plastic containers like they were treasures from a deep sea chest. "Yep, that's Cook. Always surprises."

The food was delicious and I couldn't really tell what Cook had put on the sandwiches. It was some kind of sauce that was only known to her. I suppose that is what the word "concoctions" means. I was getting hungrier and hungrier as the days went by, maybe Nely was telling me something.

"Cece, please take these dishes to the stream over there and rinse them off. I'm sure Cook put in a dish towel. Yes, here it is." She pulled out a blue and white checked towel.

I gathered up the dishes and took them to the stream. The water rushed over them and I rinsed the food into the water. I dried off the dishes and put them back in the crate. What a feast!

Angela didn't seem to want to teach me how to do this fence mending on my own. I was still handing her the things she needed. Maybe that's the way she taught: you had to watch many times first. It didn't seem that hard to me but maybe it was. It was OK with me. I knew she was a lot stronger than I was because I saw her picking up those bales of hay. I wondered if I would ever be that strong Maybe after Nely was born.

"Let me check the time. Wow, almost 5 o'clock. That was a good day's work, Cece." She was reaching over me and dropping the tools into the tool box. I took the hint and started gathering the things we had brought for the job and followed her to the bed of the truck.

"Let's see. We did one, two, three chunks today. That's pretty good." She was smiling, but I thought that we had barely touched a fence that was about three miles long.

"What's a chunk?"

"It means a piece, a kind of fat piece."

"OK, thanks but we didn't do any fat pieces today."

"Well no, not really but I was looking at the parts of the fence that needed to be fixed right away, like chunks of the fence, that's all. Other repairs can wait until later. We're going to town now. There's a little department store there that you might like to visit while I go to the hardware store." She was driving the truck in the opposite direction now, away from the house. It would be my first time seeing something outside of the farm. I felt myself getting excited.

The trip to town took about thirty minutes. We really were way out in the country. The town was like one of those deserted towns you see in movies about poor people in America. It had a little sign welcoming you that had long ago fallen apart so you couldn't even see the name of the town. You drove in past a Dollar General, a gas station, a small school, a fire house and then the main square. There was a small stone building that was the city hall. All of the parking down the main street was pull-in parking so Angela pulled the truck in to stop in front of the hardware store.

"I'll meet you back here, Cece, just go across the street there and take a look at the department store. I'll be about twenty minutes."

I did as I was told. The store had a wooden door and when I opened it, a small bell rang with a loud clank. The floorboards were wooden so I didn't understand why you needed the bell. You could surely hear anyone stomping across that floor. It was an old-fashioned store with everything stacked in drawers up to the ceiling. It fit in with Angela's farm and the rest of the town that seemed like it came from the past. There was a ladder on wheels that the sales clerks could use to get up to those top shelves. It was really nice there. It was like many little stores arranged inside of the big store.

There was a section when you first came in that had bolts of cloth and little drawers in a spinning bin on the counter. I opened up a few of the drawers and found needles and thimbles and snaps and hooks and eyes. There was an array of scissors hanging on the wall alongside the fabric. Little poles stuck out of the wall and held ribbons and other trimmings. I had done a lot of sewing and I recognized everything that was there. A lady came out of the back.

"May I help you?"

"No, ma'am." I stood very straight and looked her in the eye. I wanted her to know that I was someone who could be trusted. "I am waiting for Angela. She thought I would be interested in your store. It's really nice." I hoped my English was good enough for her to understand me.

"Well, that's very kind dear. What's your name?"

"Ros—uh, Cece." I put out my hand to shake hands like

Richard did. It must have been all right because the lady took it and shook it. No hugs. No kisses.

"Welcome, Cece. I'm Mary Lou Patterson. Pleased to meet you. How long will you be visiting with Angela?"

"Oh, for several months. It's nice to meet you, too." I was getting the hang of this. It was easy, really. "I love sewing. My mother taught me and I have sewn all my life. We even had a little sewing school in our house."

"I love it too. It's very soothing, isn't it? You can just relax and sew all day long. That sewing school is a really good idea. Well, look around and let me know if you have any questions." She left me then to return to the back of the store.

PLEASED TO MEET YOU. I wrote that in my notebook. It was my first question. I walked around the store then. There was a section with things to buy for the house like napkins and tablecloths. The colors were all pastels, muted, nothing vibrant like Mexicans have. DULL COLORS. I wrote that in my notebook too.

The store fanned out in the back and had a lot more room. There was a section for men's clothing but all of the clothes were casual clothes—underwear, work shirts, t-shirts, and blue jeans. The women had a special section for bras and panties. The mannequin had a strange head with hair painted on and a bra that didn't fit right. It was much bigger than the breasts it was supposed to support so it had little dents in the extra fabric. There was also a section for baby things and I found myself spending most of my time there. The clothes for the babies were beautiful with little dresses and bibs and tiny shoes and socks. There were rattles and toys and miniature blankets with beautiful smiling babies on them. Most of the toys were in little plastic packages that hung on pegs. There were pictures of the way the babies would use the products. I wrote this in my notebook: BLUE-EYED, WHITE BABIES. Why were all of the pictures of white babies with blue eyes?

This store was very different from the one in Dallas where I tripped and fainted. It was small and homey and I felt that I could talk to Mary Lou Patterson like a friend. Each section of the store felt like a place I would want to visit. I went to find Mary Lou Patterson to say goodbye.

"Goodbye, Mrs. Patterson." I saw her picking up boxes in the back of the store.

"Goodbye, Cece, come again when you can stay longer." Mrs. Patterson nodded to me from the top of the bundle of boxes she was carrying. "Wait a minute." She put the boxes down and walked past me into the store. She went toward the dry goods area. "What's your favorite color?" she asked while she marched on.

"Purple," I said. The royal color.

She got to the notions counter and took out scissors, walking along rolls of trimmings until she found a beautiful roll of purple ribbon. She cut a piece from it and handed it to me.

"For your hair, as a welcome gift to America." She smiled at me and I smiled back. Was it that obvious that I had just arrived?

"Thank you so much. I'll come by and see you when I'm wearing it." I curled the ribbon around my fingers and put it in my pocket. We separated in front of the door and I waved goodbye to her. I walked over to the truck and stood outside. Angela was still not there. After a few minutes, a boy carrying a big box came from the store and loaded the box into the back of the truck.

"Hi," I said when he went by me. He nodded his head. *NODDED*, I wrote in my notebook

"Hello," I said again. I smiled at him but not too big a smile. I didn't want to encourage him for any reason. He still didn't answer me. Angela came back and we got into the truck.

"What do you think of our town? Do you want to see some more?" She didn't wait for an answer but backed the truck into the street and turned away from the road we had entered. She drove down the main road. "I love this. This is a mural that the kids of the town painted about the Wild West. New Mexico used to have cowboys and Indians, and the kids painted those here. It's nice. Here is our little town park. It has a swimming pool and some places for the kids to play baseball and soccer. And there are picnic areas. See them, over there." Her finger pointed at an area at the back of the park with benches and tables. It was nice.

"A couple of times a year we have celebrations like Fourth of July, or Independence Day, like you have in Mexico, and there are games and dances and things. I don't think anything will be coming up before the baby comes but it will be fun to go if you're up for it."

"Yes, even our little town in Mexico has a fiesta each year. Everyone dances."

"Well, everyone tries to dance here but it's mostly pathetic. People jumping around with no idea what's rhythm or what's the beat. Or worse, people dancing in couples with the men stepping on the feet of the poor women desperately trying to follow them."

"We don't have that problem in Mexico because all of the Mexican men dance the same way. They just move side to side and the women move with them. It always hurts my back after a couple of hours of that dancing."

"Oh, yeah, I've seen that kind of dancing. I think it turned into the Texas Two Step here."

"Is that a dance?"

"Yeah, it's not too bad if it's done right. It looks nice watching couples do it."

She drove out of town now the way we had come. I guessed the tour was over. It wasn't much of a tour but it isn't much of a town. Before we got to the edge of town she swung around.

"Do you want to go to the library and get some books? We're really close to it."

"Can't I read the books you have at the house?"

"I guess so. We'll look. I have to find you something that's easy enough to read in English so you get some vocabulary."

We took a different route home and I paid attention to it. You never knew, I might actually have to drive it myself one day. The sun was setting now and the hills were glowing.

"Mrs. Patterson seems nice." I was staring at the hills while we were driving.

"Mary Lou? She is a lovely person. Does a lot of good for the Mexican illegals. Oh, I hope I didn't offend you, Cece, but you're going to have to get used to that word, I'm afraid. It's just what's going on in America now."

"It's OK, I'm not offended. It's true anyway. We Mexicans usually say we have papers or we don't have papers, but it's true; I am illegal. I already feel like I've been here forever but I know it's not real. Maybe I'm just scared. Getting that green card, those papers, is the goal for all of us."

"I'd be scared, too, if I had gone through what you have. You are one brave girl."

"Really? I thought you were so tough."

"There're many types of tough—physical, spiritual, emotional, psychological. I think I'm physically tough, not so emotionally tough."

"Maybe that's a good thing for a woman."

"Maybe so." We were arriving at the house. Angela stopped in front of the barn and went around the truck to get the new supplies.

"Shall I put away the tools for the fence fixing?"

"That's a good question. But no, Cece. We'll be working on that fence all week. Let's just leave them in the truck. You can take the plastic containers in to Cook. I have to do the other chores."

"I'll help you."

"I don't have time to explain to you how to do everything today. I have a meeting in town tonight."

"Don't worry. I know what to do."

I had watched her carefully just the day before. So I followed her exact routine. I got the slops from Cook and fed the pigs. I put the four bowls out and watched as the dogs came and sat before each of their own bowls. I put the food in with the scoops and hoped I wasn't overfeeding. I went to the coop and scattered food for the chickens. By that time, Angela had put all of the horses into their stalls for the night. She prepared the food for the horses and put it into each of their stalls. I hadn't seen her do that the night before so I watched to see how it was done. There were four different dry foods and one of oil. So I had to pay close attention. Angela went through them in super fast time and I watched.

"I have to take a shower and get ready for the meeting, Cece. I don't know what time I'll be home. You can watch some television or find a book to read, whatever you want. I'll check in with you if I get back in time." She was going up the stairs two at a time.

XIV

"Hi Cook." I popped a fresh cookie into my mouth. "How was your day?"

Cook was peeling fruit and putting it in a plastic container. "Good day. Not too much work because I made a simple meal for you. Hamburgers and French fries. What do you think of that?"

"I think it sounds great. Can I ask you some questions?"

"Depends what they are. I don't like personal questions."

"No, they aren't personal. They're about American customs."

"God, who can explain American customs? Go ahead, I'll give it a try."

"OK. I have some things written down here. Let's see. PLEASED TO MEET YOU. In Mexico we usually shake hands and then give a little hug. We say different things when we meet someone like *enchanted* or *at your service*. Do you say anything else here besides *pleased to meet you*?"

"Well, we don't say *enchanted* or *at your service*; people will think you're loony or gay. We say some other things: *How are you? Glad to meet you. Nice to meet you.* That's about it."

"OK, what about the dull colors? I was in a department

store and all of the colors of the napkins and the tablecloths were beige or brown or white, nothing with bold colors or bold designs like Mexican colors. Why is that?"

"Hmm. I never thought about that. It's true though. We like subdued colors. I've seen pictures of Mexican houses that are painted all of these colors. We paint our houses white or soft blue or beige. We think those bright colors are in bad taste. Sorry. Maybe not in clothes though. We seem to wear colorful clothes." She perked up here like she was offering me something good in the face of the possible insult she had just thrown on Mexican taste.

"OK, now BLUE-EYED BABIES. I was walking around that same store and I saw lots of things for babies. Rattles and pacifiers and stuff like that all wrapped up in plastic packages and hung up on the board. They all had pictures of little babies on them and all of the babies had blue eyes. Even the diaper babies had blue eyes. Why is that?"

"Oh my God, child, how would I know that? Maybe the advertisers have blue-eyed babies? I think when you watch some commercials on TV you'll see some babies who have eyes of many colors." She was finishing the fruit salad and washing her hands in the sink.

"How about nodding?"

"What about it?"

"Well a boy passed me today taking a box of supplies to Angela's truck. He nodded at me. I've seen other people do it. They nod instead of saying anything. What is the nod for?"

"Nodding? You do go on, don't you? I never thought about nodding. I think we do nod. Well looky here, I'm nodding myself while I'm talking to you. I think we nod to say hello and maybe just to let you know we're listening. That's about all I can think of. Do you have any more of these questions?" I sensed she was frustrated with my questions.

"No, thanks so much."

"Come back in an hour and I'll feed you in the kitchen." She dried her hands on a towel and finished them off on her apron.

"OK, thanks. See you later." I walked out of the kitchen into the living room. I started at the far end and read the titles of the books as I walked down the bookcases. The books were everywhere in an otherwise very neat house. They were stacked up and on their sides and upside down. I started organizing them as I went because I was sure that Angela would love to have them organized if she ever got the time. I guessed that, with an extra pair of hands now, she would have some more time.

I moved down the shelves reading the titles, taking out the upside down books, putting them back properly and picking up the books that were scattered on the floor. They made a tight fit in the shelves but I made them accommodate each other. There were hundreds of them and they took up every nook and cranny in the room. I remember reading that phrase in a book and this is the first time I ever got to use it. I smiled. Was I starting to think like an English speaker? I finished the first bookcase and moved on to the second one.

I finally found the book I knew I should be reading: *The Catcher in the Rye*. I had heard about this book but didn't ever see it on the shelves in our school. I knew it was about a boy who really loved his sister and spent a lot of time inside his head. That sounded so much like me. I knew it was the book for me. I clasped it to my chest like a found treasure and retreated to my room to read. What a fantastic treat to be able to just lie down and read. No worries. I thanked the heavens again.

"I'll be going now, Cece. Cook will get you anything you need. What're you reading?" Angela was standing in the doorway, clearly anxious to get going.

"*The Catcher in the Rye.* Have a good meeting. I'll be fine. Cook's already helped me."

"That's great. Good book. Have fun. Bye." She waved and bounded down the steps.

I read my book, following the thoughts that floated around inside the head of Holden Caulfield. It was so much easier to read English, to dwell on the words, than to have a conversation and have to create my own words on the spot. He created a world and then let us into it. I was with him. I could hear Cook in the background but her sounds didn't disturb my journey into Holden's mind. It made me think about how rich the internal lives of people could be. We pass them every minute of the day and never know what is going on inside them. I lost myself in Holden's thoughts.

"Come have some dinner, Cece," Cook called from downstairs. Her voice pulled me out of the book and I came back into the world of the farm. I swung my legs off of the bed and stood up feeling disoriented and light headed. Was that the pregnancy or the deep reading? I didn't really know.

"Coming," I yelled down to Cook.

I could smell the hamburgers from the top of the stairs. In the kitchen there was a plate with a big, juicy burger, French fries, and a fresh salad piled on it. Salt, pepper, catsup, and mustard were set out on the table. It looked great.

"Thanks, Cook, this looks so good." I sat down at the table and put the napkin in my lap.

"Do you need anything else now, honey?"

"I'm sorry to be a problem, but do you have any hot sauce?"

"Oh, of course. I forgot we have a Mexican in the house now." She got the hot sauce from a shelf on the wall. I made a note of where it was kept so I wouldn't have to ask her again. She put it on the table in front of me. "There you go, Cece. Enjoy."

"Does everyone usually say *enjoy*?" I asked her with my mouth already full and hamburger juice running down my chin. It was so good I didn't even mind.

"They do when they're about to have their food. All of your questions are sure making me think. Don't know if that's a good thing or not." She was putting on her jacket and gathering her purse now. "See you in the morning. Don't wash the dishes please. I have a job here." She waved and was gone.

Suddenly, for the first time since I came here, the house was absolutely quiet. No one clomping around. No one bustling in the kitchen. If the food hadn't been so good, I would have put it down for ten minutes and taken in the silence. I could hear the crickets from the outside and an occasional owl hooting. I ate in the silence, savoring both.

I went back upstairs after I piled the dishes in the sink and added hot water for them to soak. I took off my clothes and wrapped up in a big towel and sat in the window seat just looking out at the moonlit fields. There was a white shadow cast across the meadow like a silver cloud.

I ran the bath and, for the second time in my life, I took in its pleasure. This time I was prepared for the bloated stomach of the creature who presented herself in the mirror. I knew Nely was getting safer and safer. I was so lucky.

Then, I went inside my head like Holden. I searched around my feelings and my thoughts like someone inside a maze. I was feeling safe. This was my first feeling—safe. It was an amazing feeling. This was followed closely by secure. Funny that all of my life before in Mexico, when we were always looking to make some money, I never felt secure. After the *narcos* started all of our trouble in Mexico, I felt even less secure. With all of the corruption too, who could you trust? Never the government. Every political party was as bad as the next. Every politician would line his pockets. The police? They were a joke too. I had that returning sense of dread.

Was I happy? I had been happy in Mexico with my family and my lover, Guillermo. Now I wasn't happy. I still didn't know what I would do with my life. But I was content. I was OK. Not happy but OK. Confused? I was very confused. There were many things that Americans did that were just like what Mexicans did, but I had a feeling that every day I would be seeing things that Americans did differently. Look at the drinking water fountains with their clean cool water. Look at the Walmart manager who was so afraid that I would sue. Look at the gas stations where you have to pump your own gas. Look at the weird things on the roads and in the towns that people make pilgrimages to see. How strange is that? Yes, confused, but not in a bad way.

I finished the bath and went back to bed with Holden

Caulfield. I curled up inside his head and took his journey with him. I stayed with him until I fell asleep cradling the book in my arms.

The rattling of the dishes downstairs woke me up. I got dressed and went down. "Shall I make the coffee, Cook?" I asked carefully, not wanting to interfere with her kingdom.

"That would be nice, dearie. Angela came home from her meeting last night and left us a note about making muffins for a morning meeting so I'm really swamped. She's going back there today. Any help would be appreciated."

"OK, I will make the coffee only if you tell me what 'swamped' means." I took out the coffee and started scooping it into the filter.

"Let's see, 'swamped' means that something is rolling over you like a big wave. It means you have too much to do and too little time. Like her, right now." Angela came into the room combing out wet hair.

"Good morning, ladies. Coffee ready?" She saw me adding the water to the carafe. "OK, not yet, but soon."

"How did your meeting go?" I asked.

"It didn't really go very far. We are meeting again this morning; that's why I saddled Cook with extra work. It's a tricky situation."

"Why? What's it about? Do you want to talk about it?"

"It's about water, Cece. Water is so precious and we all have to share it. That's what we're talking about. The number of wells needed for irrigation has been steadily growing for more than a hundred years and we have to decide how we are going to conserve. It's the usual fight. One group wants to be left alone to dig wells and irrigate all it wants. Another group, our group, wants to work together to determine how best to share water among all of us. I think there's a lot we can do to share. We just ended up in a shouting match last night. So we disbanded and are going to come back together this morning and decide what we can do. I invited a water expert from the university to come and talk to us. Maybe that will help. We usually wait until we're in a mess before we do anything. We're not big on prevention."

"I don't think I ever heard of anyone talking about conserving water or having meetings like that. In our town there is no water. We have to use cisterns to catch the water during the rainy season."

"What if that water runs out?" Angela was frowning now.

"That is the way it is. The villagers use their pick-up trucks and go and buy water in big bottles, and the families use that."

"But what about baths and laundry?" Her frown was deepening now.

"We just make do. We would make one bath and everyone would share it. It's not so hard to understand, Angela. Water is scarce in Mexico."

"I really had no idea. We see commercials to conserve water but most of us have no idea that we would ever have to share a bath. I wish you could come before the group and explain how you had to live; maybe it would make an impact. Ahh, don't worry. It's always the same; it doesn't matter what the issue is. There are people who want to look after themselves only and people who want to try to do what's best for the group. I guess we can't change human nature."

Angela was very frustrated about this. I didn't really know what to say. In my family we had trouble enough just looking after ourselves. Yet everyone in the village helped each other out. No one would take his pick-up to get water without asking his neighbors if they needed it too. So many families were like ours. We didn't even have any paperwork that said the land we lived on belonged to our family. It was just tradition.

"Go and sit down, Angela. Cece will bring you some coffee. There's an article in the local paper about your water meeting. That should frustrate you more." Cook smiled at Angela who took the paper and went into the dining room.

I brought the coffee in and sat down with her. She ignored me and continued reading her paper. Little frown lines appeared between her eyes. I sighed. I looked out at the rising day and left her in peace to get her frustration out.

"Shit. The damn newspaper sounds like a call to the militia. What a mess."

I made a mental note to look up the word "militia." Angela wasn't really talking to me. She was just talking to the universe. She looked off into space and slammed her coffee cup down on the table. She went inside her mind, looking for an answer to this problem, or so I guessed. She looked at the ceiling and got up and went to the windows.

I didn't talk. I couldn't help. I got up to leave and went outside. At least I could do something useful. I got out the four dog bowls and filled them up just before each dog came to claim his food. I walked over to the barn and got up my courage. I had watched Angela feed the horses and I knew that each of the four types of food took only one scoop. So I did that. I was careful to put each scoop into the bowl and then add the oil. I put the food in the horses' food pan. The first horse trotted over and started eating right away. I must've done something right. I was very proud of myself. I heard the screen door slam and Angela passed by me into the barn as I was coming out.

"I've gotta feed the horses and then I'm going to the meeting, Cece." She rushed past me.

"I did it already," I said quietly.

She stopped in her tracks. "You fed the horses? What did you feed them?" Those little frown lines appeared again between her eyes.

"One scoop of each of the four barrels and one cup full of the oil. Was that right?" I knew it was right but, for a second, I thought I might have overfed the horses and they'd get sick or something.

"Well done, Cece. I can't believe you did so well. I guess I'll only have to tell you once."

I was beaming now. I had been a bit anxious that I would've made some kind of mistake. It was funny how something so easy could seem so important, so crucial. I wanted to be perfect. I guess I was.

"Go to your meeting. Cook and I can take care of the farm."

"Good girl." Angela hurried back into the house. She came back seconds later carrying the still-steaming muffins that Cook had prepared. Cook stood in the doorway and I joined her. We waved to Angela as she drove away. We were her family sending her off to war. She waved back as the truck pulled into the road.

"Whew! What a whirlwind she was this morning. Now I can relax and have some coffee. Can I make you something, Cece?"

"No, I'm fine. What can I do to help?"

"Well, you know how houses always need doing? I'm sure you'll find something."

I knew there was a cleaning lady that came once a week so I wouldn't need to do that. I couldn't do the cooking. No truck, so I couldn't mend the fence. I walked around looking for a place to help and there it was: the books. I would put the books in order.

I started by taking all of the books down off the tops of everything in the living room and the dining room and stacking them up. They were of all ages and all sizes and all types. I stacked them according to size first because the small ones would fit in the book shelves while the big ones had to go on top of things. When I had three areas of sizes, I sat on the floor with the piles and started putting them into alphabetical order. The work was methodical so I got into the rhythm of it. I listened to the sounds of the farm, the neighs of the horses, the snorts of the pigs, the barks of the dogs. To me it sounded like music. If I listened really closely, I could even hear the rustle of the leaves in the trees.

"Cook, can you tell me where to find a dust cloth?" Cook was reading a cookbook at the kitchen table.

"You don't need to dust. Edna will do that on Tuesday when she comes by."

"I'm organizing the books so I just wanted to dust them while I had them all off the shelves. I might dust the shelves too."

"Well, child, you are a very hard-working girl. Go into the pantry and you'll see a box on the floor right inside the door with clean dust cloths. Take whatever you need." She went back to reading her recipes.

I found some dust cloths and took them into the dining room. I dusted each shelf and arranged the newly-alphabetized books into the shelves, dusting each one before I put it into its new home. I worked like this for several hours until all of the books were in their new places. I stood back and admired my work.

After many hours I had found so much more room that I was able to put some of the decorations into prominent places so that Angela's Indian pottery showed up so much better. I thought it was Indian pottery anyway. We didn't have any Indian pottery in Mexico. We had our own artists there and most of the Mexican homes, even the poorest ones, had pottery. I loved Angela's pieces. They had Indian drawings on them or bold black lines and were so powerful. I don't know why I thought that, I just did. Cook came in to put a fresh tablecloth on the dining table.

"Nice job, Cece. I'm sure Angela will be proud of you." She cast the tablecloth up into the air and it floated back down over the table. She walked around, smoothing it and then went back into the kitchen.

I heard Angela's truck in the driveway. She came into the house like a whirlwind. "Cece," she called to me in a loud voice. I guess she thought I was upstairs.

"Hi, I'm here."

"I've got a great surprise for you. Mary Lou Patterson was at the meeting. She's one of the *sharers*, that's what we're calling the people who want to work together to share the water. Anyway, she was asking me if you might want to start a little sewing school in her shop. She has those five display models of the sewing machines and, if girls come in and learn to sew, their families might buy machines or at least buy some trimmings or fabric or something. She was right taken with you. She also thinks you might speak Spanish. Could that be true?" She laughed at that. Cook and I laughed too.

"That's a wonderful idea but there are two problems with it: I'm pregnant and I need to help you here. How could I earn my keep?"

"I hope you don't get mad at me for making a possible deal for you, but anyhow, we were talking and she suggested that rather than pay you, I could have credit at her store or her husband's store—the hardware store. We could use the credit whenever we wanted. It would be like a bartering system. Her husband and her boy work at the hardware store. He's the boy who carried my supplies to the truck." Oh, the nodder, I thought.

"Doesn't she mind the pregnancy?"

"She thinks it would be a good situation. She says that many women learn to sew when they're pregnant because they don't want to spend so much money on clothes they will wear for such a short time. She thinks you being pregnant would actually be a positive. What do you think of that?"

"I think it sounds great." Cook had to add her opinion. "Tell her yes. When does she start?"

"I don't really know how to use those new machines. They've got computers built into them and everything. And I don't want to desert you here." I had to have an opinion too.

"Well, you wouldn't start for a month or so while she gets the place ready for you," Angela continued. "I'm sure we can get along without you, Cece, and you'll be bringing in money through the credit. There have been times when

Mr. Patterson has had to wait for money from me and now we'll have credit. That's a good deal for us." Angela smiled at me.

"I'm not sure I have anything to wear." I was nervous about this possibility.

"Great, you can make clothes for yourself and show the students how to sew. Mrs. Patterson says she has a list of girls who want to learn to sew. They've asked her in the past and she's sure some of them will still be interested. She never had the time herself so she's really glad you came in. I said you were a real polite girl. A hard worker. Come get a hug." Angela opened her arms wide for me.

XV

Angela and I worked on the fence for the next month while I grew and Nely grew, and we waited for Mary Lou Patterson to get the sewing school ready. Angela went to several water meetings and she got more and more frustrated as the time went by. She also disappeared periodically and I was left having dinner alone while she visited with Mr. Richard. One afternoon after an especially frantic meeting she came to find me while I was reading *The Catcher in the Rye*. There was so much work around the farm that I seldom had time to read so I treasured these moments.

"Mary Lou Patterson wants you to come and talk with her tomorrow," Angela launched our conversation the next morning. It was so like an American to just get right into the topic without saying "Good morning," I had to remember not to judge her as rude. Mexicans would always say "Good morning" first before tackling the main point. I had to remember this. "I'll be going into town for another of those damn meetings at nine in the morning. Her husband's going tomorrow too so she'll be in the store to talk with you."

"I'd better go look at the clothes I've got to see if anything is suitable." I put the book down, sorry to see it go.

"Take your time. Dinner won't be for a few hours."

Cook and Angela were beaming at me like I had just won a prize. I felt like that too. I could still hear them as I climbed the stairs.

"Come have a cup of coffee, Angela. I'll make you a sandwich." Cook said to Angela as they moved back into the kitchen together. "Bet that's a load off your mind." Cook cut into a big ham she had taken from the refrigerator.

"What do you mean, Cook?" Angela poured the coffee and ladled in sugar and cream

"Oh, I know you, Angela. You wanted to take in that girl and help her but what were you going to do with her? The farm runs like clockwork. You don't need nobody else here. You were going to have to find some busywork for her."

"Nah, Cook, I'd already decided to give her your job. I wanted some damn Mexican food for a change." She took the sandwich Cook was offering.

"Enchiladas coming right up," Cook barked very seriously. Angela laughed.

"You are so right. I would have had to come up with a big project for her, and her being pregnant and all just made it more of a challenge. This is perfect, works out perfectly. She doesn't even have to have working papers. No money is changing hands. It works out great for all of us. She can take the bus into town or maybe ride the school bus. Depends on the hours she'll be working. This is a godsend."

"Well, He helps those who help others, and you sure do that. I've seen you take in stray people for as long as I've known you, and we are always better off when they leave then when they got here. Things work out. Now eat your sandwich in peace. I got work to do. I need to look up a recipe. It will be *chile rellenos* tonight."

I wasn't really surprised as I listened to them while rummaging through my clothes. I knew that Angela had a good heart and she wanted to help me. But what did she really need? Another person to feed? I was going to be less and less help as time went on. This way, as a worker, I could really help her.

I laid out the clothes and I think I had enough for a start. I had two pairs of jeans and a jean skirt that would work for a while. I also had some leggings and several long blouses that would cover the bump. I had some t-shirts too. Anyway, I had at least ten outfits that I could wash and move around and make do. And I would be sewing.

I was getting excited and a bit scared. I knew that my English was getting good, and there were many people here who spoke Spanish. I couldn't rely on that, of course, because I needed to speak English. I would have to trust that people would help me, they would correct me. I would be fine. Nely would be safe. I thought I should rest for a while now. I took out *The Catcher in the Rye* and climbed inside the head of Holden Caulfield.

I woke up several hours later and heard voices from the kitchen. Cook and Angela were having a deep discussion about the water. I started the bath and climbed into the oasis looking out through the windows to the stars. The water felt wonderful and the bubbles floated around me. I could just make out what they were saying but I heard the frustration in Angela's voice.

"Ah, Cook, don't we realize that if we don't all work together there won't be enough? We can't just go off alone and dig wells whenever we feel like it. We all think that it's

OK if we just add one. It's only one. But it's like what would happen if every family on earth just added one child. It's only one. You see, it would be catastrophic. It's the same with the water. If every family in the High Plains just added one well, it would be catastrophic. We all share the same aquifer. We just don't see it. We don't see it."

"Well, Angela, you have to do what you can and then let it go. What else can you do?"

"Something to get the government involved. If the local government won't do anything then I have to get the state government involved and then the federal government." Her voice rose with her conviction.

"In my experience, the more the government gets involved, the fewer the results. Government just adds lots of paperwork and lots of hassles and very little help." Cook got up to refresh her coffee.

"We've gotta try everything, Cook. If not for us, then for the future. Water doesn't last forever. Look at what happened to the Colorado River. Look at California. We can't count on anything lasting forever."

"Sorry, Angela, I have to get these chilies on the table. They're better if they're piping hot. Don't you think?" She skillfully changed the subject. "I'll call Cece to set the table." She put the casserole dish on the counter top.

"I'm already here." I crossed the kitchen and loaded up the plates and cutlery for dinner. I carried it to the dining room. "Sounds like you are having an interesting conversation," I called back over my shoulder.

"A frustrating one, anyway." Angela frowned. She followed me to the table and sat down at her place at the head of it. "What's wrong with people?" She asked it into the air but I felt compelled to answer.

"I don't know," I said. "We had this in Mexico too. People came to help towns in the country, the *campo,* to build cisterns to catch water during the rainy season. We were all having to buy water in plastic bottles once the wells ran dry, as I told you. Some people came from a club, I think it was called Rotary, some gringos. Oh sorry, I didn't mean to offend you." I checked for their reaction and it seemed OK to continue. "Anyway this club wanted to teach us how to build cisterns to catch the rainwater, but they wouldn't teach us until we had six families that agreed to work together to build the six cisterns for each other. It was going to be free and we would have enough fresh water to drink for the whole year. My mother was so excited because it meant we wouldn't have to buy water all the time and try to find a place for all of the plastic bottles. We had 200 families in the village and no one wanted to work together. Everyone felt that it would be hard to make it fair. Like one family might get a better cistern than another family or something like that. In the end no one got a cistern. Everyone lost."

"That's exactly what's going to happen here. Everyone will lose. Maybe not today, but eventually, everyone will lose." She put her head in her hands. I was afraid she was going to cry. Instead, she jumped up and headed out the door.

"I'm going to wash up for dinner." She stomped upstairs.

"Here you go, dearie, just for you, *chile rellenos.* Do they look like the real thing?" She put the dish on the table. The stuffed chilies oozed melted cheese. They looked just like the ones in Mexico and it made me homesick. I knew she had cooked them for me.

"Thanks so much, Cook, they look terrific." I followed her into the kitchen and brought back the bread, butter, and salad. At least Nely and I were eating well.

"Do you need anything else, dearie?" Cook popped her head back in. "I'll be going home if everything is OK."

"Can I answer for Angela?" I asked, secretly hoping for tortillas.

"Oh sure, you're part of the family now, dearie. Is everything OK?"

"It looks wonderful, Cook. Thanks so much. See you tomorrow." I thought I sounded so American. They say that: "See you tomorrow." I wonder if they say the same thing if they aren't going to really see that person tomorrow?

Angela came back down then with a shiny face. She sat at the table and we dished out the *chiles rellenos* in silence. She was concentrating on something in her head, maybe making a strategy. Finally, she spoke.

"I think I'll use your story about your cisterns, Cece. Nobody won. Maybe that will help to break our deadlock. Let's talk about you. Are you ready for the job to start?"

"I think so. I feel a little nervous."

"You're a very resourceful girl, Cece. I know you'll do fine. Just be yourself and you'll capture everyone's hearts."

"Can you tell me how to catch the bus to get into town?"

"Oh, I forgot to tell you. I called Evelyn who drives the school bus. She has to pass right by here in the morning to pick up the kids. She'll be going by at eight and coming back at four. So you'll have to arrange it with her for your return. I think that might work. Just ask her when you get off the bus at the school. You know the school, we passed it the other day."

"Yes, I remember. Do you think my English is good enough?"

"It's a lot better than you think it is. You'll be fine. You have an accent and you might mess up some words but people will help you. Don't be too shy to ask."

We went back to eating the chiles rellenos and they were wonderful. I wanted to remember to tell Cook that I appreciated her making them for me. I was planning my first day at work with some anticipation. I still worried about my English but I knew it would get better and better. I had been listening to the radio during the day to help my vocabulary and planned to listen again tonight if it wouldn't disturb Angela.

"Can I listen to the radio in my room, Angela, will it bother you?" I asked.

"Sure. It won't disturb me."

"I think the radio is really helping. Since all of you speak English and I've been hearing it all day, I am starting to think in English. I had a dream in English last night for the first time."

"Oh, Cece, that is really progress. When you start to dream in another language, you know that you're thinking in that language. Keep listening to English."

"If you don't mind, I'll go up now and listen."

"Sure, sure, go." She got up and started clearing the dishes.

I helped her and took the casserole dish to the kitchen. I covered it and stored it in the refrigerator for tomorrow. It would be delicious the second day. "Good night." I left her in the kitchen.

"Good night, Cece, sleep well." She waved to me.

I got ready for bed and moved the radio onto the bedside table. I turned the volume down and listened to a man telling the listeners about the bugs that were infesting the crops this year. I didn't have much interest in it but there were a lot of words I didn't know. I wrote them in my little notebook to look up later.

XVI

"Good morning, Cook. How do I look for my first day at work?" I twirled around but the skirt didn't move. It was the idea anyway.

"You look great, Cece. You look like a real professional. Better have a big breakfast."

"Not today, Cook. I'll just have some coffee and toast." I put the bread in the toaster and sat at the kitchen table watching her. She always had something to do. I think part of the job meant that she could share each day's supper with her own family. I wondered if this was another way for Angela to take care of someone. Cook was doing a job, true, but she also had the benefit of taking the results of that work home to her own family.

"Come on, Cece, you have to go out to the road. Evelyn will be coming any minute." Angela was waving to me from behind the closed screen door.

I drank down my coffee and ran out the door waving goodbye to Cook as I went. We walked to the end of the dirt driveway and I could already see the school bus coming down the road. It pulled to a stop alongside our drive and I could see the heads of the little kids bobbing in the excitement of something new.

"Hi. Evelyn, this here's Cece. Take good care of her." She turned toward me. "Bye honey, good luck."

I smiled at her and climbed on board. "Hi, Evelyn. Hi,

kids." I smiled and waved at the kids and sat down in the front seat nearest Evelyn. Kids never sit close to the driver or the teacher or the priest. Most of them were arranged in the very back of the bus.

"Hi, Cece, welcome aboard. How you doin' today?" Evelyn beamed a sideways smile at me, careful to keep her eyes on the road.

"I'm great."

"Sorry I'm not really allowed to talk to you while I'm driving. So let's talk about the return trip when we get to the school."

"OK, sorry. You've got precious cargo on board."

"That's for sure."

I watched the scenery pass by now, still going down our little dirt road. I hadn't gone this way with Angela and for the first time I saw that we had neighbors. About two miles from our farm there was another with a similar set up: corral, barn, wooden house, and trucks on the gravel drive. The same pattern continued as we passed several farms down the road. I wondered if these farmers were in the *hoarder* or the *sharer* camp on the water issue. We finally reached the end and Evelyn had a tough time turning the bus around, but she finally managed and we continued passing other farms on the opposite side.

Now we went in the direction that Angela and I had traveled the other day when we went to town. The bus made many more stops than Angela and I had made as we plucked little kids off the side of the road all the way into town. They came aboard with their miniature backpacks crammed with books and most struggled to get up the steps without being pulled backwards by the weight they were carrying.

As we got closer to the school, the noise levels, which were nearly deafening as it was, increased. The kids started bouncing in their seats and I could hear the deals being made for lunch and recess. It was nice to be surrounded by such lively youngsters so full of promise.

"OK, Cece, do you think you can be here by 3 o'clock for the trip back this afternoon?" Evelyn had levered the door closed to give us some quiet after her charges had deserted the bus.

"I think so. I'm just going to get the sewing school started. There shouldn't be so much to do today. Do you think I could call you if there's a problem? Should I write down your phone number?"

"No, Mary Lou has it. If I don't hear from you, I'll know that you'll be here at 3. Now look, do you see those trees there? You just walk right there and at the trees there's a little path. Take the path and it will bring you right to Main Street. Go right and you'll walk right into Patterson's. Good luck."

"Thanks so much, Evelyn, I'll see you this afternoon."

I followed her directions and found my way to Patterson's with no problem. The OPEN sign was on the door. The little bell rang when I walked in and butterflies fluttered in my stomach. There was nobody in the front of the store so I walked to the back to get to Mrs. Patterson. Before I got to her she came out of the back to greet me.

"Hello, Mrs. Patterson, how are you? I'm all ready to start work. I'm so excited to be here. Thank you so much for giving me this opportunity." Cook had told me to say that. The words were tumbling out so fast that she didn't have a chance to say anything.

"Hold on, hold on, Cece, take a breath." She put her

arm around me. "Come in and sit down. Let's talk about what we're going to do here." She led me into the back store room. I hadn't been there before and it was much bigger than I thought. There were long shelves all the way to the ceiling with boxes piled on top of each other. At the back corner where we looked to be heading, was another room with a door closing it off. It was surrounded by windows on three sides so we could see inside the room. There were sewing machines set up in what already looked like a classroom. Outside of that space was an office with a desk and two chairs plus a computer. Across from all of this was another little area where a large black lady was on the phone. I waved at her like we were old friends and gave her a big smile.

"That's Jeamine," Mrs. Patterson said. "She's our girl Friday. You know what that means? She does everything: bookkeeper, receptionist, clerk. Well, everything. She doesn't really like to do the selling. She's shy around the customers. So she stays back here most of the time and deals with all of the paperwork. Thank God for her. Let's go into your area, are you ready for that?"

I nodded. "Pleased to meet you, Jeamine." I smiled and waved at Jeamine who looked up for a second and waved too. She had on glasses with a leopard print and there was a pencil stuck right into her hair.

I followed Mrs. Patterson into the room where the machines were set up. I noticed that they were old-fashioned machines so I was really relieved. It meant I would know how to use them. There were boxes of brand-new machines that had not been opened. This seemed strange to me.

"OK, Cece, this is our set-up. I had Bill—that's my

husband, Bill Patterson, he owns the hardware store across the street—set this up for me a long time ago. I used the old machines. We have six. I thought I could teach girls on the easy machines first and, if they liked sewing, they would buy a newer machine. I could show them the way to use the computer machines after they learned the basics of sewing. I never really had time to do the school though and we never used this set-up. We're the only department store for so many miles around here that I'm busy all day long with the customers. So what do you think? I thought you could do, finally, what I never had the time to do and still don't."

"I think it's really nice. Can I look around?"

"Sure. Take your time. There's some paper on the cutting table if you want to take any notes or anything. I'll go and talk with Jeamine about a tax problem we're having. The government always has its hand in your wallet, if you know what I mean." She left the room and I could see her through the windows as she walked over to talk with Jeamine.

The room was terrific. There were six machines but also all of the supplies we would need. Each machine had accessories like scissors, threads, bobbins, pinking shears, and a plastic case full of other sewing supplies which the students would need like pins and measuring tape and sewing chalk. These machines were in a circle around two huge cutting tables. This set up would allow the teacher, me, to talk to the girls and explain things and demonstrate. There were three ironing boards and irons set up in the back of the room and a sink. It looked like Mrs. Patterson thought you should iron as you went along and so did I.

I was amazed at all of the work that had already gone

into this plan. I would be able to just go in and get to work right away. That's good because waiting around would drive me crazy. I would just keep looking at my growing belly. I went to talk with Mrs. Patterson to ask her some questions.

"Yes, Cece, are you ready to talk now? I just finished with Jeamine. By the way, you two haven't formally met yet. This is Jeamine."

"Hi, Jeamine, pleased to meet you formally." Jeamine was my first chance to practice greeting like an American and I tried everything. I put out my hand to shake hers. She took it and gave it a strong shake. I nodded to her. She nodded back.

"You too, honey, catcha later." I didn't know what *catcha* meant, but I would remember to write it down in my notebook.

"Sit right here, Cece." Mrs. Patterson pointed to one of the chairs on the other side of her desk. She sat behind the desk. She pulled out a notepad.

"What do you think, Cece?"

"I think it's wonderful. It's a perfect place for a sewing school. You did a really good job."

"I thought so. I'm proud of it. Do you have any idea how you're going to do it?"

"I had some time to think last night, and I just thought I would start by making an apron. That's how my mother taught me. It would teach them how to cut out material, how to use the pattern, ironing, all the basics. Then we could get more complicated with tops, skirts and, finally, pants—they're the hardest. I would just go step by step and demonstrate and then walk around and help. That's my plan. Does that sound OK?"

"That's just how I would do it. Do you really want to get started today?"

"Yes, I'm ready to go, but we don't have any students."

"Actually, we do but not for today. I have their phone numbers here and you would need to get in touch with all of them until you have at least three students and then you have a class. You could actually run a class each morning and each afternoon. Do you think you can handle that many students?"

"Do you have that many students?"

"Yes, I think so. We had fifty students on our list, they come from town and the outlying countryside too. You would need, at the most, thirty. So yes."

"How did you think about running it? Like cost and times and all of that."

"Well, we thought we would charge $10.00 for a two-hour class once a week. That would be at least $300 a week plus they will buy supplies. We would pay you $150 for the ten classes. Or rather we would give Angela the credit. Does that sound fair? We would actually make money on the supplies."

I was stunned. In my village a bricklayer working 6 days a week, 9 hours a day, made $250. I was going to make just a little more than half of that for 20 hours of easy work. I felt so happy and I felt so ashamed that I was able to get so much money.

"I think it sounds very good. Thank you so much."

"OK, Cece, you need to call the fifty women on this list and see who actually still wants to come. I thought we would teach from 9:30 to 11:30. The afternoon class would be from 1:00 to 3:00. What do you think?"

Yes, that's good." I hesitated because I was thinking

about the amount of time it would take me to walk over to the school. Mrs. Patterson caught my hesitation.

"Is something wrong?"

"No, it's just that I am getting a ride with the school bus and I have to be there at 3 o'clock."

"Oh, that Angela is a sly one. School bus, that's good. It'll be fine. Evelyn can wait for you until 3:15. It takes the kids a bit of time to get out of their classes and board the bus. I'll have Tim, my son, drive you over each day. The kids are never on time anyway. Are we good?" I nodded. She handed me the list.

"Do you want to give me any idea about what to say?" I wasn't sure I could be so independent so fast. But I had done a good job at the farm, learning fast and helping out.

"Well, be polite. Ask for the person on the list. Explain who you are and what you are offering. That should be fine. OK, here you go. The phone is in the little sewing room. You can get started and make your calls. Be convincing. Good luck."

XVII

I went into the room and sat down. I took out my notebook and wrote CATCHA. I didn't want to forget it. I looked at the list Mrs. Patterson had given to me and it was full of names that sounded like Mexicans. I needed to organize these calls because fifty people was a lot.

I knew I could tackle this job because I am a very organized person. When I planned for the escape from Mexico, I made the plan with the timing and the supplies—although I wasn't as prepared as the three brothers—and the money. Even in university, I had to be very organized. I had to help my mother early in the morning and then walk three miles to the road to get the bus into a bigger town where the university was located. Each day had to be planned and the week had to be planned too. I knew that experience gave me good practice for planning my task now.

I made two lines down the page and made three column headings: accepted, rejected, left message. I knew some people wouldn't be home and I didn't want to keep calling people. I was anxious enough because I didn't really know how good my English really was. I tried the first name: Maria Teresa Peña Ortega.

"Hello." I tried to sound American. "Hola, Maria Teresa Peña Ortega, please." The phone hung up in my ear. I called back. "Hola, please Maria Teresa Peña Ortega."

The phone hung up. I decided to try the second name on the list.

"Hello, Luisa Cristina Garcia Lopez." The phone hung up. I tried the third name. "Good morning, Estrella Nieto Palma, please." The phone hung up.

"Hello, Silvia Rogriguez, please." Bam! The phone hung up. Maybe Americans are more casual than Mexicans. I tried that approach and called the number again. "Hello, Silvia, please."

"Who's calling?" The voice was quizzical, nothing negative there.

"This is the Patterson Department Store. I am calling about our new sewing classes."

"What's your name?" Now the voice sounded wary.

"Oh, sorry, I'm Cece." I guess I should introduce myself first the next time.

"OK, I thought Mary Lou wasn't going to give classes."

"You're right. Mary Lou doesn't have time but I will be giving the classes. Are you Silvia?"

"No, I'm Silvia's mom. Tell me about the classes, how much, when?"

"The classes will be twice a day, each day. You can have your choice between morning or afternoon. They will last for two hours and will be $10 each session."

"That sounds pretty good. Will she make something? I don't want to waste the experience. I want something to come out of it."

"Yes. I'll start with an apron that will have pockets."

"That doesn't sound too practical."

"The apron will teach her how to cut fabric and how to piece it together and how to add pockets. It's actually a good foundation. She'll make other things as the class goes on."

"OK. Does she have to buy the materials?"

"Mrs. Rodriguez, don't you think that $10 is very reasonable for a class? The materials are extra, of course. Mrs. Patterson couldn't afford to hold the class and pay for the materials for $10."

"Oh sure, you're right. OK, sign her up. I'll give it to her for her birthday present."

"Which day will she want to come?"

"Give her Mondays in the morning. I'll get her fat ass out of bed." I didn't respond to the insult toward her daughter.

"Thank you so much. I'll let you know when the class is full and we'll start right away."

"Goodbye, kid. Have a nice day."

"Goodbye, Mrs. Rodriguez. Have a nice day too."

I felt like jumping in the air. I had my first client. It was so easy. Well, of course there was a list of potential students. It's not like I had to find the students by myself. I made a little chart then with the five days and spaces to write the names of students in the boxes. I put Silvia in Monday in the morning.

"Sorry to bother you, Jeamine." Mrs. Patterson was in the front of the store and Jeamine was working with the calculator.

"No bother, Cece, how can I help?" I tried not to stare at the pencil stuck into the middle of her hair. I couldn't help staring at it because it was so odd. Her hair must have been very thick. She was the first black person I had ever met and this was the first time I had a chance to see black hair up close. It was like a little pocket of steel wool that we used to clean pots. How did she comb it, I wondered?

"I am calling people who said they were interested in taking the class and the first few hung up on me. I didn't even get a chance to ask any questions. The last one didn't, though. Can you help? What was I doing wrong?"

"What did you do different on the last one, honey? What did you say your name was?"

"I'm Cece. I'm not really sure. You know, the first ones I used their names, very polite, like Maria Consuela Torres Ballinas. I used their two last names like we Mexicans have. To be polite."

Jeamine burst into gales of deep laughter. Her face shook and all of her hair shook in one big poof like it was attached directly to her head and didn't have a mind of its own. She slapped her thighs and threw her head back.

"Oh my God, Cece, that is so funny. I can't believe the folks at the other end when all of them names came jumping out of the phone at them. They just hung up to get away from you, child!" She laughed again. I was a bit insulted by her laughter. I was doing the best I could.

"Well I must've done something right for the last one because I got a student to take the class. Of course I stopped using her long name." I looked at her with a look that said *stop laughing at me*.

"I'm sorry, Cece. It was just so funny. I know you're new here in the States. Folks here don't like to answer the phone at all. It's 'cause of telemarketers." Jeamine put down her papers and folded her hands under her chin, looking intently at me. She was serious now.

"What are those?"

"They're people who're paid by a company to call you and try to get money from you or get you to buy somethin' they're selling or vote for someone they're supportin'. We all gets calls from 'em all the time and it's so annoyin'. Most people, like the first ones you called, just hangs up on 'em. When you used the full names of them girls, it made people think you was a telemarketer just reading their names off of some list. So they hung up on you."

"So, when I asked for Silvia with just her first name, they thought I knew her and stayed talking to me?"

"That's right. At least they gave you a few minutes to talk, right?"

"Yes, I got to tell Mrs. Rodriguez about the classes."

"Good. Did she sign up her lazy-ass daughter Silvia?"

"Yes she did. Well she signed up Silvia, I don't know about the lazy part." Poor Silvia, everyone was criticizing her.

"So just keep doin' what you doin'. Introduce yourself and tell them you're from Patterson's. Be sure to ask for 'em only by their first names and that should work. You doin' fine, girl."

I didn't really need Jeamine's advice. I just wanted to make some contact with her. I had already figured out that I needed to just use the first names but I didn't know about the telemarketers. I was probably around the age of the potential students and they would not be so wary of me. It made me so proud that I was accomplishing something. I felt the fear starting to leave me. I was beginning to feel that I might actually have a chance for a better life here. I continued calling for the rest of the morning. Mrs. Patterson came into the sewing room then and sat down.

"Busy morning. The mothers are buying fabric for the school uniforms and it seems I was cutting all morning. How did you do, Cece?"

"I think I'm doing fine. Well, I'm not sure. It depends

what you expect. But I'm working through the list. Let's see. I spoke to nineteen people. Ten of them have said *yes*. I also left messages on answering machines for six more."

"What did you tell them?"

"Like you said, that I was Cece from Patterson's and called to give them the opportunity to take a sewing class."

"Oh, that's a good one, *opportunity*. I like that."

"Is that wrong? Would you say something else?"

"No, it's not wrong. It's good selling. You're a natural. You're selling the idea. Did you bring your lunch?"

"Yes, Cook prepared something. I left it in the refrigerator. I hope that's OK."

"Sure, it's fine. Jeamine and I usually go over to Dick's Diner for lunch. Do you want to join us?"

"No thanks, if you don't mind, I'll just eat lunch here. Do you want me to watch the store?"

"Not yet. You'd have to do the selling. Most folks know that we close for an hour at lunch time anyway. I think we'll wait awhile to see if you want to sell. I'm just paying you to teach the classes. If you started selling, I'd have to pay you as a sales clerk and I can't afford to do that yet. Maybe later. So we'll lock up the store when we go, OK?"

"Sure, that would be fine. I'll just stay back here."

"Suit yourself. See you in about an hour." She moved toward the front of the store and Jeamine joined her. They left together and she locked the door, being careful to flip the OPEN sign to CLOSED.

I sat quietly and ate my lunch. Cook had prepared a delicious chicken salad sandwich. I hoped it wasn't from our chickens at the farm. She included a piece of chocolate cake and some raw vegetables. She also put a note inside: "Knock them dead, Cece." I wasn't sure what it meant, but

I guessed it didn't have anything to do with boxing. Probably America's way of encouraging people.

I must have fallen asleep on the couch near Mrs. Patterson's desk. The sound of the bell on the front door woke me and I couldn't believe a whole hour had gone by. I glanced at my watch and it said only twenty minutes had elapsed. Who was opening the door?

He came through the corridor leading into the shop and stopped before he got to the back. I could see into the shop and I saw a man, oh a boy really, taking money from the cash register. I could see that it was the owner's son. I flattened myself against the wall. I hoped he hadn't seen me. What was he doing? Was he stealing from his own mother? Was he just taking money to the other store or taking money he was owed? I heard my heart beat. I pulled back and crept back to the couch. I heard the bell go again after a few minutes. I wasn't sure what I had seen. If he was just getting money from this store to take to the other store then why did he do that while we were closed and everyone was gone? Why be so sneaky?

What should I do? Should I say something? Should I ask Jeamine about this? My mind was racing. I took several deep breaths. Relax. Relax. This is nothing. He works for them. He must take money all of the time and move it between the stores. How silly I would seem if I said something and how disloyal. This woman was saving my life like so many of the women I had met had done for me. I had to protect her and honor her too. How silly. I pulled out my book and read until I heard the bell ring again and Jeamine and Mrs. Patterson came to the back.

"You missed some great sloppy joes," Mrs. Patterson said.

"What are they?" I asked. Mrs. Patterson looked at Jeamine.

"How would you describe a sloppy joe?" Mrs. Patterson asked her.

"Well, they're like a crumbled up hamburger with a special sweet tomato sauce. I never make 'em myself but that's what they're like. Like a crumbled hamburger with sweet tomato sauce. It's not poured over the top. The beef's cooked right in it."

"How do you eat it?" I still couldn't picture this food.

"On a hamburger bun. It's messy so I guess that's why they're called sloppy joes." Mrs. Patterson turned and went back to the front of the store.

I was a bit worried that all of my questions would annoy people. Jeamine didn't seem to mind but she had already gone back to her desk and was putting figures into the calculator.

I went back in and set about making my calls. I used only the first names and acted like I was a friend of the person I was calling. I didn't want to trick anyone, but I wanted them to listen to what I had to say and not just hang up on me. I was very successful in getting the calls made. I had filled most of the classes already. I had some spaces left but not a lot. I was really happy with my progress, but I had to keep reminding myself that this list was made up of people who wanted to take classes. My success was not really my own.

"Come on, Cece, Tim will drive you to the bus." Mrs. Patterson was calling from the front of the store. I hurried to go, waving to Jeamine on my way out. "He's waiting for you over there in that Ford truck." She pointed to a beat up truck with a boy sitting in the driver's seat. I ran across the street and opened the passenger's door. Pulling myself up into the seat, I turned to face him.

"Put your seat belt on." He didn't look at me.

"OK, thanks for the ride. I appreciate it."

"Wasn't my idea. Ma's orders." He swung into traffic, checking mirrors. He kept his face forward.

"Well, it's nice anyway."

"You beaners really need to get your own cars." He had a serious expression on his handsome face that detracted from his looks.

"I'll make a note of that," I said sarcastically. Too quickly. What's a beaner? I thought.

"Oh, a little feisty one. We like those types here. Mexican firecrackers."

I stopped talking then. Better to keep the fuel away from him. We rode in silence the short distance to the school. He pulled up next to the buses parked there loading the kids. I got out.

"Thanks for the ride," I said. Without answering, he drove away. I tried to stop myself from looking after him but I couldn't.

There were about fifteen school buses and of course I didn't know which one was Evelyn's. Little kids were milling about all over the place and climbing up on the buses and hugging each other goodbye as if they would be parted forever. There was a huge roar of noise and they laughed and screamed at each other. I walked down the line of buses looking at the drivers, trying to find Evelyn. Some of the buses had no drivers as of yet and I saw several of them under the trees chatting but no Evelyn. Finally, I saw her coming out of the school. She saw me and pointed to a bus I had already passed and I doubled back to meet up with her at its door.

"Welcome back. How was your first day?"

"I think it went pretty well. Anyway, I am coming back tomorrow so that's a good sign."

"Yep, I'd call that a success. OK, kids, settle down. Settle down." She screamed this into the rearview mirror and pulled the lever to close the bus door. She stood up then and counted the kids. There were thirty little bundles of energy all chatting and screaming and laughing. They were the opposite of the quiet, tired kids who were on the morning bus. School must have agreed with them because they had come alive over the course of the day.

"OK, everybody here? Let's go." She pulled out slowly in case a little kid was in the path of the encroaching bus and away we went. I watched the reverse of the scenery I had seen that morning. I felt good about myself and I felt good about life. The day was beautiful. I couldn't wait to share it with my adoptive family.

Angela was outside working on the fence when I got home. The bus drove past her. I went into the house and quickly changed into some old clothes she had given me and walked out to the fence where she was working.

"Hi, Cece, how was your day? You're just in time to hand me a nail. I hate keeping the damn things in my mouth while I work." She spit the nails out into her hands. "Not very sanitary I know but what the hell. How was your first day? You didn't embarrass her, did you?

"I don't think so," I said.

"Oh, Cece, I'm only kidding you, please tell me the whole story from the very beginning."

"The bus ride was good. I was the only one in the front of the bus because all of the kids were crammed into the back. Evelyn was nice and friendly. I walked from the school to the shop. Mrs. Patterson was already there. She showed me the sewing classroom in the back and it's great."

"She already had a room? I didn't know that. She was well prepared then. Are the machines tough to use?" Angela talked while she mended the fence.

"That's a great part of the story. I'm using old machines because the new ones are too complicated for someone that's just learning to sew. I think the girls should learn to make clothes first and then go up to the more complicated machines. It makes sense really."

"How many?"

"What?"

"Machines."

I took a nail from her and hammered away at the piece of broken fence. "Six machines. That means I can have six students. We're going to have ten classes a week."

"Sounds great. Here hold this for a minute." She handed me a nail that she was having difficulty positioning. The barbed wire kept turning the wrong way and she had to bend it back to the place she wanted.

"She was even more prepared than that. She had a list of girls who were already interested if she ever put together a class. So I had to call them to see if they were still interested. I called most of them."

"Did you have any trouble with that?"

"Yes, at first. They thought I was a tele-, a tele-, a tele-something."

"Telemarketer. We all hate to hear from them. They're a menace."

"Well, I figured out that I'm pretty close in age to the

girls who will be taking the class so if I acted like I knew them then I could get past the initial distrust. That worked like a charm. I think the parents all thought I knew the girls. Using their full names didn't work, especially the Spanish names with the two last names." She nodded toward the nail in my hand and I gave it back to her.

"Yeah, if someone calls and asks for Angela McGowan, I know it's a telemarketer. I just say she's not at home and I don't know when she'll be returning. I think they put my name at the bottom of their lists and just go on. My name doesn't come up again for a long time. So how'd you do? Did you get students?"

"Yes. I have most of the slots filled now. I'm doing really well, I think. But, of course, these were girls who were already interested."

"Don't get humble now. You did a good job. You should be proud. Did your lunch work out OK?" She was pounding that poor little nail now and it was holding the wire in place.

"Yes. Cook fixed me a delicious sandwich and put a nice note in there too. I had a relaxing lunch hour. I brought *The Catcher in the Rye* with me. Oh, that reminds me what does *catcha* mean?"

"Hmm. Don't know. I can't say that I've heard the word before. Can you use it in a sentence for me?"

"Sure, catcha later."

Angela let out such a laugh she nearly dropped her hammer. It was the second time today that I had made someone laugh and didn't even know why. "That's a good one. Catcha. Catcha. Ha-ha."

I didn't know if she was laughing at me or not but I didn't feel too comfortable. I moved back a little.

"Oh, Cece, I'm sorry. I'm not laughing at you. It's not a real word. She was saying *catch you* later. It just means I will see you later or I'll connect with you later. I can see why you thought it was a word. One thing about Americans, we use a lot of slang and a lot of contractions and lot of slurry words. You need to watch some TV. I'll get a television brought up to your room so you can listen to people in comedies. We speak fast and we use slang. It will help you. Listen, Richard is coming over for dinner tonight, let's all watch a movie together and you can practice listening for the slang. Does that sound good?"

"Do you think I will like the movie?"

"I think so. I'll tell you about it at dinner and you can make up your mind then. I'm almost finished here. Let's pack up. We've got other chores to do."

I helped her to put all of the tools in the truck and we drove back to the house. I didn't need any instructions. In fact, she didn't even wait around. She left the truck and went into the house.

"I want to talk to Cook about dinner. Efrahim is in the barn. Go and meet him. He's a special person."

I went into the barn and there was a little brown man working in the horse stalls. He was scooping up the poop with a shovel. He was obviously Mexican.

"Good afternoon," I greeted him in Spanish. He stopped his work and put down the shovel. He came toward me and extended his hand being careful to take off his dirty glove first. He didn't give me the little Mexican hug. I guess he was American now.

"Hello, *Señorita*. At your service," he said in Spanish too. "Efrahim at your service." Ah, there was the Mexican greeting. I missed hearing it. Here was Efrahim who was a ghostly presence on the farm. It was difficult to actually catch sight of him, but there was evidence that he had been somewhere because it was cleaned or picked or fixed.

"*Encantada.*" I was so happy to be able to greet someone in the Mexican way. "Have you been working here a long time?"

"I have worked for Angela, and her husband too, fifteen years at least." Like most of these shy Mexican men he looked down at the ground more than he looked at me. "It's good work. I like to work alone."

"Where are you from?" I put some of the tools from the truck up on the wall. It gave me something to do so I didn't just stare him in the face. He picked up the shovel and began to scoop again while he talked.

"Jalisco. But it was a long, long time ago. I'm from here now. Well, not legally of course, but I am American in every way but that." He sounded like he was ready for me to argue with him. I wasn't sure what it meant to be American yet, but I knew that if he was ready to deny being Mexican, then he was American.

"Nice to see you. I'll catcha later." He smiled at the shovel like he knew what that word meant.

I left him and went about the chores now. I fed the dogs and the pigs and the chickens. I hummed while I worked. Life was good. I thought the job would work out well. Nely and I would have a better life here.

"How was your first day as a working lady?" Cook beamed at me.

"It was good. I got to call a lot of people and see the sewing school."

"Yes, Angela was telling me you have a really nice space to work in. Mary Lou is a great gal. And, Jeamine works there too. She's a corker. 'Bout the only black anywhere near this place. I really like that girl." There was a sauce bubbling on the stove and Cook was putting together a salad.

"Do you want some help?"

"Sure, you know I never turn down another pair of hands." I went to the pantry and got out other vegetables for the salad.

"So how did it go? I mean how do you feel about it? I know the basic work but I want to know your feelings." She continued to chop the onion, wiping the tears on her apron.

"I feel good. I had to make some calls and talk to strangers and I think I did pretty well. Several people hung up on me—"

"They probably thought you were a telemarketer."

"That's what everyone says. Jeamine explained how to make some changes so that people wouldn't hang up on me. She was nice. So I made some adjustments and I had a lot of success getting through to people. Mrs. Patterson was nice. Jeamine was nice. Oh, by the way, thanks for the lunch, it was delicious. And the note. It made me feel special."

Cook nodded.

"I think it's going to be a good experience for me. I'm nervous. I just need to go slow, one day at a time," I continued, thinking about how I would organize myself to be a working woman.

"How was Evelyn? Did you have any trouble with the bus?"

"She was good. I got a ride from Mrs. Patterson's son."

"Hmm, that little shit."

I was surprised at Cook. She had never used words like that before.

"He's trouble, that one. Always causing his parents grief. Lying. Cheating. Stealing. He was always avoiding school and causing trouble. Ran around with the wrong kids. Drugs. He's a little shit."

"He works at his dad's store now. He seemed OK. Maybe he's changed now."

"Of course he works with his dad, no one else will take him. His mother thinks he's just a little misunderstood boy and he's just a typical teenager. He's closer to twenty and he still sucks up all their energy. He's a waste of space, that one. Did he give you a hard time?"

I thought about the lunch time when he took the money from the register. I thought about the ride to the school.

"No, he was fine. He drove me to the school to get the bus after work. I think he's going to be doing that every day so that I don't keep Evelyn waiting."

"I'm sure he didn't volunteer to help you. He was in school with my Rafael. Rafael worked hard and got himself into university to study computers. Tim did nothing and ended up having to work for his dad. You figure it out. He was always picking on the other kids. A typical coward disguised as a bully. You watch out for him, you hear." She sounded agitated.

"I'll be careful. Thanks for the warning." We prepared the salad in silence then. Chopping sounds mixed in with the animal sounds.

"I hear that Mr. Richard will be coming for dinner," I broke the silence.

"Yes, everything is ready for him. We are having

spaghetti Bolognese. Have you ever had it?"

I didn't answer her immediately. I just looked at her and she laughed. "OK, I guess that was a stupid question. I think you'll like it. It's spaghetti with meat sauce. Then the salad and a dessert that is Italian too. Tiramisu. It sounds Japanese but it's Italian. It's like the cake you all have, what's it called? Oh yes, *tres leches*. I bet you don't think I know what that means, *three milks*. Hah! I love that cake. Anyway, you'll love it. Better go get ready for dinner. It's always a special occasion when Mr. Richard comes."

She was right about that. As I passed the upstairs bathroom and Angela's bedroom, beautiful fragrances filled the air. The steam from the bathroom carried lavender and vanilla. Angela's room had a fresh smell of oranges; not the typical farm smells of musty animals and dung. I knew it was a Mr. Richard night.

Angela came out of her room dressed in a beautiful long dress with an Indian turquoise belt. Her hair was piled on top of her head with a few curly strands hanging down. She had on a big necklace with lots of amulets hanging on it. She looked like an Indian princess. I smiled at her when I looked at her and her eyes crinkled up.

"I know, I know. I'm overdoing it, do you think?"

"I think you look wonderful. And you smell like a flower garden."

She blushed. I wonder what it would be like to blush. "I don't want to seem like a silly old woman." She said this seriously as if she could ever be an old woman.

"You look beautiful."

She waved at me as she went down the stairs. I went into the bathroom to have a flowered bath too.

XVIII

I could hear them walking around downstairs as I dressed after my bath. It was hard for me to desert the bath as I was looking out at the stars but I had to go to relieve Cook so she could go home to her family. When I got downstairs they were already at the table.

"Hello, Richard."

He stood up and gave me a shy hug. "Hi, Cece. How's our working girl?" he asked.

"I'm good. How are you?"

"Good. Good." He sat down and busied himself getting food and passing the bowls to me. Cook had already left. Angela was intent on being hostess and everything had these wonderful smells.

"Do you like Italian food, Cece?" Richard was actually making conversation.

"This is my first time," I said. "I'm looking forward to it."

"First times are always exciting," he said.

"I've had a lot of those lately. First time crossing the border. First time on an American bus. First time in a Walmart. First time seeing a pig on wheels, a spaceship, the world's largest paper airplane. I've had a lot of firsts." I didn't say that it was the first time I got raped. I didn't want that to be the beginning of a list.

"I'm sure there will be many more first times to come."

He smiled kindly. Angela put her hand over his.

"What's going on with the water controversy?" Richard asked.

"Ah Richard, it's like all of the difficulties humans have with each other are being played out in the water debate. The *hoarders* vs. the *sharers*."

"I can guess which side you're on just by the names." He twirled his spaghetti on his fork using his spoon to hold the strands. I did the same.

"Well of course, it's the only side to be on. It doesn't make sense not to share. We share it anyway whether we want to or not. It's not like the *hoarders* have their own private planet with their own private water supply. It makes me crazy."

"Do you see any possibility for success?"

"I think I just have to wear them down. I just have to get them educated. I have someone from the geology department coming to talk to us and explain the water situation."

"So you think if they just understand more, they will change their minds and become *sharers*? Why not be stronger *hoarders*?"

"Ahh, Richard, I can't be that much of a pessimist."

"I know, darling, but I don't want you to get disappointed. We watch debates all of the time and educated people, really educated people who should know better, react with selfishness rather than intelligence. It happens all the time. It's like *I've got mine, screw you.* That kind of mentality. It's sad, but I'm afraid it's true. Look what happens in every corrupt society. The freedom fighters oust the dictator only to become the dictator. I don't know if it's human nature but it seems like it."

I watched him talk and I didn't understand all of the words but I got the general idea. Her face began to fall as the truth of his words sunk in. She was so disappointed.

"I know what you are saying is probably true but I have to try. I can't give up. The *sharers* have to stick together or we really will be lost as a community."

"I am very proud of you and the merry band of *sharers*."

"Let's change the subject. Cece, tell Richard about your first day at work."

The mood shifted abruptly then. I recounted the day's activities. Richard listened as he usually did. When I was finished, he only asked one question.

"So what do you think of Tim Patterson?"

"He seems nice. Kind of quiet."

"Like a snake," Richard said.

"Now Richard, be nice." Angela was clearing the dishes. She was defending Tim Patterson now; maybe she thought about her earlier criticism.

"I'll be nice, but watch out for him Cece. Spoiled rich kids in America can be a problem for everybody. They think they deserve to be any way they want to be. No one stops them. Tim is the son of the richest people in town so he thinks he is entitled to act the way he wants. Just be careful."

What else could happen to me, I wondered? The picture of him stealing from the cash register flickered into my mind. What should I say about that? Should I tell on him? Should I tell Richard?

"He's a kid, Richard, don't be so hard on him." Angela was carrying in the coffee pot.

"He was a kid in school when he got in all that trouble.

Even getting poor Jennie pregnant and having to have an abortion and what about the stealing incident? He's not a kid anymore. He's nearly twenty and he needs to take some responsibility. I'm not saying anything about him that isn't true. I'm just warning. That's all. Look at Cece, she's the same age as he is and she's running her own life."

"Well I'm just saying that we should be kind and give him the benefit of the doubt that he might have been growing up and out of all of that immature behavior. That's all." She poured us the coffee and then went to turn on the TV and the VCR. Richard drank his coffee, reverting back to his shy self. I was lost in thought.

"OK, let's watch *Babel*. I love this movie. Have you seen it? I think the director is Mexican."

I thought about all of the movies I have seen in Mexico. Alejandro, the owner of the bodega near my house, had pirated copies of all the movies. Every kid in town got to see all of the major movies without having to pay to go. We saw everything. *Babel* was a movie that made us so proud to be Mexican. The writer was the director, too, and he was also named Alejandro. Alejandro Iñarritu. He made everyone proud to be Mexican with his movies. Of course I had seen it. I didn't have the heart to tell Angela I had seen it. She was so enthusiastic to give me another first.

"He *is* Mexican," I offered.

"Oh of course...he's wonderful. Don't you think so, Richard?"

"I think he is so wonderful that I am watching this movie for the third time with you instead of preparing my lesson plan for tomorrow's class." He nuzzled into her shoulder.

"I'm looking forward to seeing it." I felt I should add

something to the discussion. "Oh I forgot. What's a *beaner*?" I asked.

He stopped nuzzling for a second and directed his eyes at me. "Not a nice word, Cece. It is a derogatory term, do you know what that means? It's negative or really hostile. It's a hostile term that some people use for Mexicans. Where did you hear that?"

"Oh, I just heard it from kids in the schoolyard." I lied. Why was I protecting Tim Patterson?

"Don't worry about it, Cece." Angela gave me a defiant look. "You'll hear many words from people designed to undercut your confidence. Don't worry. You're a strong woman. You swam the bloody Rio Grande for chrissakes, who is going to put you down? Ignore the name callers. Don't call them names. We say, *take the high road*. That means don't get pulled down to their level."

"Says the queen of the *sharers*," Richard added.

"Tout chez." Angela bowed to him.

"Oh, now she's speaking French to confuse you," Richard said. He put his arm around her and pulled her closer.

"I didn't know you could speak French." I was surprised at her many talents.

"Oh I can't speak French. That's a phrase that people use when we realize that someone has made a point that we can't refute. We have to concede the point. I think it's French for *I guess I have to concede the point, you rat bastard.*" Everyone laughed then. Now I had to learn French words as if English were not enough.

I had forgotten how great this movie was. *Babel* was all about people being outside of their cultures and caught in places that confused them. I watched the characters struggle like I was struggling. We didn't feel secure. We were in strange lands and we had to find our footing but we didn't even know how. None of them had guides like I did. I had so many guides: Angela, Richard, Cook, and now even Mrs. Patterson and Jeamine. I felt like all of these people were on my side wanting me to win and wanting me to succeed. I didn't feel alone like Holden Caulfield, the hero of *The Catcher in the Rye*. He was in his own country. His own culture. Yet he was all alone. He felt like he had to save everyone else. I felt very lucky at this moment. Nely stirred inside me. I guess she was feeling protected as well. Why did *The Catcher in the Rye* flood back into my brain so much? Could a novel live inside of you? We watched *Babel* until the very end.

"Richard and I are going for a drive, Cece." She turned on the lights and turned off the TV. "Do you want to watch TV?" She pointed the remote at me.

"No, I'm going to bed too. Good night, Angela. Good night, Richard." I hugged Angela and, for the first time, Richard too. He didn't shrink from the hug. He held onto me.

"Good night, Cece. Take good care," he said.

"Hey, I'm taking care of her. She's in good hands." Angela was pulling the drapes against the morning sun.

"I know, honey. She's in the best hands." He winked at me over the top of her head.

I waved as they left the house, letting the screen door slam behind them. It reminded me of Tim Patterson letting the store door slam behind him. This situation with Tim Patterson was getting more and more complicated. Cook and Angela and Richard all warned me about him. Was he dangerous or just one of those ignorant people you wish would go away? I climbed the stairs to the bedroom. I heard Angela's key turn in the lock of the front door. I knew their drive would last all night.

The next day went well. I took the bus with Evelyn who, I guessed, was never late. The kids were all waiting outside of their houses on the road and she swooped down and scooped them up into the bus. They all continued to cram themselves at the very back while I sat up front and enjoyed the scenery. She dropped me off at the entrance to the schoolyard to save me some steps.

Mrs. Patterson had opened the store already and Jeamine was at her desk buried in her figures.

"Can't look up, Cece, I'll lose my place. Good morning anyway." Her big glasses peered down at a page of numbers on which she was totally concentrated. She had two pencils stuck in her hair and one in her hand. She waved her other hand to me and the fat under her arm jiggled in the air. I tried not to laugh.

I didn't see Mrs. Patterson but I knew what I had to do. I went back to the back and got out her list of numbers. It wasn't quite 9 o'clock which was the hour I had decided was my starting time to call people. I got a cup of coffee and wandered around the sewing room inspecting the set-up. It looked very complete to me.

At nine I started making my calls. I remembered to ask for the girls by their first names and it worked. I talked to someone in their families and I got to make reservations for the class or identify those who weren't interested. At least not yet.

"Jeamine, can I bother you a minute?" She wasn't putting any numbers in her computer that minute.

"Sure honey, what's up?" She turned her full attention on me.

"I wonder if there's an internet cafe somewhere in town. I might want to use a computer."

"Sorry, honey. No internet cafe. But there's an extra computer over at the desk there." She pointed to a desk in the corner I hadn't even noticed before. "Sometimes we hire part time help and they all use that computer. It works. No password neither. How d'you know how to use a computer? I thought Angela told us you was from a tiny town in Mexico. Do they have internet there?"

"No one had internet in their houses like you do here, but we had an internet cafe in our village and the owner taught us all. If he taught us then we would use the cafe, right? Then I got to use one at the university."

"I didn't know you went to university. Ain't you a smart one?" She said it like it was the most natural thing in the world, not bigoted, not an insult.

"Yep. Even in my village it was possible to take the bus to the university. The church had a scholarship fund and I was able to get some money to pay for my education."

"What studyin', honey?"

"Education. I wanted to be an English teacher."

"Wow, now you gotta be an English student, right? Well you just use that one there whenever you want." I nodded a *thank you* and went back to my calls.

By the end of the day I had more reservations and almost enough students to start the classes. Tim Patterson did not steal from the till that day, thankfully.

"Put your seatbelt on." He didn't look at me as he barked his order.

"It's nice that you care about my welfare. Thanks." I

smiled at the side of his face.

"Don't really. Just the law. Don't want to get no ticket. Don't expect you'd get in any trouble. We'd just deport you back to where you came from." He did look at me then with cold eyes. He was waiting for me to deny this.

"How long has your family lived here?" I looked out the window and let my question hang in the air.

"Forever—and a lot longer than yours. Here's the bus."

I got out and felt a chill run up my spine. Was he dangerous? Evelyn was inside her bus and I hurried there, suddenly thankful for a refuge. I felt unsettled. The old feeling of dread passed over me.

The kids clamored aboard and stashed themselves in the back of the bus and I, as usual, had the front all to myself. I pushed the thought of Tim Patterson to the back of my mind.

When I got home, I changed my clothes and started the chores. There was a lovely rhythm about farm life. The animals had such a routine that you had to have a routine too. They needed to be fed and often needed vitamins or medicines. The dogs were always fun, running around or playing. There was Cook and there was Efrahim who continued his ghostly sightings.

When I went to the corral no horses were there. I checked their hay bin and put in some hay anyway. I found Angela in the barn. The horses were tied up in their stalls.

"Hi, Cece." Angela had a plastic syringe which she was rubbing against the nose of one of the horses. "Bet you think this is a strange way to give medicine."

"I wasn't sure what you were doing." I came closer.

"You rub it around their mouths to get them used to the feel of the syringe before you shoot it in. It just helps them to relax a bit so they don't get so uptight. A calm horse is always better. Then you just push it here, in the back of their teeth, and push the plunger and voila! Your horse is wormed. You don't want any of the little buggers running around inside their stomachs, do you?"

"I think I better watch you do this a few times before I try. We didn't have any horses on our land in Mexico. We had dogs, but we gave them pills," I answered.

Angela gave the horse a friendly pat and untied her. "Here, you can take her out to the corral."

I took the horse by the reins and walked her out to the corral and let her go. She trotted across to the hay bin and chomped on some hay. I walked back into the barn and got out the horse dishes and started getting the food ready for later. Angela continued to work on each horse and I watched her. After she finished each horse, I took it out to the corral and let it go. We made a good team.

"Want to go to town for pizza tonight? I let Cook go because one of her kids has a birthday today and she was making a big feast."

"That would be great. I had pizza in Dallas delivered from Pizza Hut."

"You'll probably like this even better. It's owned by an Italian family and they make their own pizza right in the restaurant. I'll take a quick shower after I finish this and we'll go in about an hour and a half. We have to feed the horses before we go."

"I'll do that. I started it anyway. I'll read my book until you're ready."

"Oh *The Catcher in the Rye,* huh? The book for every teen rebelling from the world. Do you like it? You seem to be taking your time reading it."

"Well it's interesting and it lets you into Holden's head, that's for sure. He really is sweet. He just wants to protect his sister. I am reading it slowly to appreciate it."

"Yes, he is sweet. How'd you do at work today? Are you getting along with Mary Lou?" She was rubbing the syringe up against the horse's nose.

"I didn't see much of her today. I was working on the phone trying to sign up people for the class. I have enough to start the classes for Mondays and Tuesdays. There are many more who are interested, but I think I should get a few classes to try first and see how it goes. The more students, the more store credit."

"Yes, it's great. Mr. Patterson sells me everything I need for the farm including the food for the animals and the parts for the farm equipment. Everything else we buy is from the department store. Don't worry, we can spend it. In fact, I think I should give you some cash each week. You need some spending money."

"I'd feel bad about that. I'm living here for free and eating for free too."

"It doesn't cost me anything to have you here. Cook just puts a little more food out and the room is empty anyway. No cost at all. Let's think about it, we can decide later on an amount."

I went into the house and washed up a little. I curled up with Holden Caulfield but my mind drifted to Tim Patterson. He challenged me, letting me know he knew I was illegal. I supposed this was the start of the bullying. Everyone else had been so friendly and helpful, so the contrast with him was stark. Nothing about him was good.

We rode into town and Angela showed me a bit more. There was a park on the other side with a little swimming pool in the center for the kids in the summer. I had already seen the city hall and it was nothing special, not like the magnificent colonial buildings of Mexico, that's for sure. The town had several schools, not just the one where I went in the morning. There were also some small dress shops and jewelry stores. Two beauty salons were at opposite ends of the street and a barber shop was in the middle. Restaurants were on Main Street and along the side streets too. Just around the corner from Main Street there was a store selling cosmetics. Finally, there were three different grocery stores. In all, this town had everything you needed.

The pizza parlor was beautiful. The walls were decorated with murals, not as wonderful as Mexican murals but nice anyway. They were scenes of Italy, I guessed. I know one was Venice because there were gondolas in the water. We sat at a booth in the center.

"Hi, Angela. The usual?" The waitress had her order pad in her hand.

"Wait a minute, Sheila. I think we'll need a menu so my friend here, that's Cece, can have some choices." Sheila put out her hand.

"Pleased to meet you." I shook her hand. It was soft.

"You too, honey. I'll be right back."

"So what do you think of your first pizza parlor?" Angela played with the placemat.

"It seems nice. I guess these are pictures of Italy, right?"

"Seems like it."

"Here you go, girls. I'll give you a minute." Sheila left two menus and two big glasses of water with ice. It was a treat to just have the water. I looked around and everyone had water glasses and were drinking other things like Coke and lemonade and Sprite. I wondered if they all drank the water or if it was wasted. I was still being shocked at so much water.

Angela was reading the menu. I read it too. There were so many choices of pizza. So many of the words I didn't know. I made a mental note to look up food words in the dictionary.

"What looks good?" She looked at me over the top of her reading glasses.

"I don't know a lot of these words, so I can't really decide."

"OK, no time like the present. Which words?"

"Anchovy." I hoped I had pronounced it well.

"That's a little tiny salty fish. It adds a fishy, salty flavor. Here I'll go through them with you. You know what tomatoes, cheese, ham, bacon, shrimp, peppers, onions. Do you know what *pineapple* is?"

"That's the fat yellow fruit with the green leaves coming out of the top like an agave cactus?"

"That's a pretty good description. How about mushrooms?"

I shook my head *no*.

"Those are the spongy white vegetable that grow in the shade."

"OK, *championes*," I said.

"Yeah, I guess. I don't know the Spanish words so you'll have to describe the food to me when I translate it for you. What else?"

"Oregano, basil, olives, parmesan." She just read me the list. "These are spices mostly. You'll just have to taste them to see if you like the taste. I don't know how to describe spices. Olives are the little round things that are green and have the red kind of little tongues in them, pimentos we call them or they are black and have pits. Parmesan is a kind of cheese. So what do you think?"

"You decide. I like everything."

"OK. I like pepperoni pizza. It's a sausage that's a little spicy and then there are some vegetables on it. Does that sound good?"

"Yes, thank you. It's only my second pizza."

"Oh no, I hope we're not finished with the *firsts*. I'll have a Dos Equis and we'll have a medium pepperoni pizza. What do you want to drink?" Sheila had come back and was writing down what Angela was ordering.

"Coke, please." I was thanking American movies for teaching me how to act here.

"So how was Tim Patterson today? Any problems?"

"No. He was not very friendly."

"That is an understatement. You know, that's not the half of it. He is downright nasty. He can be hostile and aggressive too. He was always beating up kids when he was in school. They finally kicked him out and he had to finish his high school by taking tests. He doesn't have any friends either. Just keeps to himself."

"How does he keep his job?"

"He's the boss's son, first off. He seems to be able to keep it together because he works in the back in the warehouse and doesn't interact with people much. He lives with his parents. No one else would hire him so he has to work there or else he'd just get in trouble."

"How did he get that way?"

"I'm not sure but I would guess his parents just spoiled him rotten. Mary Lou had a really hard time getting pregnant. She had a couple of miscarriages. She lost a baby late in her pregnancy. Very tough. Then along came Tim and she and Bill were thrilled. She must have been nearly forty when he came along. They doted on him and gave him everything. He was the rich kid in town so he got all of the new stuff first and let everyone know it. He bragged that he could do anything and his parents wouldn't stop him. He got into drugs and had to go to rehab for awhile too. He got a girl pregnant and she was only fifteen—that is a crime here in the States in case you didn't know that. He could have gone to prison, but they bought her off and he never got arrested or anything. Even when he beat up other kids, there were never any consequences. He just paid somebody and got away with everything."

"He sure doesn't like Mexicans, he let me know that."

"Don't take it personally. He doesn't like anyone. He's just a bully."

"Is he dangerous?"

"Hard to say. He might be. Nobody really knows how many times his parents have had to bail him out. We all know some, but we think there were many more. He was bounced out of school at sixteen and he wasn't working all day. It's pretty reasonable to assume he was getting in trouble. His first reaction to anything seems to be anger. He has a quick temper and quick fists. I guess you would have to say he's dangerous. Luckily, he's not real big so the damage he does isn't as bad as it could be. He has kicked some people, though. Yes I guess that means he's dangerous. Does he scare you?"

"Kind of."

"Don't worry, I'm sure he won't hurt you. You're only together for about five minutes getting to school. I'm sure you'll be fine."

"But why did you defend him with Mr. Richard?" The pizza arrived then and Angela pulled the pieces apart and let them cool.

"I just wanted Richard to keep a balance. He doesn't talk much so when he talks everyone listens. I wanted to make sure he understood how critical he was being and how important his words are."

The pizza was a wonder, not really like the pizza that was delivered in Dallas. It was like a giant, stiff tortilla, but much chewier. It was covered by a spicy tomato sauce much thicker than salsas and loaded with other spices I had never tasted. Melted cheese covered the sauce. On top of the cheese were pieces of spicy pepperoni and onions and peppers. I imagined this was how they made pizza in Italy.

"I had a terrible experience when I got to America." I started this conversation so softly, so much lighter in tone than its message. "I was raped by one of the boys in Dallas."

"Oh my God, Cece, why didn't you say something?" She got up and came around to my side of the booth and hugged me. I felt protected. "Do you want to talk about it?"

"There was a strange thing that happened. I fell over a box in Walmart and the store manager let me take home anything I wanted that I could get into two carts. I thought I had won a great prize but the boys told me I was stupid because I could have done something legal to the store."

"Yes, you could have sued them. But go on." Angela was looking at me directly.

"I got everything I could think of like a wide screen TV and tons of food, tequila, beer, everything. Cruz, that's his name, got drunk. His cousin, from my village, is shy and sweet. Cruz is not. He had been flirting with me for days. He sometimes rubbed up against me like an accident, but he was really touching my breasts.

"I couldn't get involved with any of those boys then. Or now, or maybe never. That night the boys were celebrating all of the things I brought into the house. They were drinking a lot. Everyone got drunk. It was the day before I was supposed to leave. I went to bed, as usual, and I actually locked the door. That was really silly because the room where I was sleeping was Cruz's room and, of course, he had a key. He came in while I was asleep and he pushed me down into the bed. He held my head into the pillow and got on top of me." I started to cry and Angela held me tighter.

"You don't have to talk about this, baby." She stroked my hair. "It's OK now."

"No. I think it's better. I have to get this out of my mind. I don't even know why I'm telling you this but there must be a reason." I took a sip of the delicious water and continued. "He rammed himself into me. I could smell his horrible breath and feel his stinking sweat. He rammed and rammed. It hurt so much and I was so worried about Nely. The *pendejo*! The *asshole*! It made me feel so helpless and vulnerable. Like I couldn't even protect myself or my little baby.

"I finally whispered *pregnant* over and over. It was hard for me to talk with my head smashed into the pillow. Finally he heard me and he knew what I was saying. He jumped off of me then and ran out of the room. I got up and staggered to the bathroom and tried to wash him out of me.

"How could he just take what he wanted? How could he just use me like that? I was already ready to leave and I just took my things and left. I would have slapped him over and over if I was near him. I didn't do that because I didn't know what he would do. What would he do to me? I just left."

I cried again then and it went on forever. The people in the restaurant looked at me with curiosity and then looked away. Some looked like they were sorry for me. I didn't have any self-consciousness. I had to get it out. I just cried and cried and cried until it was over. The whole time Angela rocked me in her arms. She stroked my hair. She held me tightly as if protecting me from all of the pain the world was throwing at me. At that moment I didn't feel so alone. I felt the strength and warmth of my Mami. I missed her so much.

The waitress brought over a fresh glass of water. Isn't it strange, I thought, that people give you a glass of water when you're upset? I drank the water and it made me calm down a bit. I was OK finally. Angela gave me a hug and then moved back to her side of the booth. I got up and went to the bathroom and washed my face. The people I passed looked away. How do you give someone privacy in a public place?

"How are you feeling, physically I mean? Do you want to go see the doctor? It's about an hour away. We could make an appointment and drive over there." Angela was looking at me with concern, her piece of pizza in her hand.

"No one in my village ever went to a doctor. Is there a midwife here?"

"Yes, there is an Irish midwife. She comes to the house to deliver the babies. Is that what you want? What about an examination from a doctor to make sure everything is all right with Nely now?"

"No, I'm sure I'm all right. No reason to worry."

I didn't want to spend my money. I would only be making a little money each week that I could keep for myself and the money I had left in the shoe. I didn't know what it would cost to have a baby. Then we had to move to LA. I had to be careful with money.

The drive home was quiet.

"Do you want to watch some TV with me?" Angela was closing the drapes in the living room.

"No, I think I'll take a bath and read my book. Is that OK? Do you need the bathtub?"

"No, you go ahead. Good night. Sleep tight."

"Good night, Angela. Thanks for everything. You saved my life."

"Well then, it will be your job to save someone else's in the future." She smiled at me and sat down on the couch and turned on the TV.

After the bath, I curled up in bed with my book. I felt drained after the big scene in the restaurant. It surprised me how quickly it had come on. I didn't know all of those feelings were still trapped inside of me.

In the back of my mind I had fears about Tim Patterson too. He reminded me of Cruz. The same feeling. Guillermo had been such a sweet boy, so gentle. Now I was meeting boys who were the opposite. Grabbers. People who just took what they wanted. Even if it was precious to you. I knew Tim was one of those. How far would he go? I went to sleep with those thoughts in my mind and had a troubled night.

XIX

"How is the list going?" Mrs. Patterson was standing over me in the back of the store.

"I'm almost finished and we are nearly full. I think some of the girls will still have to be on a later list. What do you call that?"

"A waiting list. It's because of the uniforms. The Catholic schools require kids to wear uniforms and they are really expensive. If the families have a lot of kids, which they usually do, then the cost is really high. So the girls want to learn to sew to help the family. Why don't we have the first class and make sure it is going well before we add a lot of classes?" She put her purse up high on the shelf over her desk.

"Why don't we have any boys in the sewing classes? I know there are girls in the shop classes."

"Good point. I think the girls are looking to be equal. The boys are already privileged, although they don't even know it or care about it. So the boys don't ask for anything which might be considered extra. They just assume they can do anything they want. I bet if a boy wanted to be in the sewing class he would just call us and assume he could come in. No questions asked. Men set the rules in this world and no one even questions it."

I thought that was true in Mexico too. Even when the men are gone for many years trying to save money in the

USA, they are still setting the rules for their families back home. The women run the house for years and when the men come back, they just assume they are in charge again. It's a time when many women get abused. You see black eyes around Mexico all the time. The men don't like to be challenged. I wonder if women get beat up in America too? I was thinking all the time about America now. There was so much that was the same, so much that was different. When I was thinking about America I was comparing it to Mexico in everything. I had so much to learn.

Tim Patterson picked me up at the end of the day and stared out the window. He looked over at my lap. I buckled the seat belt across my swelling stomach.

"Did you have a good day?" I asked him. I looked right at him, but he didn't turn his face to me.

"I ain't dead yet, that's a good day." He checked the rearview mirror before driving out in traffic, keeping his eyes looking directly ahead.

"We are doing really well getting students for the sewing classes. I think we'll be a success."

"If you think for one minute I give a rat's ass about what you're sayin', you're wrong. Shut the fuck up, will you? Girly sewing classes don't interest me at all."

I didn't say anything for a few minutes. I tried to explain myself. "I just thought you'd be interested in your family business, is all."

"You mean the business of my mother and my father. It ain't mine."

"I just assumed you were part of it, that's all. You don't have to get angry about it."

"Ain't anger, dipshit. It's righteousness. I got a right to feel this way. I'm the son, not no hired hand. Get the fuck out of the truck." Mercifully, we had arrived at the school and I climbed out of the door.

"Have a nice day." I managed to get the words out before he sped away. I was happy to see the smiling face of Evelyn and to hear the end of the day chatter of the school kids. I still felt the chill of Tim Patterson on my back.

Efrahim was in the garden when I got back and I changed clothes and went out to help him. Judging by his earlier non-conversation with me I guessed he didn't want to talk so I just stood next to him getting the watering can filled for him while he watered the plants the hose wouldn't reach. He worked methodically, taking extra care with each plant. Did he count to ten for each plant to make sure it had enough water like my mother did? I missed her. After we finished he nodded at me and moved on to his next job. How does a person live a life in virtual silence? I wondered if he went home and turned into a magpie. That's what Americans call people who talk a lot, also chatterboxes, very colorful language.

"Come on, Cece, let's play Scrabble." She was taking a long skinny box down from the shelf. "It's fun. You'll like it." She put a board on the table and gave me a little piece of wood with a shelf on it. "Now we need to turn all of these over so that the letters are facing down on the table." She started turning over the little blocks with letters on them. I did the same.

"Now you choose ten tiles, these little blocks are called *tiles*, and put them on your shelf so only you can see them and I can see mine." She chose her tiles and put them on the shelf. I did the same. I looked at the board and it was covered with boxes like a checkerboard only smaller. Most of the boxes were white but some were blue and some were pink. The colored ones had words in them.

"Good, now you are going to arrange words on these little boxes here on the board. You need to spell words with your letters in the boxes. You want to try to get a letter to land on one of the special blocks like *double letter* or *double word* or even better, *triple word*. We keep score and the winner gets an extra piece of Cook's apple pie, OK?"

"We're playing in Spanish, right?"

She looked at me and laughed. I laughed too. It was the first joke I could remember making since I came from Mexico.

"It'll be good practice for you. You go first. Just choose your letters and make some words. You have to start in the middle where the star is and put your letters one by one in the boxes to spell out your word." I put my letters in the boxes and spelled *cat.*

"That's good, Cece, but it doesn't get rid of your letters and it doesn't get you a lot of points. Can't you make a longer word with your letters?"

I added -*cher* to my word. "Catcher," I said. "I learned that word from my book."

"Good job. Great. That's seven letters. I'll write down your score. You can choose seven letters to replace those. My turn. You see I have to add my word where there are already letters. I can't just put my word anywhere. I want to get some good points so I'm going to use the extra point spaces. Listen to how I figure out my score, this one is complicated. I'll add *U-R-R-I-E-D* to your *H* and that gives me 13 points because I have the *D* on a double letter giving me 4 points and with your *H* worth 4 points, that gives me 13 points and I used the double word score which gives me 26 points. I'll take six tiles to replace the ones I used. You get it now, right? It makes a big difference if your letter or your word falls on a special score, the extra bonus boxes, like double letter or double word. Your turn."

We played for three hours. I couldn't believe how the time went so fast. Angela was a very good player. She used the extra bonus boxes almost all the time and got a lot of points. She was very happy to have those points so I saw a competitive side of her I didn't know was there. I also learned that my spelling was terrible. There were many words that I thought I knew how to spell and I was absolutely wrong. I had a lot to learn. Angela was a generous and patient teacher. It was getting late then and since she had so clearly won the game we finished and put everything away. She didn't say anything to make me feel like a loser though; I just felt we had had fun together.

"Good night, Cece, that was fun." She pulled the drapes and turned out the lamps.

"Only because you were the winner. I thought it was a torture chamber." I gave her a pout.

For a second she thought I was serious and a look of concern passed across her face. "You're kidding. You always seem so serious, Cece, I didn't even know you were a teaser."

"I'm only serious when I'm hiding from the immigration police." I said it with such a straight face that she looked at me again.

"You are a very interesting woman, Cece. I think I will have to keep an eye on you." She hugged me then and it felt so good to be safe in her arms. "Wow, that baby is growing. We're going to have to find you some bigger clothes. Good night, sweetie."

I climbed the stairs and found I was in a light-hearted mood. My English was getting so good that I was starting to make jokes in a second language. I was proud of myself.

*

The first day of our practice sewing class was full of little challenges. Three girls joined the class: Monica, Patrice, and Silvia. Monica was beautiful in the way of so many Mexican girls: straight white teeth against mocha-colored skin and long lustrous hair. She walked with confidence almost like she was modeling clothes. When she was in the room everyone stared at her.

Patrice was shy and bookish with big thick glasses and her hair tied back in a ponytail. She spent most of her time looking down and seldom made eye contact. She spoke in soft whispers and I had to practically sit in her lap to hear her.

Silvia was a bubble of personality, talking at a mile a minute and always smiling. She was the one everyone thought was lazy so I knew I had to keep an eye on her. She was short and plump with a head of curly hair that looked like tiny snakes trying to find their way.

I spent the class getting the girls used to the machines. Teaching them how to put in a needle and how to lead the thread through the machine properly took a lot of time. I also showed them how to fill the bobbin with the matching thread color. After each small lecture, they practiced what I showed them and I walked around correcting. I tried to imitate my favorite teachers who always corrected but never criticized. I wanted them to be proud, not ashamed.

Monica and Silvia were easy to correct because they

were both confident girls. I had to be delicate with Patrice because I could tell that the correction made her feel bad and she would sit back in her chair, avoiding my eyes. I gave her a lot of praise when she did something correctly so that she would build confidence in her abilities.

The surprise was that I was actually good at this. You would have thought that I had been doing it forever. I guess I would have been a good teacher if I had finished my degree. I thought that I would like to teach but I had no idea I would love it. I was surprised again when the little light in their eyes flashed and I knew they had understood. I know it was only sewing but anything learned is worth it, I thought.

The time sailed by and the girls were excited when they left. I felt like I had accomplished a lot. After they were gone, I set about putting the supplies away in the drawers under their machines and taking the thread off the bobbins to get ready for the next class.

"So you like working with little girlies?" Tim was asking in the truck on the way to the schoolyard. Why was everything he said so negative? A person had to always be on guard around him, waiting for the next attack. He had so many secrets he must live in constant fear that someone will find out about him. But a person who has fear is like a dog with fear—they attack. No matter how innocent his question I knew he was on the attack.

"Teaching anything to anyone is rewarding in itself." I wasn't taking the bait.

"Such a fuckin' goody two shoes." He spat out the words.

I would write those in my notebook to ask Cook to explain them to me. She was getting patient at last and was enjoying explaining her culture to me, at least I thought she was. I don't think she had ever thought about it before. My questions made her think, strange that it was someone from outside her country who made her think about it. I guess I never thought about the Mexican culture until I had to explain it in comparison to the American culture I was experiencing. It's like you have to be somewhere else looking back at your own culture to understand it. At the moment, I wasn't looking at anything but the scowling face of Tim Patterson.

The mornings were a routine now as the weeks went by. I added feeding the dogs to my schedule of activities. Cook had breakfast ready for me and a packed lunch every day that I worked. Sometimes she put an encouraging note inside the bag for me. So sweet. Angela was up for breakfast too, of course, and sometimes she'd ask me to do something after work or to bring something home with me from the store. I liked these little jobs because it made me feel like I was contributing and part of the family.

At lunch times, I used the opportunity to go on the computer and get lost in the internet world. It transported me far beyond this little town in New Mexico like it had in my little town at home. I could travel all around the world on the internet and learn all there was to learn. I used this time to look up words I had heard that morning. I also read a side-by-side text in Spanish and English and looked up the words. I was really sorry I couldn't translate word for word but I knew that living here I would soon start to think in the structure of the English and no longer be held back by the structure of the Spanish language living in my head.

One day when Mrs. Patterson was back from lunch,

she crossed over and stood behind me. "Ah, reading in English. Good girl. What is this, like a bilingual book online?"

"Yes. It's called *side by side* or *parallel* stories. You can see, here is the story in English and right beside it is the story in Spanish. It's a great way to practice."

"Such a smart girl you are, Cece."

"Thanks so much for letting me use the internet. It is such a big help." I logged off and went back to work.

I guess that Tim thought I went out to lunch with his mother and Jeamine, the next time he came in the store. He never went in the diner, or so they told me, as Dick banned him years ago for causing so much trouble. So I guess he never checked that I wasn't with the other two there. He surely didn't know that I had seen him steal. He probably didn't know that I stayed in the store, in the back during the lunch hours. He didn't know I was there in the dark working on the computer. I heard the little bell. I knew it was him.

I waited about five minutes: long enough for him to take the money and leave. But the bell was silent. He was still there. What was he doing? I waited a few more minutes and finally crept to the corridor where I could see into the store. He was there. He wasn't stealing from the cash register. Instead he was doing something very different. Something that had to be done in the dark when no one was around. He was putting on the women's clothes. He was buttoning one of the frilly blouses over a long skirt when I got to the corridor. He had already put on a hat and gloves, the old-fashioned kind that people wore with formal clothes. He wore a big hat with a feather. After buttoning the blouse, he moved the hat around admiring himself in the mirror until he had placed it at an angle.

He moved to the jewelry counter then and passed several minutes trying on earrings and necklaces. The store still carried the old clip-on earrings and he had many choices. He experimented with about ten pairs of earrings before settling for some pearls.

Next it was to the cosmetics area where he used all of the testers not on his hand, like you're supposed to do, but on his face and mouth and eyes and cheeks. He painted his lips ruby red and air kissed himself in the mirror. He smeared shiny blue eye shadow on his lids and deep red rouge on his cheeks. When he was finished, he picked up a purse and then carried on his own fashion show. He pranced down the length of the store, arriving at the mirror for an appreciative look and a spin like the models do on the runway. He even pouted like they do. He was a very handsome boy and so he made a very pretty woman.

I watched the whole show from my position in the shadows. Here was the bully; the macho pig who fought and stole and pushed everyone around was hiding his secret. Something that probably made him act like he did. Something that was the deepest.

Suddenly he glanced up at the clock and hurried around the store returning all of the merchandise to its place. He hung up the hat and the purse and put the gloves back on the shelf. The blouse got hung on a hanger and re-buttoned. Finally the skirt got clipped to a skirt hanger and put back on the rack.

He tore through the store to the men's room and I heard the water go on. I was guessing that he was washing the makeup off his face. He came out, quickly throwing a paper towel into the waste basket as he reached the front of the store. At last I heard the bell as he left, locking the door behind him. The store closed around him, burying his secret. I fell back against the wall. Dumbfounded. A second terrible secret I had to keep about Tim Patterson.

I was also sad. It was obvious by his need for security and privacy that to him, this was not something to be celebrated. This was something that had to be kept away from everyone else. He was isolated in a small town in the middle of nowhere. I wished that I could reach out to him. In our culture *muxes* are revered. They are treated as a third gender—a gender which plays an important role in our culture. Even in our small village there was a *muxe*. She was a large man with big hands. Very tall. Very strong. We would see her walking around the village always dressed in a very feminine style with jewelry and skirts. She always wore makeup. There were rumors that she had several boyfriends in the village who were married and had families. No one bothered her because, like many *muxes,* she took care of her elderly parents. In fact, everyone treated her with respect and liked her. I thought that Tim should talk with someone like her, or me. At least I would not be condemning nor judging him; we could talk. I could explain the importance of our third gender in Mexican society, maybe he could be proud of what he is. I would never know.

At the end of the day this same person came to drive me to the school. I got in the truck without saying a word. What should I say: "I saw you dressing in women's clothing"? No, I had nothing to say. I acted as if there was nothing strange. Nothing wrong.

"Did you have a nice lunch at Dick's Diner today?" He

asked it like a normal person would have asked. He asked it as if we were friends having a little chat. I wondered what bait he used when he went fishing for real fish instead of facts.

"No, I wasn't there." Such a small statement which carried so much potential for panic.

"Oh." He said it so nonchalantly. Like he had so little interest in where I actually was. "Did you go to another restaurant?" His voice rose a bit in pitch. It was hurried and nervous.

"No. I don't have the money for restaurants." I did not give him any more clues. I did not relieve his suffering. Let him sweat a bit longer. I wanted him to worry. Was I there? Did I see him?

"So where did you eat?"

"Why do you want to know so much all of a sudden? You never talk to me. You just bark." I got out of the truck. I started to move away.

"Sorry. I'll be nicer. I'm shy. So where?" Now I could feel his panic. I walked farther away.

"At the park," I said over my shoulder as I got to the edge of the space where he could hear me. I turned full around and saw him fall back in his seat and look toward the heavens. God was not going to help him. I had two of his secrets now and I hoped I would never have to use them against him. For now I would file them away for use if I needed them. I got no justice with Cruz. I might need to find justice for those who Tim could hurt, including me.

"Hi, Cook. I wrote something in my notebook today. Are you ready?" I was sitting at the table watching her make another pie.

"Go on then. I swear you are one girl full of questions."

She smiled at me over the mess she was making with the flour and the rolling pin.

"I looked these words up today in the dictionary so I know what they mean, but I want to know how people treat them."

"You are talking to me in riddles, Cece, spit it out," Cook responded impatiently.

"What about the transvestites and the transgender people? How do people treat them here?" I asked directly

"Oh my God. What are you sayin'?" She stopped rolling in mid-stroke. "My God in heaven, Cece, you do go on. Why would you want to know about such a bunch of confused people?"

"I was talking to Jeamine about it today," I lied, "and I just wondered. Mexico is very tolerant of people's beliefs." I picked at the edge of the raw dough and rolled it into little balls and ate it.

"Now you listen to me, girl." She pointed the rolling pin at me. "Don't go talking about things like that. Me and everyone else thinks this is a sickness. These people are sick. I don't care what the courts say and no one else cares either. We are all God-fearing people and we know that God never meant for strange combinations of men and women. Men are men and women are women and that's the way it is and the way it should be. Simple as that. I don't want to hear nothin' else about it." She began to violently roll the poor unsuspecting dough under the rolling pin.

"I was just wondering, is all." I sneaked another piece of dough.

"Listen, Cece, case is closed here. Go do your chores." She faced down at the table and wouldn't look up as I left the kitchen to go out to the barn. No wonder Tim Patterson hid his real self, who would want to be around him?

My relationships continued to grow with everyone I met except for Tim, of course. After what I had witnessed it was strange that I wasn't scared or worried. Why did I feel so happy? Ah yes. I knew why. In the back of his mind Tim Patterson thought he had something hanging over my head. He knew that I was illegal. He knew that I was pregnant. In his twisted mind he must have felt the power he had over me. He knew I was vulnerable. Now that power shifted. I saw the panic in his eyes when he thought, for just a second, that I might have seen him. Even when I lied and told him that I had gone to the park he was still nervous. He knew and I knew that he had lost the power. Sometimes this made bullies more dangerous. I would have to watch my back. I had to have a plan to protect myself.

I felt good and I was eating great, thanks to Cook, so things were fine. The students were eager to learn and they got really good at sewing in a relatively short time. I insisted that they iron the pattern and they iron their pieces as they made each one. They hated this part but it makes for better sewing. The seams are better. They smiled widely when they modeled their aprons and their tops.

I learned more and more about running the farm and I think that I was a great help to Angela and Cook and maybe even Efrahim. I tried to make sure that Angela didn't have to give me any direction, that I did the jobs on my own. I knew this would take some of the burden of planning off of her and she would be more free. The water debate was taking up more and more of her time and she was grateful for my help. Anyway, she didn't say much but she seemed pleased.

XX

"Just let the clutch out slowly with your left foot and push down on the gas with your right foot." Efrahim was coaching me with what was probably the longest speech he had ever given at the farm. "That's it. *Bueno.*" The engine began to race but the car wasn't moving. "Let the clutch out with your left foot, Cece." I lifted my foot higher so the clutch would come out. I didn't really know what that meant but Efrahim had told me that the clutch and the gas pedal needed to work together or the car wouldn't shift through the gears. I guess a car has gears like a bicycle. So I lifted my left foot. The car immediately bucked like a horse and died.

"I was letting the clutch out," I said sheepishly.

"Yes, *joven*, you did good," he lied. The car had bucked and died. How could that be good?

"You need to think of it like a balance that you work with your feet. One side goes up while the other side goes down. When they meet in the perfect place everything is in balance and then you can take your foot off of the left side, the clutch side. It means the gear is in place. So you push down on the gas with your right foot." He was pushing his right hand down. "At the same time you let up on the clutch with your left foot." He was raising his left hand up. "When the two are together, you can feel it. There is a little sense of it giving way and then you know you can take your foot off of the clutch and just drive with the gas pedal." He put his two hands side by side now. They were together. "You just need to practice. Let's do it again."

We did it again and again and again. I sat in the driver's seat and either revved up the engine or the car bucked like the horse Angela was breaking and then the car died. Efrahim, the god of patience, told me to start the car again. Do it again and again and again. I knew how my students felt when I told them to rip out a seam they had sewn crookedly and asked them to do it over. They had to do it over until they got it right and I did too.

Efrahim worked with me all morning long. I started the car and the engine raced or it bucked and died. The car never moved forward. At long last, after about fifty attempts, the car suddenly felt like it was making a small connection, like the two hands of Efrahim were lined up side-by-side—it moved forward. I was driving. He let out a cheer like I had scored the winning goal in the world cup. He even pumped his hand in the air before folding back into his shyness.

There was a real difference in the feel of the clutch and the gas when they worked together. I could feel the car make the connection and it was at this point that everything was right as it should be and then the car made progress. I thought that was probably true about everything in life. If things are working together as they should, everything would make progress. If the people in Angela's water problem worked together there would be progress. If the kids in my classes worked together we would all make progress. And even if Tim and all of the people he hurt worked together there would be progress.

For the moment, I was enjoying the progress of the car as it moved down the road. I kept my foot on the gas so that it made progress. Every once in a while, Efrahim would reach over and move the steering wheel if he thought I was heading in the wrong direction. I guess that's all we needed, a little help from someone who cares.

By the end of the day I was a driver. All day long Efrahim worked with me and we practiced the start and the stop and the turn. We hadn't done any of the hard stuff yet like parking but I felt I could say that I was a driver. Unlike my mother and my aunts and my grandmother and all of the women in my family—I was a driver. I had the most precious gift of all: I was independent. I remembered how easily Raquel had taken over the driving from Jose Cruz when we were going to see the roadside attractions. She was independent too. Finally, after our day of triumph, we drove into the driveway.

"I have to go do some work in the barn, Miss Cece." Efrahim bowed and started to try to disappear into the barn. I ran around the car and before he could stop me I grabbed him in a big hug and kissed his cheek.

"Thank you, thank you, Efrahim. You have given me a wonderful gift." My smile practically fell off of my face. I know if he could have blushed, he would have. He did not say anything but kept his progress toward the barn.

"Congratulations, Cece. Thank you for leaving the house and the barn in one piece." Cook was making bread.

"What do you mean?"

"Well, you didn't hit anything, did you? The house is still standing. The barn is still standing. We're still standing. Even Efrahim looks uninjured, although it's hard to tell with him. He is a bit of a ghost. I guess I should alert the world that there is another woman driver to watch out for."

"Ahh. Cook, I feel like someone let me out of a cage." I gave her a big hug and she leaned into me. "I think I will write a letter to my Mami and tell her." I went up the stairs to my room.

My mother's letters were in the purple ribbon Mrs. Patterson had given me the first day for my hair. I arranged them by date and they looked beautiful. I took out the last one so I could answer it. I wished I could write to her in English now because I was getting so good but I had to respect her Spanish and mine.

Dear Cece,

I am so happy that you are doing well. Of course, I miss you terribly. The boys and their wives and the grandchildren are all well and I love being with them. But you, my precious, are my own little angel and what we have together is special.

It sounds like you are having a wonderful time and are learning every day. Even when you get your green card you will be able to teach sewing. After the baby comes maybe you can teach in your home and then stay with the baby all the time. It's so special to be connected to your baby as each day there will be something new in her life and it is such a gift if you will be there to share it. You will know the magic of this soon.

Nothing changes here. The boys still work so many jobs to make things work for us. Lidia, your sister-in-law, has a great opportunity to attend university with a scholarship like the one you had. She will study accounting. I am so happy for her but how will she use accounting here? We will have to move to some place bigger so that she can get a job, I am sure. I take care of Jesus, the little one, while she studies and your brother works. I love being with him because, at seven years old, he is so bossy and fun. You would love him.

There is some talk that the government is going to put the road to the beach just to the side of our village. This will bring so many people through the town that maybe we can have some small businesses selling mangoes or cocos or nuts and it might help us to make some money. I don't trust it because anything that is done by the government means someone is getting his pockets lined with our money. You know how it is.

Take very good care of yourself, Cece. It is not long now until you have your little Nely in your arms. I am praying for you.

Bless you my child and all my love, Mami

Each time I got a letter from home I had two reactions: relief and sadness. Relief that I was no longer there, and that I had actually begun to have a better life for me and for Nely. Sadness that I was not there helping my mother. I answered her immediately.

Dear Mami,

Thank you so much for your letter. I am so excited to be hearing from you. Angela has promised that when the baby comes we will figure out some way of calling you on Skype so you can see the baby. You will have to go down to the Internet Cafe and Rico will show you how to get on the computer. We will call and you will watch us on the screen just like you were watching a video. It really is magic.

I am doing very well at the store. My classes have been going for months now and the girls have made many outfits. They get so excited when they model the outfits they have made. Do you remember how excited I was when I made my first top even though I sewed the sleeves on backwards?

We recently had a fashion show for the families at the store and all of the students modeled the outfits they had made. You should have seen how proud their parents were. Almost everyone in town came to the fashion show and many more students signed up for classes in the future. I even got a raise. I make $15 US dollar an hour, Mami, can you believe it? After the baby comes I think I will be able to send you some money because I do not have any big expenses here. I don't know how much it will cost to have the baby so I am saving my money until then. If it is not too expensive, I can send you some money right away.

I am getting better and better like I told you in my last letter with the work on the farm. I have been worming the horses and I even met with the vet to learn about problems that a sow is having with her pregnancy. Don't worry I am not having any problems and I am going to the doctor with

Angela soon. She says there is some special fund of money to take people to doctors in the United States and I will be using that.

The best news Mami is that I can drive a car! Efrahim, you remember I told you he is the handy man here? Efrahim taught me how to drive. I drove all over the farm and I made turns and everything. Of course, I can't legally drive on the road but when I finally get my green card, I'll be able to drive then.

So Mami, I will write you again when I see the doctor. Maybe I can send you a picture of Nely. We are going to take her picture. I don't know how that works yet but I'll let you know.

I miss you and I think of you every day.

All my love, your daughter,
Cece

I was actually nervous about the appointment with the doctor but Angela said it would be fine and Cook said she was a good doctor. On the morning of the appointment I took a long time in the bath because I wanted to be extra clean for her.

"Do you know this doctor?" I asked Angela in the truck on the road to the doctor's office.

"No, but I checked around and all of the ladies who had babies recommended her. You'll have a midwife for the delivery at home, like you wanted, but you need to see a doctor now to make sure everything is fine."

"What if everything is not fine?" Was I worrying for no reason? I was still hardly showing and I was seven months pregnant. I had that old sense of dread come over me again.

"Everything will be fine, Cece. I can tell you not to worry but of course you're going to worry, and that's why we're going to the doctor, to make sure. Settle down and watch the scenery."

The doctor had a shiny office. Everything was shiny. We were reflected in the shine of the floors as we came in. The countertop at the reception desk glistened. There was no dust in the corners or in the railings or on the floor. Even the scale where they weighed me was clean.

"Cece, come in now." The nurse stood in the doorway holding the papers we had filled out and held the door open for me. I looked at Angela.

"You go on now, Cece, you'll do fine." She continued to look at her magazine.

"Good morning, dear." The nurse looked kind and gentle. "Follow me and we'll get your information." She led me down a hallway with little doorways on either side with red, yellow and green arrows on top of the doors. Some of the doors had red arrows sticking out and others had the green or the yellow arrows sticking out.

"What are those?" I pointed to the arrows.

"Those are a very clever signaling device for the doctors. The red arrow means that a doctor is with a particular patient and no one should bother them. The yellow arrow means *waiting* so a patient has already seen the doctor and is waiting for a prescription or the result of a test. The green arrow means it's safe for anyone to enter. It usually means you've got your clothes on." I laughed at this. "Step up on the scale, honey."

She looked at the number on the dial and wrote it down on her papers. "Sit right there and we'll get your temperature and your blood pressure." She wrapped a black band around my arm and pumped air into it and watched the little dial move when she let it out. She wrote some more numbers on her papers. Finally, she rubbed something across my forehead and wrote other numbers down.

"Now, Cece, I want you to urinate into this cup. This is very important."

I gave her a strange look.

"Wait, I'll go with you into the bathroom and explain it. Follow me." She moved back down the hall with me trailing after her. "Come in, come in." She went into the bathroom and I followed. This felt strange. There were two of us in a very small bathroom.

"OK, now I'm writing your name on this cup. See, it says *Cece*. Here is a wipe in this little packet." She showed me a packet that looked like a condom wrapper. "Open it up and take out the wipe. Wipe yourself down there really well." She pointed to my genitals. "Then go to the bathroom. About three seconds after you start urinating stop. Just stop. Put the cup under you in the toilet and continue urinating in the cup. Take the cup out and put it on the sink. Then you can finish urinating if you need to. OK, so far?"

I nodded.

"OK, then put this top on the cup and wipe the cup off so it's clean for the technician. Then come here, see this little door, just put the cup in the door and close the door." She pointed to a tiny door like an Alice in Wonderland door that was on the wall. "You see those people in there. John, give us a wave?" A man on the other side of the little door had on blue plastic gloves and a blue shower cap and a blue shirt. He smiled and waved. "Those are people who work in the lab. When you close the door, your cup is in the laboratory. Then we can make tests to make sure you are good. Any questions?" I shook my head. "Oh yes, well, we ask you to catch the urine after a few seconds of going so we get a really clean sample. When you're finished wash your hands. Always wash and dry your hands and come back outside. I'll wait to take you to the doctor. Don't forget to dry your hands too, the germs can still be there after just the washing."

I didn't look at John. I washed my hands and came out. The nurse was waiting.

"OK dear, you'll be in here." She led me into an office. She handed me a piece of material. "This is a hospital gown. Take off all of your clothes and put on this gown with the opening in the front. You can hang your clothes over there. Sit on the examining table and the doctor will be in to see you in a minute." She left then and I heard the little arrow clicking on the outside of the door. I wondered which color she had put out there for me. I did as she requested and sat waiting for the doctor. There was a knock on the door.

The doctor entered but first I could hear her moving one of the arrows on the outside of the door. I expected it was red. "Hi, I'm Doctor Cynthia." She extended her hand. I liked her right away. She was very young, maybe ten years older than me. She had a broad open face with a beautiful smile and twinkling eyes. I had never seen such friendly eyes. She was a small lady, like me. But she didn't look like me at all. She was blonde and had blue eyes and there were freckles all over her face. This was my second time seeing freckles. I think I stared at them.

"I understand this is your first examination even though you are, let's see, over seven months pregnant." She looked at some papers on a clipboard she was carrying. "Can I ask why you waited so long to come and see us?"

I wasn't prepared for this question so I just told the truth. "I was coming here, to America, to give my baby a better life and I didn't have any money."

"I see. Well let's make sure that baby has a better life. I'm going to do several things today to make sure both you and the baby are in good shape. Did you give the urine test?" I nodded. "Great. We'll be looking at the results of that test to make sure you don't have any infections or any other issues that might upset the baby. Let's see here. Your blood pressure is normal and your pulse is good. You haven't gained much weight but every person is different and if everything else is OK we won't worry about that. You might have seen women who are really huge and you are rather small but that's normal too. It depends on where you are carrying the baby. If the baby is out front then the woman gets really big. So no worries there. Let me take a look at you to see if there's any swelling now."

She checked several places on my body: my hands, my face and my ankles. She turned the ankles and the hands to give a good look and touched them.

"That's good. This looks good." Whenever she said the word *good*, I relaxed a little more. She had a gentle touch and a soothing voice that helped to calm me down as she went about her business. I liked her. She was a woman.

"Have you ever been to a gynecologist, Cece?" she asked.

"No, this is the first time." I said.

"All right, then I will explain everything I am doing so you will understand and it will be easy for us together. OK, lie down for me please on this table and I'm going to ask you to put your feet up in these strange metal things here at the end of the table. These are called stirrups. Just pretend like you're riding your favorite horse and not in some god-awful position on a doctor's table." She laughed. There was a knock on the door and I jumped.

"Relax, Cece. It's just the nurse."

A nurse entered the room, wheeling a small machine. She stood at the foot of the table and handed things to the doctor who didn't even have to ask. I felt like I was a car and a mechanic was working on me. She poked and prodded and shone a light on me and just generally checked that everything was as it should be. Even though in my mind I knew this was good, I was still embarrassed by it. She turned off the light and pushed it out of the way and peeled off her plastic gloves.

"Everything looks really good, Cece. We'll hook you up now to the sonogram. You can take your feet out of the stirrups."

The nurse hooked up a machine. At the same time, she moved the gown aside and rubbed jelly on my stomach. "Take a look here, Cece." She pointed to a screen like a tiny television. There in a black and white grainy picture was a little baby floating inside a cocoon. I heard a thumping sound that reminded me of the racing engine when I was trying to drive the car. It filled the room.

"That thumping sound you hear is the sound of the

heart of your healthy baby, Cece." My eyes welled with tears. "And on the screen for the very first time may I present your little baby girl. Take a look at your Mama, little girl." The nurse moved the wand around on my belly so I could see the baby sleeping there.

"Nely," I said through my tears.

"Excuse me honey, I didn't hear you," Doctor Cynthia said.

"Her name is Nely."

"Oh, Nely. Well welcome to your first introduction to little Nely. She seems very fine." The nurse handed me a copy of the image I saw floating on the screen. It was a picture of my Nely. She really was there, right inside of me.

"Could I have another copy?" I wanted to send one to my mother.

"Sure, honey. Here you go. Have several." The nurse handed me three copies as they came out of the machine.

"You can get dressed now, Cece. Everything looks absolutely normal. Just keep doing what you are doing and have a wonderful baby." Dr. Cynthia left first and the nurse followed, wheeling the machine out in front of her and bringing great joy to another mother in another room. I didn't get dressed; I stared at the black and white photo of the great gift Guillermo had given me. I held her against my heart and whispered her name. Finally I got dressed and walked out to the waiting room to meet Angela.

"Angela, look at this." I handed her the photo. "It's Nely. She's a girl and she's perfect and she's mine."

"Mine too, I am going to make a great aunt." Angela hugged me. "I think she looks just like you." She laughed. I did too.

"Let's get going then. I think everything is fine, right?" Angela gathered her belongings.

"Right." I took the pictures and carefully slipped them into my bag. They were precious. Angela walked up to the desk and the nurse told her how much it was for the visit. I heard hundreds of dollars mentioned. Angela presented her credit card.

"I thought the special fund was paying for this." I was confused.

"Yes, yes, it is but I have to pay first and then the fund gives the money back to me. Don't worry, it's all taken care of." She patted my hand.

Nothing could ruin this moment so I smiled and we moved outside into the bright sunshine arm-in-arm. "Let's go get a non-alcoholic beer to celebrate," Angela said. This sounded really good to me.

"Cook, Cook, look!" I ran into the house waving the picture of Nely. Cook was washing her hands and had already put her apron away. She squinted at the picture with her arm totally extended.

"Yeah, she's got your nose all right." Angela and Cook laughed. I didn't laugh. "Yes, yes, Cece, she's a beauty. She looks like a plump little baby. I'm sure she'll be very healthy. I hope she likes American food."

"I'm sure she will. I knew she was a girl all along. Guillermo would have been so happy." I put the picture on the refrigerator with one of those magnets. Nely was lying down, floating comfortably, looking very relaxed.

"Did everything go well?" Cook looked a little concerned.

"Fine. I had so many tests. I even had to pee into a little cup and put it in a window and there was a lab on the other side of the window. Everything is good. They said it was normal that I hadn't gained much weight and my tummy wasn't so big."

"That's a relief, isn't it? I know you feel good but it's a relief for a specialist to tell you that everything's normal." She was cooking hamburgers on the stove and the smell of the meat was floating through the air.

"Yes. It's comforting in a way. I wasn't really worried about anything but you know, maybe underneath it all, I was. You think you're so strong."

"You just keep thinking that, dearie. Better to think you're strong than to think you're weak. Folks will take advantage of someone that seems vulnerable. Sorry to say I've seen it my whole life." She was turning the burgers over on the stove. I went upstairs to change my clothes to do chores. On the way, I passed the refrigerator and put my fingers on Nely. She was safe.

When I came back, Cook and Angela were staring at me with big smiles like they had a secret.

"Sit down, Cece. Cook and I have a little present for you." She handed me a box.

"What's this? I took the wrapping off the box and there was a picture of a phone. "A phone for me? Thank you so much." I smiled at them.

"Not just any phone, one of them smart phones, they're supposed to make you smarter, I guess. Not sure why they call them smart phones." Cook looked at Angela with that question in her eyes.

"It's because the phone gives you so many options. You can make videos, take pictures, look up information. Oh yeah, if you are really desperate, you can make phone calls!" Angela and Cook laughed. "Seriously, we thought you should have a phone as you are getting closer to your due date. You need to be able to call us if there is an emergency."

I wrapped my arms around them. "Thank you so much."

"You'd best spend the rest of the week trying to figure out how the damn thing works," Cook said.

"Or you can do like all of the rest of us and ask one of the six-year-olds on the bus to explain it to you." We all laughed again and hugged. I went upstairs to learn about my new treasure.

XXI

I was sitting in the truck parked at the curb on Main Street. The streetlight overhead was out and only the moon cast a light into the alleyway. It was called a Thunder Moon because it was so strong. I loved this kind of moon; it didn't come out often. Angela would be finished with her meeting soon so I just passed the time playing with my phone. I had become quite an expert, I was proud to say.

Suddenly, I heard a muffled sound coming from the direction of the alley. I looked over and saw a figure doing something. At first I couldn't tell what was going on and then in the light of the street lamp, I saw it was someone kicking at something. What was it? It was another person. The person was down on the ground and the one over him was kicking and kicking. What could I do? I couldn't get involved. Couldn't do anything with the police. I had enough people keeping my secret. But I had to stop it. I also had to do something else. I had to record it.

I slid across the seat lying low. What could I do, how could I stop it? I started breathing heavily. I was scared. The kicking just kept going. I opened the door slowly and crept to the side of the alley. With the phone, I recorded the beating for only a minute, just enough to record what I saw.

I crept back to the truck and slammed the door, maybe the noise would stop the beating. I jumped into the back and lay down on the floor. I held my breath. Sure enough, someone came out of the alley and passed along the street beside the truck. The sound had startled him. I knew who I had filmed. It was Tim Patterson. He moved quickly past the truck, not looking inside. He was escaping, putting distance between himself and his actions. I knew the other person was hurt badly. I sat up. What to do?

I saw Angela coming out of her meeting and I got out of the truck to meet her. I hoped there would be some way to tell her what had happened. She was walking with another woman.

"This is Pastor Alice from the church." She pointed to the woman beside her.

"Alice, this is Cece, she's my niece from Texas."

"Nice to meet you." I probably said it too fast as we were coming to the truck and my mind was racing. Pastor Alice gave me a strange look, I guess because I hadn't said anything more.

"Oh, sorry. I was a bit distracted. Did you hear something? It sounded like a moan." I hadn't heard anything. I was sure the person was long past moaning but I had to do something. "Listen. Do you hear it?"

"No. I don't hear anything, dear." Pastor Alice listened intently to the growing silence.

"I don't hear anything either, Cece. What do you hear?" Angela was still on the sidewalk as we arrived at the alleyway in front of the truck.

"I think I see something in the alley." I pointed down the alley into the darkness.

"Where? I don't see anything." Pastor Alice peered into the alley.

I strode into the alley. "I'm sure I heard something. Let

me just see. Look. I think I see something. It's an animal or something." I knew damn well what it was. Angela and Pastor Alice followed me, Angela striding and Pastor Alice tentatively stepping along like she might step on a spider in the dark.

"Oh my God, it's a boy!" I had positioned Angela to find him first and she didn't disappoint me. "Alice, call an ambulance."

She bent down to inspect the unconscious boy. His face was barely recognizable, having been so badly beaten. His eyes were swollen shut and big black and blue puffs took the place of the features on his face. He was breathing in raspy breaths but he was alive.

"Put your shawl over him, Cece. We have to keep him warm." She rolled up her own shawl and put it under his head while I covered him. His blood seeped into our clothes. I could hear Alice talking to the ambulance.

"It will only be a few minutes. Greg Allison is on duty with the volunteer fire department and he'll be here soon. Do you know who it is?" Pastor Alice still stood some feet away as if she would catch some disease if she came any closer.

"I can't tell. He's too badly beaten. I wish Greg would hurry." Angela crouched over the boy, protecting him from further harm.

As if someone heard her plea the ambulance arrived. Two men got out with medical bags in their hands like the men I had seen in the Walmart in Dallas. They came toward us.

"Better bring the stretcher, Greg, this is bad." Angela instructed them.

"OK." They turned around then and got the stretcher

out of the back of the ambulance. The two men ran up to us pushing a stretcher on wheels.

"Oh jeez, that's bad, huh? Move away now, Angela, let us take a look at the boy."

Angela reluctantly gave up her protective place and moved out of the way. Greg and the other man bent over the boy and went to work. They touched every part of his body and cleaned off his arm and put in a drip of some medicine. They looked at him with a flashlight but mostly by touch. The boy did not seem to respond. They gingerly lifted him onto the stretcher and piled on blankets. They put straps across him. They began to roll him to the street.

"Greg?" Angela began to talk.

"Not now, Angela. He's in bad shape. Definitely some broken bones. Maybe some internal bleeding or other damage. He needs to get to the hospital as soon as possible. I'll let you know."

They wheeled him past Pastor Alice who was standing at the mouth of the alley where she had stayed the whole time. They hoisted him up into the ambulance and as we watched they were gone. The siren was wailing.

"Oh my God." Pastor Alice had her hand on her mouth as if she was stopping her words from coming out. "What could have happened to that boy?"

"Somebody obviously beat the crap out of him, Alice." Angela sounded frustrated. "Let's go, Cece." She strode out to the truck and climbed in and started the engine. I was surprised she hadn't said goodbye to Alice or offered her a ride. It was dark.

"Good thing you have young hearing, Cece. Neither Alice nor I would have ever heard his moaning. You probably saved his life. He looked so beat up. Shit! Poor

Mario."

"Mario? I thought you didn't know him. You know him? Who is he?" And what is his connection to Tim Patterson, I wondered.

"I only know by the bandana. He had a yellow bandana around his neck. It was covered with blood but you could see it was yellow. Mario is a gay kid in the village. He's a quiet, gentle soul. His father is a macho Mexican, no offense, and doesn't want anything to do with the kid. He's about sixteen. He doesn't go to school, but he's a great artist. He painted almost all of the signs you see in the streets, over the stores and stuff. And the mural on the wall of the building with the pharmacy. I think he lives in one of the boarding houses. No one bothers him. I'm sure there are plenty of homosexuals in town but they keep a low profile. We're a very conservative town when it comes to a lot of things. Gender stuff is one of them. So for the gays, nobody bothers them and they don't bother anybody. Until now. This was a hate crime I'm sure of it. Some bastard beat him up just because he's gay. Poor kid. I hope it's not as bad as it looks."

I was afraid it was worse than it looked. Tim was kicking him. How could it not be bad? The fury and the violence were overwhelming. I didn't know how long it had gone on before I stopped it. Hopefully, it wasn't too long. Was Tim Patterson dangerous? I had asked that question many times and there was no answer; now there was.

We got home and said good night. There were deep troubles in our hearts and neither of us seemed to want to talk them out. I went to bed and had fitful dreams of people pursuing me and angry mobs and people screaming. I woke up scared.

Cook had breakfast ready when I got downstairs the next morning. The coffee was still brewing when I sat down at the table. I heard a car pull into the driveway. A door slammed. Cook went to the window.

"It's Greg Allison in the ambulance. I wonder what he wants. Call Angela please, Cece." She wiped her hands on her apron and went to the screen door. "Howdy, Greg and Andy. Come on in. I just got some coffee made." I went up the stairs and called Angela.

The two men entered, carefully wiping their feet on the mat like they could keep out the dust. "How do, Cook?" Greg said this. The other man, Andy, just nodded. Did everyone call her Cook?

"I'm fine, Greg, sit down and I'll get you some coffee and biscuits." She bustled around the kitchen setting out cups and sugar and cream. The men pulled out chairs and sat at the kitchen table across from me.

"Hi, I'm Cece, Angela's niece." I stuck out my hand and the two men shook it. Cook shot me a glance. Angela came in with her hair all messed up and wearing a bathrobe. I never saw her so disorganized in the morning.

"Good morning, Angela," Greg began.

"Hello Greg, Andy, what's the news?" Angela sat down, agitated. Cook gave them cups of coffee and biscuits and butter and jam. The two men heaped teaspoons full of sugar into their coffees and slathered butter on their biscuits. They were both fat. Between bites and gulps they told us what was going on.

"First off, here's your shawls. I guess these are yours. Very smart to cover up the poor kid. He was definitely in shock." Greg handed us the bloody shawls.

"Oh my God, these are yours! What happened?!" Cook was scooping up the shawls and looking at the four of us with horror in her eyes.

"I'll tell you, Cook, you best sit down," Greg continued. He took another biscuit and absently started to put butter on it.

"We got to the hospital in record time and we had called ahead so everyone was ready. He has some internal injuries like we thought so the doctors had to operate right away. Nothing is permanent inside so that's the good news. He has a fractured skull and broken ribs and his arm and leg are broken. He'll be in traction for a while but it looks like he'll survive. He isn't talking yet because they put him in an induced coma to give his body time to rest. I've never seen anything like it."

During all of this, Cook was pacing the kitchen behind the men. She refilled their coffee and gave them more biscuits which they gobbled us up as fast as she offered them. Finally she couldn't stand it anymore.

"What happened?" she asked, her eyes as big as golf balls.

"We found a badly beaten boy last night in the alleyway near the pharmacy." Angela was pulling her hair back into a ponytail. "Cece heard some moaning. We were with Pastor Alice when we heard it. We went to investigate, thinking it might be a dog or something and we found the boy. It's a good thing Cece's hearing is so good." Angela poured herself a cup of coffee.

"It's really surprising, actually." Greg took another big bite of the biscuit. "You must have heard his last moan before he passed out completely. He was really beat up and was unconscious when we got there. Lucky to be alive really. Who would do such a thing?"

I knew exactly who would do such a thing. I flashed on the movie inside my head of Tim kicking that boy who was so vulnerable. Not moving. Not talking. I wonder the horror that had flashed through his mind when Tim came up on him. He must have been terrified as the pummeling began. Did he cry out? Did he beg for mercy?

"Oh that's so terrible. That poor boy." Tears were in the eyes of Cook. "Do you know who it is?"

"It's Mario Godigez." Greg looked down at his biscuit as if saying the name of a homosexual were a shame in itself.

"The queer kid?" Cook blurted out. "Sorry. The gay kid?"

"Yes," was all Greg said.

"We think this might be a hate crime," Andy added. He reached for another biscuit.

"Of course it's a hate crime." Angela took a biscuit from the basket and pulled the butter dish to her side of the table. She pulled the robe tight when she reached in front of the two men.

"He's the only kid in the town who had the balls to tell the world who he is. His own father threw him out. But he was strong. Look what he did. The signs hanging above the sidewalks are his. The mural is his. He gave the town beauty and we couldn't even protect him."

"I don't think that's fair, Angela. Let Sheriff Dayton do his job. I'm sure you'll be called in today to make a statement. Trust in justice. Well, we better be goin'." They got up then and put on their hats and shook hands with all of us.

"Please let us know how he's doing, will you guys?"

Angela stood in the doorway drinking her coffee as they pulled away.

"Wow. So sad." Cook still fought back tears.

"Cece. When you get home today, we need to talk about this. We'll need a back story for you that won't raise any suspicion. Think about our relationship."

"What do you mean?"

"I already told them you were my niece from Texas. They might ask you some questions like where do you live and all that. We need to think this through. We need to make sure there is no way they can investigate you. So think about it. I'll drop by the Sheriff's office in town sometime today and make a statement and see what they want to do about you."

"OK. I didn't realize that, but of course, I need to think about this." Cook shot me a worried look. I gave her a *don't worry* look in response.

On the school bus I thought about Tim Patterson. First he was a thief and now he is a potential murderer. What was I going to do? If I accused him of doing this then my life underground was completely blown. I'm sure the police would ask for some kind of identification from their star witness. How can I get justice for Mario without getting myself deported?

The day crawled by. I had a hard time concentrating on my classes. It was getting close to lunch time anyway and I was looking forward to the treat that Cook had prepared for me. I didn't hear him come in then so my heart stopped when I turned and saw Tim standing in the doorway of the door from the alley.

"This is your space, huh? Bit far away from the front of the store, isn't it?" Was he fishing for something? Was he trying to figure out if I could possibly have seen him? I wanted to look away. He scared me but I didn't want him to know it. I had the secret. I had the winning hand. He couldn't intimidate me if he didn't know what I knew. He was fishing.

"I like it back here. It's private and the girls can make mistakes without anyone seeing us. I had class this morning and it went well. No one bothers us back here. The front of the store seems a different world." I was putting the scissors away. I liked having them in my hands. "What do you want, Tim?"

"Nothin' really. I'm just droppin' by to see Ma. Yeah. You're in a cave here. Must feel like home to you beaners." He waited for his little insult to hit the mark.

"Do you know the girls in the classes?" The scissors got stowed safely in drawers.

"I don't give a shit about little girls. So I don't even know if I know them. Or care. They're all stupid little girls to me."

"They're very nice. Eager to learn and patient. It was nice teaching them." I kept putting away the supplies, hoping to distract him from whatever sick mission he was on.

"Ain't that nice. You say *nice* for everything. Don't you know no other words?" He sneered then. He looked pathetic to me. He must have practiced that sneer but it was empty without any power behind it.

"I know many other words. At this moment *nice* is the best word to describe what I am saying and *nice* it is."

"You are one big bore to talk to." He spun on his heel and walked away. I was glad to see him go. I hoped this wasn't the start of a pattern of visits. Mrs. Patterson came in a few minutes later as Tim vanished into the alley.

"How you doing, Cece? I see my son came by for a visit. He's a good boy." How can she not know anything about her only child? I hoped I wouldn't be so blind to Nely. "How are the classes going? Any problems?"

"Everything is fine."

"Good girl, see you later." She hurried to catch up with Jeamine.

All of this drama with Tim brought back my long-held sense of dread. It washed over me like a dark wave. I didn't know why, but I felt I had to do something for Nely. I had to tell her about her mother. I had to share what I would share if I were there with her. For the first time, I felt that the better life would be for her, without me. Maybe because I saw Guillermo killed in such a flash of time. Maybe because I had seen the *narcos* do that to so many families. Maybe it was because I saw Tim Patterson's brutal attack. Whatever the reasons, I knew that life was precarious. I knew that none of us was ever really safe. I might not be there for Nely. Tears welled up in my eyes as I had this thought. I cried for something then that might not even happen, but what if it did. What if she never got to know me at all? The sadness engulfed me and I sat in the back of the store, crying to myself.

I buckled up immediately at the end of that day when I got in the car. I didn't look at him. I wasn't saying anything either. What do you say to a beast?

"Cat got your tongue? Oh I forgot you probably don't know what that means, do you? It means *ain't ya got nothin' to say*?" He turned his full attention to me then and found the side of my face turned away from him.

"I don't really have anything to say today." I listened

to how cultured the words sounded coming out of my mouth and was pleased.

"Suit yourself. I don't want to talk with you anyway. Bitch."

Like his words would hurt me. I knew him now. There were no secrets between us except for the big one: I knew what he was. It seemed that America was not so different from Mexico. Bullies the world over are cowards. He was a coward running in the darkness away from his crime. I knew his type. We had them in our village in Mexico. We had them in our schools. We even had them in our universities. We had them on a bed in Dallas. People visiting violence on other people. How do we think that is OK? On what planet could that possibly be OK?

I never met his gaze. I never said a word. I just got out of the truck and did not look back at him. He revved the engine and sped away with black smoke coming out of the back of the truck. He gunned it at the corner, small kids scattering everywhere. What an *hijo de punta. Son of a bitch* worked in every language. I was making my plan to take him down. I just needed a little time and a little opportunity.

At home I changed quickly and did the chores. The horses got fed and the chickens. I picked up a bucket of slops from Cook and fed the pigs too. I put the food in the dog bowls for giving to the dogs a bit later in the day. I went to check on the garden but Efrahim was there quietly working on weeds. He nodded at me. The whole world was bobbing its head.

"Angela's in the office and wants to talk to you. There's sweet tea in the refrigerator." Cook was chopping as usual.

"Thanks, Cook." I put some ice in a glass and poured

some tea for me and added more to her glass on the table. She nodded. I went to the office to see Angela.

"Hi, Angela." I settled on the small sofa in her office. She pushed her reading glasses onto the top of her head.

"Hi, Cece. How you doin', honey? Yesterday was a tough day. Mario wasn't a pretty sight to see."

"Terrible, but I have seen worse, I'm sorry to say. *Narcotrafficantes* leave decapitated heads on fence posts."

"Oh Jesus, I forget about that. Sorry. Well I wanted to let you know that you don't have to testify. I went to see Sheriff Dayton, Jim Dayton, at his office. He took my statement. He wanted to know how we found him; how we even chanced to look for him. I told him you heard a moan. He wanted to know where you were standing and where I was standing. I think he might have found other footprints but how that'll make any difference in such a heavily traveled alleyway, I don't know. He wanted to know, let's see, what we did with Mario. I told him about keeping him warm with our shawls and using a shawl for a pillow in case he went into shock. That's about it really."

"Why doesn't he need me to tell the story too?"

"Well I told him a little white lie that you were only sixteen and that means you're a minor. Oh, because of Pastor Alice. She already made a statement and hers corroborated mine so everything is good. He thought two witnesses whose stories matched was enough. Terrible things, right. We also got a call from Greg Allison. He says that Mario is still in critical condition but they moved him from the ICU, that's the intensive care unit, where the really serious patients go, to his own room so he is doing better. He's going to be OK. Thank God he's so young."

"Corroborated means that you both agreed, right?"

She nodded.

"So I don't have to go to the sheriff?"

"No. He has everything he needs. I hope we catch the guy. He was nearly a murderer."

I hoped we would catch the guy too. I hoped he had left enough evidence; the spit that was probably coming out of his mouth, the footprints from his pointy-toed boots, the soil from his mother's garden, the bits of hair that flew from his head. I hoped he had left everything we might need to put him in jail forever. He had taken a lovely boy and made him look like a monster. The real monster was Tim with his thieving and his lying and his anger. He had secrets that no one knew. What kind of pressure do those secrets cause in a person? What if the whole town knew that this tough guy, this bully, liked to wear lipstick and gloves and women's clothes? What kind of pain did carrying such a secret cause? Did it cause him to lash out like he did? Do we forgive the monster because he has his reasons? I had a plan. My plan. Tim would never hurt anyone else.

The town was full of nothing but the beating. The churches held meetings to discuss homosexuality. The kids had t-shirts printed that said *We Are All Gay*. The newspapers published a list of the names of young people who had written in to say they were coming out of the closet. There was even a gay pride parade down Main Street. I am sure Tim Patterson wasn't in it. The parade passed by the Pattersons' two stores.

"Look at those young people, so sad, what a waste." Mrs. Patterson was looking out the window as the parade passed by.

"Why?" I asked innocently.

"Why, Cece, those young people will never have the sacred relationship of a husband and wife. They will always be outsiders in the sight of Our Lord. Certainly in Mexico that must be true as well." She had her fingers knotted in the pearls of her necklace.

"Mexicans are pretty tolerant of such things. There are people who dress in the clothing of the other sex and they are often in our national parades." I watched her twirl her beads.

"I'm sorry, dear, but I find that utterly disgusting. If God wanted women to be men He would have made us men. Dressing in each other's clothing is a sickness, if you ask me."

I nodded emphatically as if this closed the discussion. "Well there are a lot of rights for gays in our country. They can even get married. They don't have to miss out on being parents like they used to have to." I watched the twirling increase.

"My point exactly. How in the name of Our Lord can you let unnatural couples raise children? In some cases they are even having the children. It's just not right. Mark my words, Cece. You haven't seen the last of these beatings. God-fearing people will be expressing their anger. It won't end with poor little Mario." She turned away from the parade with a final look of disgust.

I walked to the back of the store with Jeamine who had taken a break to see the parade too. "I think it's great." She put her arm around my shoulder. "Live and let live is what I say. If it works for them then they should be free to do it. I would get pretty pissed if the government climbed into my bedroom and told me what I could and couldn't do. No sirree. Live and let live. Fuck, we been on the bad end of the stick for two hundred years. I know how THE MAN treats folks. Bein' black in America ain't no picnic. You get what I'm sayin'? Uh hmm. They've got a right to be as they is." She took her arm away and went back to her desk. Americans were confusing.

XXII

I had a new group of classes but I had the same problems.

"Allie, you pushed down on the pedal too hard. Look, you've bunched up the thread on the bobbin." I showed her the knotted thread. "You'll have to rewind it now and see if you can get the thread back on the spool. Then take your time and push gently on the pedal. Class, gently," I said over the hum of the sewing machines. Allie smiled up at me.

"Clara, you need to iron the pattern first." Clara was attempting to pin the wrinkled pattern pieces on the material spread out on the table. "Remember that I said you had to iron the pieces as you go along? Class, listen for a minute." Three heads turned toward me. "Please don't skip steps. It's important to iron the pattern pieces as well as the material because you can have a flat fabric to work with. There are plenty of stations to iron and lay out the pieces so take your time." Clara walked over to the ironing board and plugged in the iron.

"Ahh! Shit." Ginny was crying out in pain.

"What is it? What happened?" I rushed to her side and saw that she was cradling her finger. There was a long needle poking out of it. "Oh dear. Wait a minute. I'll take care of it." I didn't like doing this. So many of the girls sewed right through their fingers and then pulled back their fingers and broke off the needles. The solution was to pull the needle out and no one liked this.

"Shit! Shit! Look what I did." Clara and Allie were crowding around Ginny now and watching blood start to come out of the wound around the needle that was still sticking out. It looked terrible to have a needle sticking out of your finger. I ran to the cabinet where I kept a sterilized needle-nosed pliers. Unfortunately I had to learn the name of these pliers the very first day of class. I took it out of its plastic bag and went back to Ginny.

"No! No!" she shrieked these words. "It'll hurt too much. Don't!" She yelled. The needle protruded from her finger and I knew from experience that it would be an easy removal. As she continued to yell I grabbed the finger and in one quick jerk I had the needle out.

"Yuck, yuck," Allie said. She made a little tremble on the way back to her machine.

"Come on, Ginny, let's get that washed and disinfected." I took her to the bathroom and washed her finger in soapy water. We dried it thoroughly and I put an antibiotic cream on it and a bandage. I had to wrap the bandage because, of course, the wound had two sides. She had stopped crying. I hugged her close. "There you go Ginny. Now listen. Leave your finger like this until tomorrow and then once a day put Vaseline on it and a clean bandage, after you wash it. Also, when was the last time you had a tetanus shot?" I had learned this information from the internet on my smart phone. I had to know how to fix these kinds of wounds as a sewing teacher. I loved that phone.

"We had to get one this year for school. Why do I have to put Vaseline on it?" She wiped the tears from her eyes.

"Because it's a puncture wound. It's deep. You want it to heal from the inside so you want to keep it moist. If you don't, a scab will form and it won't have healed from within."

"Thank you, Cece." She went back to her machine. I followed her.

"Let me put a new needle in for you. Do you want to keep working today?"

"Yes, I'm all right. Or I will be anyway."

There were little dramas like this all the time. Someone spilled a coke inside the machine. Someone broke a needle in her finger. Someone dropped the iron on the floor. Someone burned the fabric. It took a lot of energy to teach. How did Richard do it with all of the welding machines and cutting machines and probably electricity running all over the place? It was a miracle anything got done and all of us lived through the day.

Cook fixed me wonderful lunches every day and I often had fresh biscuits or soups when she made a big batch. I used this time wisely to hatch my plan to stop Tim Patterson. And, of course, to do something so that my daughter would know me, no matter what happened. I had to hold the sense of dread away from me for a while.

"Been doing well." Tim wanted to make conversation with me now. I guess he felt he could get on my good side. I wasn't sure if it was a question or a comment. Either way I didn't want to talk to a thug. I was watching television at night now and learning many new words each day. 'Thug' was one of them, and a perfect word for him. I pulled my backpack close against my chest.

"Everything's fine." I looked away from him, ending the discussion before it could begin. He took the hint and drove me to the school in silence. I barely got out the door before he gunned the engine and peeled out.

Later that night I decided to broach a sensitive conversation again. "I'm confused about how Americans feel about gay people," I said. Cook was peeling potatoes and I took a knife to help her.

"You're not the only one, Cece. We are all confused about what we are supposed to feel." She didn't stop peeling. "What do you want to know?"

"How do people feel about gays? How do they treat them?"

"I think the gay thing is a mess. You best ask Angela. That's something for serious thinkers. I didn't even want to talk to you about those trans people. No, not me. Ask Angela." She continued to peel potatoes but with more energy now.

"Ask me what?" Angela came through the door and wiped her feet on the mat. She sat down at the kitchen table.

"Our unusually curious Cece wants to know about gays in this country." Cook peeled faster and the potato peels flew around in the air.

"Hmm, gays. Cece, you've been here for a while now. You know that Americans come in all sizes and colors and cultures. We're not a homogenous society; that means we're not all the same. Look at the people running in elections. You couldn't believe they're from the same country much less from the same planet. Some people treat gays like they are their own families. Some people beat them up. Some people even kill them. We had the same actions with blacks in the sixties and I guess, still. Some people treat them differently and some people beat them up and some people kill them. There's no set answer to the way Americans do anything. We are only held together by an accident of where we were born. Or like you, by a belief that something could be better than what we had somewhere else. Really confusing, huh?" I could barely hear her over the water she was putting in a big pot for Cook's potatoes. She put the pot on the stove. "Wish I could make it easier for you to understand."

"What happened to Mario was horrible. I guess it happens in Mexico but I never heard of it." I helped Cook carry the potatoes to the pot of water.

"Of course it happens in Mexico. It happens everywhere. People fear what they don't understand and when there is fear, there is aggression. That's what happened to Mario. An aggressive son of a bitch attacked because he felt threatened by a young sweet boy who would never have harmed him. At least physically. There was something there that caused the fear. Can't say what it was." She reached for an apple from the table.

"I think in Mexico we're more tolerant. We have parades where all of the cross-dressing people, mostly men, can come out and be proud of how different they are. We have some ranches where men and women can go for sex with each other—the same sex or the other sex. They aren't ashamed. I think. I'm not really sure. What about cross-dressing? Cook didn't really want to talk about it." Cook sent me a disapproving look.

"I don't think there's so much shame anymore. There have been movies and TV shows about people who are transvestites and those who have operations. The lesbian, gay, and transgender movement is gathering steam. But like most waves of change in the US they start in the big cities. Things take a while to drip down to us. Maybe that's why Mario's attack was so shocking. We thought we were part of the change and we seem to be going backwards." She went to the larder and returned with a handful of beets.

"Beets for dinner." She held up the plump red vegetables like a trophy. "What do you think, Cook?"

"I think it's a great relief that you are here to answer her infernal questions and in answer to the last one, give me those and I'll fix 'em." She grabbed the beets from Angela and went over to the stove to prepare them.

"What could be better?" Angela said as she was heading out the door to feed the animals.

I didn't feel like the question had been answered. Of course I was specifically thinking of Tim Patterson and how he liked women's clothing. If it wasn't a big deal in America anymore, why was he so scared that someone would find out? Why did it cause him shame and make him attack other people? Why did he seem like such a caged animal all the time?

The next weeks were busy ones for me. I ran the classes and the girls progressed. At night I read something from Angela's library or watched the television to practice English. A big part of my time was taken up with my secret project every day at lunch. Since I had discovered that the telephone let me make movies, I had been practicing with it. It wasn't really complicated; you just had to use things that were already built into the phone like the camera and the microphone.

I made little videos and experimented with the lights so that I looked good on the screen. I even took to wearing more make-up to the store so that my daily movies were more glamorous. I made sure only my face showed in the movies, I didn't want any tummy bump.

The midwife, Yvonne, was coming for regular visits now. She was from Ireland and had red hair and freckles and the most amazing eyes. They were sky blue and had darker blue circles around them. She had a very gentle touch and she made you feel that you were safe with her. She would take my blood pressure and poke around inside me and she said that everything was just as it should be. I still didn't have much of a tummy but she explained like Dr. Cynthia had that this was normal so I thought it was OK.

"Come and help me, Cook, please, I've got some supplies." Angela was at the door of the kitchen where I sat reading my book and Cook was working. Cook wiped her hands and followed Angela through the banging screen door.

"I'll come, too." I put my book down.

"No, Cece, watch the rice so it doesn't boil over." I went to the stove and there was no rice in the pot just the boiling water. Odd I thought. I didn't quite know what to do because there was no rice so I foolishly stood and watched the boiling water.

"Hold the door then, Cece, got it?" I grabbed the door just before it closed on her.

"Yeah, go on then."

Both women entered the kitchen, one following the other, loaded down with huge colorfully-wrapped packages. Most of them were really big and had to be carried in one-by-one or dragged in. I was watching, fascinated, and keeping an eye on the stove at the same time. I don't know why, because there was still no rice there. "What's all this? Someone having a party?"

"Yes, you are. Sit down." She arrayed the packages at one end of the kitchen table. Cook went over and turned off the stove and I sat down.

"What's all this?" I looked at the wrapping paper and it was covered with tiny drawings of babies and balloons and teddy bears. I had an idea what was happening.

"This is called a *baby shower*. We are sparing you the stupid parts of baby showers where women sit around and talk about the labor they went through having each kid. We are also not playing any stupid parlor games, that's a fancy word for just plain stupid games. We are just giving you things you will need for the baby with love from the bottom of our hearts. Don't worry, there's not too many clothes because we will be shopping for baby clothes at yard sales. Babies don't stay in their clothes for long and so we will be getting a lot of bargains later. Open your packages." Angela was smiling broadly, moving the packages around the table.

Cook and Angela took their seats beside me and I dove into the pile of packages. I decided to start with the biggest first. I tore off the paper and it was a lovely pink stroller. They had actually wrapped it with wrapping paper and taped the paper all around the bottom next to the wheels.

"Look here, Cece." Cook got up and came over to the stroller. "Here's a little roof that folds out to cover the baby's face and protect her from the sun. Isn't that nice? We didn't have strollers like this in my day." I pulled the roof out and pushed it back several times, staring at it admiringly. "Go on, keep opening your presents." She was smiling so much it felt like the party was for her.

There was a big box that they had put on the table and

I tackled this next. It was a beautiful baby carrier. There was a picture of the baby in the carrier being lugged by a happy man. On the other side there was a picture of the same carrier in the car and the baby being strapped in. I knew there were all kinds of laws here about babies in the car, as I had seen all of the mothers in town strapping their babies into and out of cars and carrying them around.

The whole time I was unwrapping I kept up a chorus of appreciation. *Thank you, oh so beautiful, how wonderful, terrific, oh wow* filled the air with my gratitude. I was touched by their thoughtfulness. I wasn't surprised. Their kindness was limitless in my life and this was just another example.

The diaper bag was covered with pink balloons and pink babies. There was something called a *playpen* that looked like, from the picture on the front of the box, a net corral for the baby. There were baby bottles and bibs and little all-in-one suits. There was even a box with a hand-crocheted hat and booties from Evelyn. I felt like a kid at Christmas but instead, I was a mom at Christmas.

I hugged Angela and Cook. "You know I can never thank you for all you've done. I am so blessed to have found you. You welcomed me, a stranger, into your home and have taught me and protected me from the minute I found you. You never made me feel for one second that I shouldn't be here, that I didn't deserve to be here."

"Everyone deserves the best life they can have, Cece. We just wanted to help you get that life." Angela folded me in her arms.

"Don't forget about me." Cook encircled us both with her little fat self and we made a human ball in the middle of the kitchen. I had some tears in my eyes and so did

Cook.

"We better take this stuff upstairs before it gets dirty here in the kitchen. There will be a cake later made especially for the baby shower. There's usually some cake and cookies and stuff. I haven't been to a baby shower in about twenty years but I remember those dumb afternoons as an excuse to give the baby some presents. So there is good and bad." She was hauling the stroller up the stairs. It took several trips to get all of the loot up.

"Better rest up for dinner now, Cece, and don't break any of these things before you use them. I have one more surprise." Angela left and went across the hall to her room. I heard some squeaking coming across the floorboard. She came back wheeling an old baby crib.

"This was my crib from when I was a baby. It took me awhile to find it and clean it up but I think it'll do nicely for Nely. I saved it for the baby I was going to have but you know that it didn't happen and it makes me very happy to see that someone I love will be using it."

I took the end of the crib from her and wheeled it across the room near the window where I had planned to keep Nely. She would be able to look out at the meadow and look up at the stars. There was a big green bow tied to the top of the railings on the crib. Tears came to my eyes.

"Thank you so much. This is really a better life." I buried my head in her shoulder.

"You're more than welcome, sweetheart. You deserve everything good you get in life. You earned it. Now rest up and play with the baby's things. See you for dinner. We're having beets. I'll be going to Richard's later." She walked out of the room and ran the bath.

I did as she had suggested. All of the things for the baby

had pictures and instruction booklets and big boxes to unpack. I had not seen many of these things up close and it was fascinating to me to read the instructions and see how the playpen and the baby carrier and the stroller all had features to make life for parents and baby easier or safer. In all of the pictures there were blue-eyed babies, the American specialty. I worked through all of the instruction booklets for each item so I could understand how they worked. The manufacturers had thought about everything. None of them had little pieces which babies could break off and chew. All of them had special plastics and coverings that had no harmful chemicals for the baby. They had straps to secure them and bolts to hold them together. So much care had been taken to protect the tiny wards who would use them. I wished they would have taken such care in the rest of the things they make to touch our lives. I went down to dinner then to share more time with my family.

It was unusual for Richard to be there early in the morning but I could hear him having a quiet conversation with Angela at the kitchen table as I padded down the steps in my bare feet. I stopped before I got too far because I heard my name. I sat on the steps and listened.

"I still don't think she'll be able to get it. Why should she? She has no special skills. She's not a relative. So why?" Richard was talking.

"Well, I think she could make a good case about being afraid for her life. Those drug cartels are terrible. Her boyfriend was already killed by them." Angela was answering him.

"I know sweetheart, but everyone in Mexico has probably had a family member whose been killed by the cartels. It's not a compelling case. If it were, then everyone south of the border could be claiming asylum and applying for a green card. It's not enough." I heard his chair being scraped across the floor. I guessed he was leaving. "It just isn't easy to get a green card, that's all. Don't get your hopes up. Maybe we can adopt her."

"This is serious, Richard, we have to help her." I heard the other chair then and the boots walking across the kitchen floor and the screen door slamming.

What did this mean? I thought I would be able to get the green card when I found work and when I proved I was a good citizen like Jose Cruz explained that he had done. Raquel acted like it was pretty easy. They did say that everything had changed, didn't they? I couldn't worry about this now. Too many things were changing. Too much was happening. At least Nely would be safe. She would come into this world an American and no one could take that away from her. I couldn't worry about this now. I had to stick with my plans. I had to finish what I started.

XXIII

It was bound to happen, of course. I had been living such a wonderful life and had been so protected and nurtured by my American family that I let down my guard. I was even able to tolerate Tim Patterson's annoying visits to my life. My English was growing better and better so I was connecting with people. I wasn't as self-conscious. The sense of dread should have warned me.

It happened while I was practicing making movies on my phone during one of the lunch hours. I heard the bell and was pretty sure that it was Tim. I didn't get up right away but I crept down the hall to see him.

He was in the bridal section of the store. I know he felt completely safe and alone. He took off his shirt and his pants and just stood there in his underwear. He went through the racks making his selection like any Midwestern housewife. For Tim there was a small difference: he caressed the material as if it were the finest silk. He ran his hand along the satins and pressed them up against his cheek. He gently touched the silks and put his hand inside the sleeves running his fingers down their length until he got to the cuffs. He picked up the softest dresses and rubbed them up against his chest. His face was like a baby nuzzling its mother. He looked dreamy and was in a trance.

Finally he made his choice. He slipped a super plus size

satin dress over his head and zipped it up the back. He chose a tiara with a veil attached and put it on his forehead. He spun around in the mirror and admired his reflection like any bride-to-be and then he stopped. He stared in the mirror as if he had seen the devil and whirled around to face me.

"Who's there? Who's there?" He screamed it out while hurriedly unzipping the dress and returning the tiara to its rack and scrambling out of the veil. I didn't see these actions because I had run back down the hall at the first possibility that he had seen me. I plugged ear buds into the jack and sent *hurry, hurry, please hurry* messages to the Spotify site to open up. I heard Tim clomping across the floor now in a full fury to find the spy. My heart was blasting inside my chest but on the outside I was a young girl listening to music on my phone. I heard him come up behind me.

"What are you doing here!!!? Why are you here!!!?" His face was red and contorted. His bottom teeth stuck out like a wild animal. He shot spit at me. And me, I was calm as can be.

"What's wrong with you?" I demanded to know why someone was coming at me with anger when I was just listening to music. I made a very big show of taking the ear buds out. He bounced around me, livid with anger.

"How long have you been here? What have you been doing?!" He raged on.

"Tim, I don't know why you are so mad. I'm just spending my lunch hour listening to music. Here listen to this, it's Adele. You probably won't like her." He could hear the music coming out of the ear buds in my hand. I handed it up to him but he looked away. My heart was racing but on the outside I was calm. "Sorry, I didn't hear you come in." I lied with such a calm voice, such a straight face, that anyone would have believed me.

"Well, you should stay back here where you belong." He continued to bounce but his face lost its redness and his teeth returned to their usual place.

"I was just listening to music back here where I belong, like you say. I was sitting here minding my own business. You're the one who came in all mad. Leave me alone." I put the ear buds back in my ears and turned my back on him. My heart was pounding but I hoped that I looked calm and unconcerned like someone who turns his back on an aggressive dog. I hoped he wouldn't attack from behind.

He didn't attack. Instead he walked away. He believed his secret was still safe. If he had talked to me about what he did, he would have found someone without prejudice or judgment who would have listened to him. But he did not have the possibility of talking to another human being with such openness, even if it meant he might get some compassion. Tim Patterson had no empathy for another person so he didn't think anyone had it for him. I felt so sorry for him at that moment. He was imprisoned in a web of his own making.

I heard the bell ring. That was the sweetest sound I had ever heard in my life. I sat back in the chair and put my head on the desk. I was likely the only one who knew what Tim was capable of. I flashed to the scene where he was kicking poor Mario. He was like a person possessed. I sighed a huge sigh of relief once he was gone; only then did I start to shake.

Several days later I found it was too good to be true. He had retreated after that interaction too calmly. Too confused. He had had time then to think about it. Time to consider what I might have seen. He couldn't let it go so easily.

The next time I heard the bell again, I knew he was coming for me. He had me cornered in the back of the store. I had heard the bell but didn't really feel like watching him steal or dress up, so I had stayed in the back. I was coming from the bathroom when he went for me. I tried to go around him but he grabbed my hands and held me. He shoved me up against the wall and held his hand on my neck. I couldn't breathe.

"I know you saw me, you bitch. I know you wasn't listenin' to no iTunes. You saw me in the fuckin' weddin' dress."

I tried to answer but his hand was on my throat. I tried to shake my head and deny it but I couldn't move. My heart was racing. I tried to push him away but he was too strong. His breath was filled with alcohol and it was flaming at me with little flecks of spit. His face was red and his bottom teeth were out. His face was so contorted in his rage that he didn't look human. I struggled but he had me pinned against the wall.

"You bitch! You fuckin' whore! Why'd you come here? We don't want your kind. You don't bring nothin' to us but trouble. Why didn't you just stay in your own fuckin' country? They's so many of you comin'. You're like a tidal wave of grabbers. You just want to come here and take from us. You fuckin' bitch. You bitch!" He was screaming louder now. Ranting.

"You saw me. You was spyin' on me! You was tryin' to get somethin' on me, wasn't you? Fuckin' beaner goin' to blackmail me or somethin'. You cunt!" He still had me by the throat. I struggled. He didn't tighten his grip, but he didn't let me go either.

Finally, he flung me to the ground with one flick of his hand like I was a piece of dirt stuck there. I sailed across the room and landed on the floor. He came running after me then. I turned over, trying to get away, trying to get out of the line of attack. It was useless.

The kick came then, landing directly on my stomach. Its pain shot through my whole system like the burst from fireworks. It lit up the nerves in my whole body like an electric storm. I put both arms over my stomach and rolled as far over as I could. I got ready for the barrage that was to follow. He kicked again and once more and then, he stopped. Miraculously, he stopped.

"You fuckin' wetback! You better keep that secret, bitch, or I'll kill you." He stomped out of the room and I heard the bell. The wonderful bell telling me that for the moment at least, it was over. I turned over on my back and stared up to the ceiling. He would kill me. He had just kicked me. Had he already killed Nely? Had he killed her?

I stayed there forever. I put my hand on my belly tentatively. Everything hurt. Was she moving? Was she alive? I left my hand there. I waited. After some minutes, I felt her kick. She was getting back at him. She kicked up a storm. My little fighter was alive.

I turned over and got up on all fours and finally stood. My back was killing me and my stomach hurt too. I went to the bathroom to try to see how I was doing. The face I saw in the mirror was like a ghost. It was so pale. The eyes were squinty. So this was the face of fear and pain? I washed it with cold water and the color began to return. I sat on the toilet and waited. I went to the toilet. At least I could do that. Everything seemed to be working. No blood. Here I was again sitting in the bathroom after some man hurt me. I sat back on the toilet and sighed. I thought Nely was all right. He hadn't killed her after all.

I got up slowly as there was some pain in my back. Such a strong kick. Was that all it took? One kick from a mad man in full fury. Such was the power of men in full rage. They were like nature gone wild. Like all of those shows where some animal rips another animal to bits. I had seen it so often in Mexico with men punching, kicking, dragging. Most of the time it was man-on-man like two stags or two elephants in a furious fight. It was like those Roman gladiators. But when it was man-on-woman it was different. For these kinds of fights, it wasn't a contest; it was an act of destruction. Nothing was fair. Nothing was even. The woman was reduced to something less. The power of the attack made me less. Even if I ended up not too physically damaged, I now had another damage: I was scared. I remember the women in my village whose husbands hit them. The women always seemed frightened after that, all the time. They were nervous and jumpy. They were forever scared of life. Not me. I came here for a better life. I was going to get it.

I didn't tell anyone what had happened. Why admit to being the latest in a long line of Tim's victims? Besides, I didn't need pity. I needed two things: safety and justice. I could get safety by being on guard now. He wouldn't ever sneak up on me like that again. The bell would signal me and there was a back door. I was never alone in town and I was totally protected on the farm. I would make sure I was safe. Justice was something else. I was hatching my plan and it would be awhile before I could put it into practice. I would have justice, though. In the end, there would be justice.

After this, I was more on-guard when it came to Tim Patterson. I kept an eye on him when I saw him across the street at the store or riding around town in his truck. He was always alone. Angela, Richard, and I went to the movies from time to time. Tim Patterson was never there. I never saw him at the park or the diner or on the street with another living soul. He lived in a bubble all alone. Strange really that an immigrant like me was surrounded by people who loved me and a boy who had been here his whole life was totally alone. His parents didn't even spend any time with him. His mother never mentioned him in the way that mothers do…"Oh my son Tim…" Nothing.

"I saw Tim Patterson lifting the feed bags this morning. That boy works hard. He's always working." I said this as I was hanging up my purse and watching Jeamine making coffee.

"That boy is a total waste of space. The only reason he's not in jail is that he's the son of the richest people in town. Anyone else would be in the slammer." Jeamine actually sounded angry and she nearly threw the coffee into the filters. "Don't get me started on Tim Patterson. I don't want to ruin my day."

I didn't say anything else about him. I guess he did something to her too. No one ever said anything good about him. His mother didn't boast as mothers do and I never even met his father. His name didn't come up in conversation.

The three girls came in then and the day started. I followed them into the sewing room with a piping hot cup of coffee in my hand. "Good morning, girls."

"Mornin', Cece. Hi. Hello." They greeted me. It was interesting to me that each set of three girls tended to be a lot like the last three. I never got three outgoing girls or three shy girls or three talented girls. I usually got one shy, one outgoing and one in between. It was as if nature puts people into three categories and then makes up groups that have each.

"Please pick up where you left off last week with your projects. We are putting on the waistbands like I showed you. I'll be around to help you." I put the coffee on the table. I sounded just like a professional teacher now.

"Cece, can you come and take a look at this, please, to see if I'm doing it right?" Teresa was the outgoing one. She was a cheerleader in the middle school. We didn't have sports in our schools—too expensive. I never heard of a cheerleader in Mexico. Teresa was very proud of being one so I guess it was some kind of honor. Angela and Richard and I went to the high school games because some of Richard's students played on the football and basketball teams. We went to the running and jumping events too. We didn't see many girls in competition but they were there as cheerleaders. I thought it was an odd role for girls. They were on the sidelines cheering for the boys. Was this our role in life? It was even stranger when we watched professional teams on television when Richard came over. Grown women dressed in little skirts were on the sidelines still, rooting for men.

I went to check out Teresa's work and of course it was perfect. Teresa just needed attention. Maybe that was why she was a cheerleader.

"Well done. Nice ironing. You have a beautiful straight line that you can easily sew. Keep up the good work." She flashed me her dazzling cheerleader's smile. I walked over to Susana's machine.

"Susana, I think it would help if you ironed the waistband a bit before you started sewing. It looks good but it'll be better after it's attached if the piece is crisp." Susana was the one in the middle. Neither pretty nor ugly. Neither smart nor slow. Neither outgoing nor shy.

I hesitated to go to Maria Elena right away. Instead, I walked over to the table and took another gulp of coffee, walking around Maria Elena. She was the shy one, the third category of people. She was plump and thick in the way of Latin women. She almost never looked me in the eye. I always had to point to the fabric when I talked to her because she wouldn't look at me. I did that now.

"Great job, Maria Elena. See how you've attached the two pieces perfectly. When you iron the finished project, you'll have a nice connection and there won't be any bulges or puckers. I wish I could say that about myself." I pointed to my baby tummy and the three girls, even Maria Elena, burst out laughing. In this way the morning went by quickly.

"Goin' to lunch, Cece, last chance if you want to come." Jeamine had stuck her head in the door.

"No thanks. Enjoy." I sounded so American to myself. I wanted more than anything to go to lunch with them. It would make me feel safe to be there. Here, I was at the scene of the crime and I didn't feel safe at all. I took precautions though. I had to set up some traps and some escape routes in case Tim returned for more.

When the ladies left, I double locked the door with a bolt. I thought Tim might have that key too but every second gave me more opportunity to get away. Next, I put the umbrella bin with the three umbrellas right in front of the door. Finally I unlocked the back door. None of these were major obstacles but each bought me a little time. He would not catch me again.

While Mrs. Patterson and Jeamine were gone, I was at my phone making my preparations. Everything was so easy these days. It wasn't surprising that people were glued to their phones. The whole world was in our hands. I worked on. I wouldn't have to face him until the end of the day.

*

"Don't fuckin' say a word." Tim stared sullenly out of the window of the truck. I buckled my seatbelt and turned away from him. I was not about to talk to him and thanked God for the silence.

"Not a fuckin' word, I mean it." He raised his finger and shook it in the air. "Nothin'. Don't say nothin'."

It would've been funny if it weren't so sad. He was having a one-sided argument with himself. He was talking like I was making objections to his words. I wasn't saying anything. I wasn't even involved in the conversation. I was a million miles away in my head having an imaginary picnic with Nely. Why would I want to be in a truck with this terrible boy when I could be in a meadow with my little girl? I made his talking into background noise and closed my eyes. Tim Patterson disappeared.

"So what's up with Tim Patterson?" I tried to ask Cook innocently. She looked at me over the top of her reading glasses, pausing her newspaper in midair.

"*What's up* did you say? Look who's getting all American on us now?" She smiled at me. I hadn't even noticed that I was using American expressions like I had been saying them all my life.

"You've asked me about him before. What do you want to know about the little bastard?" I had never heard Cook cuss before and the little anger in her voice surprised me. "There's a whole lot to tell."

"Just that he's always alone and he seems angry all the time. I just wondered if there was something wrong with him, beyond what you have already told me."

"I'm not really sure about that boy. He has been miserable for a long time. If I want to be an amateur psychologist, I would say it had to do with jealousy."

"Jealousy? Why?" I took a seat across from her at the table now.

"You see Tim had a little brother, Ben. Ben was about two maybe three years younger than Tim. When Tim was born he was showered with everything you could want in life. Like all little rich kids. He was spoiled rotten. Then along comes Ben and Ben is the new baby. Before Ben, Tim was a little angel. After Ben, Tim was the devil come to life. Ben was a doll. A very easy baby, according to Mary Lou, and just a doll. Tim couldn't share the attention. He started acting out. He wet the bed, you didn't hear that from me, and I didn't hear that from their housekeeper. He set fires all around town and was caught several times but it was always hushed up.

"Well this went on for two, three years, I can't remember. Tim got worse and worse. They took him to a child psychologist. He was hitting Ben when the parents didn't see it. Once again you didn't hear that from me. He was getting into fights at his pre-school. He would pull the hair of the girls and punch the boys and kick them too. He was always a kicker.

"Well as things were heating up for Tim there was a terrible accident. Ben was out playing in the garden at their big house. You've seen the house, the McMansion we call it. Anyway, he was playing like toddlers do and there was a big concrete urn. A planter thing. He somehow pulled it over on himself and he died. It was terrible. Here was this beautiful little angel and suddenly he was gone. Everybody was so upset. I'm not saying there's any proof of this, mind you, but it's a lot easier for a bigger boy to pull over an urn than a little toddler. I'm just sayin'. As I said, everyone was upset. Except for Tim, of course. He wasn't even sad at the funeral. He didn't try to hide his happiness. He just laughed and cut up and played like it was any other day. It was kind of eerie. Like a little evil was living inside the boy.

"So things went on. The parents became icy to him. The housekeeper told me, you didn't hear this from me, that they never eat meals with Tim. The parents eat alone and she serves Tim in his room. They almost never talk to him. He's isolated. It's like they are still punishing him for his jealousy.

"Over the years he's gotten worse, I think. The town has been plagued forever by some gruesome animal murders. The carcasses are found nailed to town signs or crucified and put up next to the *Welcome* sign. We all know who's done those.

"He's actually a star athlete. He runs track but he had to be barred from the games. He actually broke the bones of some of the runners. He's pushed them or stepped on them. He always says it's an accident. But once is OK and maybe twice. But too many accidents if you ask me. Way too many to be by chance. You know how the criminal always blames others for what he did. Well that's it for Tim too.

"Honestly, I think he's probably done a lot worse. He never gets caught. He's smart. He could have been anything in life. He's talented. He's rich. Instead he took the low road every time. I know for a fact he steals. The families of the kids he punched got paid off. The pregnant girls got paid off. Everything got paid off. The Pattersons didn't do that kid any favors by covering for him. So that's Tim Patterson. If I were you, Cece, I would try to stay as far away from him as possible. Anyone who gets close to him gets hurt." She shook the newspaper and went back to her reading.

I went up the stairs to read. I knew that what she was saying was true. I was afraid of Tim Patterson for what he had done and for what he was capable of doing. When he came for me there was no reason. I didn't do anything to him. What would he be like if I really stood up for myself? I had seen him in his full fury with Mario. Would he do that to me?

In Mexico, the sons of the rich and powerful are under a protected umbrella like Tim. They don't have to follow the ordinary rules. I never met any of them personally but the gossip mills are full of stories about everything they get away with. All of the things they've done and they never got punished. They cover for each other.

I thought about the terrible things happening in Juarez. I had heard that many young women like me had gone to Juarez on the other side of El Paso, Texas to find jobs in the American factories that opened on our side of the border. The police found thousands of them murdered over the years since these factories opened. My mother told me there were never any arrests for the people who killed these girls. At first, the papers called them prostitutes. Later, the papers started to tell the truth, that these were just young girls, usually with tiny kids, who just needed to make some money to support their children. The prostitutes were probably trying to do the same thing. These girls went to work in the factories and were murdered. No one was ever even arrested

We Mexicans knew that this was because the judges and the police and the politicos were all involved. There was sex involved too, because most of the dead girls were beautiful and all of them had been raped. Juarez was not a place I ever wanted to go in my life. I think my mother told me that there were now thousands and thousands of girls who had been murdered and still no arrests. How could that be? They all covered for each other.

So Tim Patterson would just keep going until he was stopped. How many more Marios would there be? How many lives would he stomp on? I was sorry to hear about Ben but imagine what it would have been like for that little boy to grow up as the brother of Tim? It might have been much worse than it was. Maybe it was a blessing that he left life so soon.

XXIV

The pains shot through my system in the middle of the night. I began by moaning but very soon I was screaming. The light flew on and Angela was at my side in her nightgown.

"Cece. Are you OK? Is it starting?" She propped me up in bed but I could hardly look at her the pain was so bad. "Let's see, honey, let me check. Yes, look, your water broke."

Cook burst into the room. "It's starting, is it? Did her water break?"

Angela had asked Cook to stay with us for a while until Nely arrived. Her husband promised to take care of the kids, but who was going to take care of him?

"Yes, Cook. Call Yvonne." Cook ran out of the room to call the midwife. "Come on, Cece, let's get you out of those wet clothes." She turned me over and took the wet nightgown over my head. I held up my arms to help her but I didn't feel like helping anyone do anything at that moment. She got a fresh gown from the dresser. "Now let's move to the single bed over there and everything will be clean and sanitary. We can't have you giving birth in a wet bed." She smiled.

That sounded funny to me because this was not going to be a clean bed for long. She helped me up and I waddled across the room to the bed that would be the operating table. We had put a single bed with a lamp with a strange neck there and a stack of clean towels on top of a dresser. We were prepared with our plan, Cook, Angela and I, so that we had everything ready for Yvonne. I lay down on the bed and Angela got out the stopwatch to time the contractions. I felt very calm and capable.

"This'll be easy, Cece, you should see all of the drama that surrounds the birth of ten pigs or six dogs or a colt. This is a piece of cake." I wondered if she felt so tranquil. She didn't know about the kick in the stomach. I did. A flash of worry flew through my mind.

"Take some deep breaths now. Just relax." I let out a blood curdling scream.

"OK, I'll clock that. We'll just time the contractions, honey, breathe deeply."

The pain came in waves like an earthquake starting in the top of my stomach and crashing down to the top of my legs. It felt like a period cramp, only one hundred times more terrible. Someone was trying to smash a bowling ball through my stomach. I cried out. It took forever for Yvonne to get here. She came into the room in a rush.

"How often are the contractions?" she asked.

"Every twenty minutes." Angela clutched the stopwatch.

"Where can I wash up?" Angela got up and escorted her to the bathroom. I could hear them talking as they walked out of the room but I couldn't hear what they were saying.

"Cook is boiling some water, Cece. Take it easy. Breathe, you'll be fine." She wiped my forehead with a cool washcloth. It felt good.

Yvonne came back into the room. "Let's take a look,

Cece." She spread my legs apart and sat down at the end of the bed and turned on the strange lamp. "Good light. These goose neck lamps work a treat. Well done girls." She peered into the light's beam. "Looks good here. Let's give it a feel." She stood back up and pushed around on my stomach.

"Good little girl you've got here, Cece. She's just in the right place." It was odd to hear the Irish accent in the middle of New Mexico. Angela had already explained that the Irish made the best midwives and usually that's what they did around these parts. Yvonne was the first Irish person I had ever met in life so I had no idea what they did. I just wanted the pain to stop.

Cook came into the bedroom then, carrying a pan of boiling water. The steam was clouding her glasses and she laughed as she walked right into the dresser. "Can't really see, you know." For the only person among us who had given birth to three children Cook was the most nervous.

"We're going to have to wait a bit, girls, I'm afraid. Nely isn't ready to give up the security of her mum, right now. The cervix isn't really dilated that much. I'll just have a little nap if you don't mind." With that, she fell instantly asleep sitting up in her chair beside my bed. I was a bit tired myself and dozed off as well.

I slept in fits. Suddenly, I was stabbed in the back, not literally, but that is the pain that woke me—a sharp stab in the back. I sat up and let out a scream. I'm not sure how much time had passed but after that first stab there was a definite change in the pains. They started coming much faster now and I let out a yell at each one.

Angela and Cook came back into the room and Angela starting keeping the time again. The three women were busy around me but I couldn't tell what each was doing. I knew Angela was time keeper but Cook and Yvonne were just being busy. I couldn't focus because the pains were greater now, hitting me in my back and the tops of my thighs. Yvonne came back to the bed and put the light on to examine me.

"Yep, she's dilating a wee bit now. Well done, Cece, you're fine. You've got a ways to go, girl."

I didn't feel fine. Hours had gone by and the pains were coming every few minutes now but there was no baby and there was no end in sight for this pain. The waves of pain ran down to the tops of my thighs and I cried out with each one. Sometimes my screams were long moans of pain. I was so happy that we were in the middle of the country—the whole town would be awake.

Angela was by my side asking me to breathe and pant. I wanted this to end. I huffed and I breathed when she told me but it didn't seem to make any difference. The agony dragged on.

"I need to go to the bathroom," I said. All three women jumped up and tripped all over themselves helping me to the bathroom. It would have been funny or sweet or cute if I felt any of those things at that moment. What it felt like was pain. I waddled to the bathroom and plunked down on the toilet and went. Angela and Cook helped me back to the bed and I lay down on the bed and waited for the next wave of pain to come crashing in. It did.

"I'm so tired, Yvonne. I'm just so tired. Look at this." I held up my hand that was shaking.

"Sure, that's normal, little one. The girls always feel tired. Think of all the work your body's doin', a'course you'd be tired. Those shakes. Those are the little shakes of love your body's gettin' ready for your wee one. All's fine. You're just gettin' ready to be a mum."

"It stings down here." I pointed to myself with my shaky hand.

"That's good. The baby will be movin' around now tryin' to find you *down there*." She let out a great raucous laugh. "Don't push down. I know you'll be wantin' to push down. Don't do it!" She had a finger pointed in the air and a serious look. I felt a strong need to push but her stronger warning against it stopped me. What would happen if I pushed down? Why would I feel like I need to push down if I wasn't supposed to push down? Was this some trick Mother Nature was playing on me? I hated the pain.

Angela reported that the pains were coming between every one and three minutes now. How could she tell that? To me, the pains were continuous. No breaks. I thought they were intense in the beginning and they got worse and worse. On top of that, I had to push. I had to push. But the image of Yvonne with her finger raised stopped me. I wanted to push.

"Let's have another look," Yvonne was saying as she moved the hot light. I was barely conscious now. Six hours had passed since I'd woken up that morning. I wanted to throw up or sleep and I just kept shaking. I wanted to push so bad and Yvonne wouldn't let me. "We're ready to go, little one. Listen to me now. Push!"

I was so relieved to be able to push that I did it immediately. I pushed as hard as I could. Nothing. I don't know what I expected. I guess I thought one push and Nely would be welcomed into the world. But nothing. The pain was unbearable. My vagina was on fire. I was panting and so tired. When would this end? I heard her voice in the background as if I were underwater.

"Push! Push!" I had wanted to push so badly just minutes before and now I was pushing and nothing happened. I just got more sweaty and shaky and nauseous. Nothing was happening with the baby. I breathed and pushed and pushed and breathed. Still, Nely would not come out.

"Here she is. Here she is. Look at that hair. Oh, she has a lovely head of hair."

Lovely head of hair meant that she had a head. She was a baby with a real baby's head. I had been protecting her for nine months. I had been cherishing her as the only thing remaining of Guillermo and now she was here, at last.

"Here she comes. Here she comes. Push! Push!" I heard the cheer of Yvonne and I pushed. Suddenly, there was a rush. I felt a great weight swoosh out of me. She was here.

Yvonne scooped up Nely and gave her a little squeeze and Nely gave the world her first cry. It was a strong one. My little girl would be fine. Cook cleaned her up and put the tiniest creature in the world on my chest. I had her. I had my Nely.

"Oh my God, Cece. You did it! What a little angel you made!" Angela was standing over me, wiping my face and smiling down at Nely.

"I did it. I have her. I am so happy." I couldn't close my eyes because then I couldn't see Nely. I was just staring at the miracle that was her.

"A little darlin' that's what she is." Cook was beaming too. Her smile was the widest I had ever seen.

As I looked down at her, I sighed deeply and tried to

sleep. She was cradled in my arms and she knew, as she had known for nine months, that I was there for her. She would be protected forever. We had found our better life.

The midwife was massaging my stomach and I held Nely close to me as she slept. For some reason, after so much agony and so much effort, I couldn't sleep. Something was nagging at the back of my brain. Something was nagging inside me too. The sense of dread returned in a torrent. I sat up terrified.

"The phone! The phone! Check the phone!" I grabbed Angela's hand and looked at her with wild eyes.

"OK, Cece, the phone, I will check your phone. Whatever you say honey. Now just relax." She held my hand, her calm gaze returning my crazed one.

"Promise. Promise," I hissed, still clutching her hand.

"I promise, honey. Don't worry, I will check your phone." Her look was puzzled. I fell back on the bed.

Yvonne worked to birth the placenta and what was coming was not tissue. It was blood. The pain was not stopping and neither was the blood. Something was wrong.

"Take Nely please, Cook," Yvonne said with a worried voice. Cook took Nely away from me even as I tried to hold onto her. I couldn't catch my breath. "I can't breathe. I can't breathe." I was gasping now. I felt so tired. So dizzy. I could hear them talking.

"Push there. Try to stop the bleeding." Yvonne had terror in her voice and she directed Angela. "Push here!"

"Stop the bleeding, Yvonne. Stop the bleeding!" Angela was hysterical. They knew they were losing me as the blood flowed. Nothing stopped it. Yvonne was giving me shots and still the bleeding kept up. It was incredible that such a river of blood was inside me.

"Stop it, Yvonne! Stop it!" Angela was yelling.

Yvonne kept moving around and barking orders but nothing was happening. I was so shaky. My heart got faster and faster and I couldn't breathe. I just couldn't breathe. I was so very tired. I had worked all night to bring Nely home, into the world with me. Now I was cold. So very cold. I could see Nely safely asleep in the arms of Cook. I knew she would be safe. It was so cold. So cold.

ABOUT THE AUTHOR

Julie, like so many of us in these times, lives multiple lives: writer, professor, nomad, collage artist, dancer, singer, humorist. She was an immigrant to England, and Cataluña, Spain and now Mexico. She tries to work through the challenges we all face day by day. Connections are welcome at hoolia711@yahoo.com or check out her travel blog www.outwardjourneys.com. Like we just found out with our worldwide pandemic: we are all in this together.

CPSIA information can be obtained
at www.ICGtesting.com
Printed in the USA
LVHW041108280820
664156LV00002B/199